In Gold We Trust

Jonathan Thomas Stratman

Front cover coin art: Mark Welch

Back cover photo of sternwheeler *Nenana* courtesy of
Alaska Digital Archives

ISBN-13: 978-1517643645
ISBN-10: 1517643643

For my dad,
Father Lee W. Stratman,
who was the priest
at St. Mark's Episcopal Church
in Nenana during the time the
Father Hardy stories take place.

CHAPTER 1

S he was nearly naked when she woke me. I'd been dreaming of her and now waking, dazed and only partway back from that other place, saw her clearly. *Am I still dreaming?*

Blue moonlight washed imperfectly through the frosty window behind her. It distorted a shadow of window grid on the knotty-pine wall, on a carved willow crucifix, and on a thumb-tacked *National Geographic* map of Alaska. I'd been sleeping in my cotton waffle long johns, beneath a goose down sleeping bag and a stack of olive-drab surplus woolen army blankets. Spring, yes. Warm? No.

"It's you," I said in the twenty-degree room, my breath a silver cloud.

"Yep." She smiled that faintly pitying smile I was becoming used to.

Slim, blond, leggy, she wore the diaphanous, peach-colored negligee I had never been able to resist, giving both the woman and the garment a gauzy, shimmery quality in the haze of moonlight

"I was dreaming about you."

"I know," she said. She shook her head, jiggling the silhouette of a shapely breast. I admit I might have been staring.

"Ha-a-r-dy!"

"Yes, what?" As always, any glimpse of her body made it hard to focus.

"You need to get up now, throw a pack together and get over the river before dawn. You hear?" she said. She waggled a forefinger. "Before dawn."

I did hear, but was reluctant to relax my grip on any moment with her in it. She was already fading. "Up now, Hardy."

"I love you," I said, to the space where she'd been.

"I know," she murmured, "but I'm still ..."

She was gone before she finished, but I knew that last word: 'dead.' I was still seeing, talking to—even taking directions from—a woman who had died of polio in an iron lung more than two thousand miles from here. That was two years ago, April of 1954.

So I had come alone, a widower Episcopal priest, to a tiny mission with a hand-hewn log church and altar vestments of beaded, bleached moose hide. The isolated, snow-drifted village of Chandelar lay almost dead center on a map of Alaska. It was seventy miles roughly south of Fairbanks and less than two hundred miles below the Arctic Circle.

Things weren't always as they seemed here. One plus one wasn't reliably two. And Mary—the wife I missed so badly that I sometimes physically hurt—could still show up to have her way with me.

I didn't really understand and had no reasonable explanation, so did the only thing I could do under the circumstances. I rolled out, turned on the light and grabbed my old canvas army pack.

CHAPTER 2

*A*m *I crazy?* Maybe. Not only did I just have a conversation with my dead wife, but now I'm out of bed hunting for clean socks to stuff in a packsack. One consolation: if crazy, I'm certainly not alone. It wasn't at all unusual for people in Chandelar to see and talk to dead relatives, to receive advice or even warnings. So I fit right in.

But deep in my heart I knew this was more than just odd behavior. Saint John of the Cross, writing in the sixteenth century, called times like these "the dark night of the soul." They certainly had been for me. I admit that in losing Mary I almost lost myself.

We planned to meet this challenge together. We would come to remote Alaska, take on a needy mission and work side by side helping people who really needed it.

I had almost finished with seminary in Tennessee, at St. Luke's in Sewanee, nearly ordained, when it happened. "I have a terrible headache," she said one evening, she who never had headaches. I fetched her a couple of aspirins and a glass of water and we went to bed and didn't think much about it. That was late on a Tuesday evening. By midmorning Wednesday, she lay almost completely paralyzed—could scarcely breathe—and a long month later she died in an iron lung. She was one of the last fatalities of the last polio epidemics in the United States.

Thanks to the new vaccine, people now talk about a future completely free of polio, maybe even a future with no dread diseases at all, like tuberculosis or even cancer. What if they'd had the vaccine just a little earlier? I couldn't figure out why someone like Mary should have to die, not so much of polio as of bad timing. One month, two months ... six months?

Taking the whole thing a step further, as a priest it made me wonder if there would ever be a vaccine for bad things people do to each other. A vaccination against evil? Could one be on the way? Maybe, but I admit to doubting it will arrive in time, like Mary's vaccine.

Across the snowy street the generator cut out, as it often did. Big as a truck and two or three times as noisy, this diesel generator provided electrical power for about a third of the town. Twice monthly, usually at this time of night someone came in and shut it down for service. I had become so used to its roar that I no longer heard it when it ran. But when it stopped I felt nearly deafened by the roar of silence. Fumbling on my dresser top in the darkness for the box of wooden kitchen matches, I lit and trimmed the kerosene lamp until it didn't smoke and went back to scrounging for socks by flickering yellow light.

The kerosene lamp enhanced and magnified what a friend called the "bachelor look" of my bedroom. Heck, the whole cabin! I slept on an old, steel-framed double bed with a single mattress supported by noisy coil springs that moaned and complained when I shifted position.

As a personal challenge I tried to be consistent about such things as making my bed daily and not wearing the same clothes too many times. And yes, I do my own laundry. Luckily most of my shirts are black and the white collars I can clean in the sink with Bon Ami and a toothbrush.

After learning to keep a fire going, one of my first jobs at the Chandelar mission was to master the ancient Maytag wringer washer. I admit Mary did all the laundry and housekeeping while I was both seminarian and night janitor at the University. A lean-to room at the back of my cabin housed the noisy piston water pump, an old-time concrete utility sink, and the Maytag. The tub filled with a hose from the hot water tap and started to agitate when plugged in. I was still using what looked like the original faded green carton of Rinso, an all-purpose detergent I inherited with the washer. Drying clothes in winter either meant hanging them up inside where heat from the woodstove slowly steamed up the whole cabin, or hanging them on the clothesline outside. They'd be frozen stiff but dry, as long as I brushed off the heavy frost.

Recently I said to a visitor—who didn't know I was Episcopalian—that my wife had previously done the laundry, but that she had died. I could tell he was stunned that I seemed to be confessing an illicit relationship.

By now I'm used to the strange looks I get if I mention having had a wife. A lot of people still think only the Roman Catholic Church has priests, forgetting Russian and Greek Orthodox, Church of England, and their American counter-parts, Episcopalians. Those priests marry, have families and somehow still manage to serve God while ministering to their fellow man.

So I came to the mission at Chandelar by myself and for a while didn't do so well. I 'failed to thrive.' As I later came to recognize, my parishioners were keeping an eye on me in their quiet, nonintrusive way. They brought me food when they knew I wasn't eating, took me along on hunting trips and to the fish camps so I wouldn't be alone too much. They generally worried about me while I—lost in grief—filled my days with mission chores and worrying about *them*.

What turned it around? Oddly enough, nearly dying at the hands of one of my own parishioners, and at the same time rediscovering the possibility of finding love again—yes—urged on by the ghost of my wife. I admit that another chance at love was something I had never even considered.

Even crazier than a midnight meeting with my dead wife was the current prospect of crossing the now-melting Tanana River on ice in the dark.

Locals, mostly Athabascans who have lived on this riverbank for a thousand years, wouldn't walk the quarter mile across thinning, rotten ice this late in the season *in the daylight*. And yet here I am, packing my bag for a predawn crossing. How dangerous can it be? Plenty.

People in the States—the south forty-eight— have heard about the mighty Yukon. Less well known, the Tanana, a major tributary, is its wild little brother. Some places it runs more than a mile wide, muddy and swirling with deadly snags and quicksand banks and bars. Most of the people who fall in, jump in, or are pushed don't come out alive. On the other hand, crossing now in early May should be safe. At least that's what I told myself. But I'm still a cheechako—a greenhorn—by local standards, with a lot left to learn about life in Alaska. If I survive. In most places outside of Alaska a simple mistake makes you late, inconvenienced or embarrassed. In this part of Alaska, simple mistakes make you dead.

Plenty of time, I told myself. After all, last year, 1955—the spring before I got here—breakup happened on May 9. How do I know that? Around here everyone knows that. It's a matter of public note because of the famous Ice Pool just upriver at Nenana. People from everywhere bet on the day, hour and minute the ice breaks up and the river starts to flow again. Winners from all over the U.S. share a whopping pool of several hundred thousand dollars. So around here, do we remember what day the ice went out last year? You bet!

Today would be only May 5, just in case that mattered, and most of the old timers were saying "another two weeks, easy," even if they were no longer willing to venture out on the ice.

Just days ago, I had safely driven my pickup truck—well, the *church's* pickup truck—across the river on the ice road. I moved it in anticipation of an upcoming trip to Fairbanks, parking it high on the far bank. Yes, I had driven through daytime melt pools, fortunately just inches deep on top of the ice. But I'd heard of the ice actually opening up with the river current running and thirty-to-forty feet of depth. Not that depth would matter if I fell through. I'd be swept away beneath the ice and maybe *never* found again. Alaska was like that. Shuddering, I couldn't even imagine being swept beneath the unforgiving ice without tensing up and holding my breath. My heart pounded at the thought.

"Knock it off and pack," I muttered, willing myself back into my cold, dimly-lit room.

In just a couple more weeks, with the river clear of ice, a small barge—made fast to a little sternwheeler—would ferry vehicles back and forth across the river. It would be the only summertime route to Fairbanks and beyond. Otherwise there simply wasn't a way to drive from here to there. That's why I'd taken the opportunity to move the truck across early.

The mercury hovered mostly above zero at night, but daytime temperatures tended to rise a bit above freezing, so icicles—some five and six feet long—dripped from the eaves while recently silent dry snow now crunched noisily underfoot. Because moosehide mukluks quickly soak through, I turned, at first reluctantly, to a pair of stateside boots I had ordered for hunting season last fall. A small company in New England, run by a man with the improbable name of Leon Leonwood Bean, manufactured a boot with rubber bottoms bonded to high, laced leather tops. They were great boots, nearly tempting me to order a second pair almost as soon as I'd received the first. But I didn't and would probably be sorry later. It seemed unlikely a small, quirky company like Bean's would last long enough for me to wear out this pair and need another.

I glanced at the bedside clock, a round-faced, ivory-colored Big Ben Jr. windup with hands that glow in the dark. Time to get out of here.

So, just after 4:30, I pulled the cabin door firmly to. I didn't lock it. This was Chandelar. In fact, I doubted—if I went house to house—I would find a locked door in the entire town. However, I might get shot for my trouble.

This far north, it would be another half hour before the sun rose. For now, the sky stood up in the last of night impossibly deep and black, layered with stars.

It felt almost warm out, likely above zero. For the first time since September, the soft breeze blew, faintly scented with trees or leaves or dirt, even though the only dirt showing was ruts in the road between formidable six-foot snowbanks.

"It's warmer than I thought," I said aloud in the soft night. I picked up my pace to the riverbank, as though these few unexpected degrees of warmth might somehow hasten breakup. It was a crazy notion, I knew, brought on by the unaccustomed crunching of my feet in the melting snow.

Off on my left an owl hooted softly, then launched itself in a nearly silent glide above me that I sensed rather than saw. In the distance one wolf howled, then more, but then the whole bunch cut off suddenly, mid-howl. A glow started in the east, the onset of what pilots call "Civil Twilight" with sunrise approaching.

The whole of the village of Chandelar lay spread like a quilt in a roughly four-by-six block pattern, with the railroad and river on much of the town's two sides. On the third side lay a broad, old fashioned main street with a couple of saloons, railroad terminal, Pioneers of Alaska meeting hall, Post Office, general store, lodge and my favorite, the Coffee Cup Café.

Of the town's twenty-some blocks, quite a few might have just one or two dwellings on them, mostly low-slung two-and-three-room log cabins or tarpaper shacks, with maybe a cache on stilts out back, or a meat shed. Here and there stood a clothesline or a drying rack for summer salmon. A few of those blocks had real frame houses for the storekeeper, CAA employees, the public health nurse, river pilots, and others—usually Caucasian.

My house, the rectory, is a log cabin that had been jacked up about a mile away at the Old Mission. Set on round logs it was skidded in by bulldozer to be set hard by the side of the small log church in a little half circle of medium-sized birch and cottonwood trees.

Chandelar had been something of a boom town back in the twenties. It was the place where the railroad met the river and gold rush gear could be loaded on barges for a stern-wheeler voyage all the way down the Yukon to the Bering Sea. President Harding drove a golden spike near here, to inaugurate a long-span bridge at Nenana, then died in San Francisco on his way back to Washington D.C. Local wags still insisted it was the trip to the Chandelar area that killed him.

The town had faded a good deal since those boom days. The early population of some five thousand had dropped to fewer than five hundred. Last fall, just before the first snow, I'd been hunting rabbits out beyond town, thinking myself well away. There, in a willow wood, I came upon a solitary ancient rusty fire hydrant, like a ghostly visitor from the past, and it made me shiver.

It was still too dark to see into the yards I walked past, but I knew them well. Here and there a dogsled stood up on its runner ends, sheltered under a broad log cabin eve, or tunneled under a snow-laden tarp. Some yards were arranged in a pattern with five or ten—or more—doghouses, since for hunting, trapping or racing, dogs and dog teams were still very much a way of life here.

So it was not a surprise that, walking gingerly in the dark on the frozen glaze of street ice, and nearly to the river, I startled a husky tethered alongside a small, shadowed square of log cabin. The dog let out a serious "who goes there" bark and lunged out hard to the end of his chain.

It's only me, I might have told him, *sent out into the night alone.* His challenge unmet, I heard the chain jingle back toward the doghouse, followed by the listless mutter of a captive creature alone in the night.

Or maybe not so alone. About a minute later I heard the challenge bark again and the chain slam, just as I was about to head down over the steep bank to the frozen river. I paused, turned for a moment to look back and try to see who else might be out early and walking down this road—which didn't go anywhere but to the river. *That seems odd.* And I couldn't back down the tiny, seed of suspicion that I was being followed.

Events last fall—the discovery of a dead man spread-eagled and frozen in a snowbank—had spiraled out of control, in the end nearly killing me and people I had come to care about. The experience left me, one who had never in my life worried about being followed, worried now. But I couldn't let it stop me.

Starting out on river ice, I sensed the huge power building beneath me, scarcely contained. Out there in darkness the river waited, as if a living, quivering being. Below me distantly, ice cracked—not the sharp surface cracking of my own weight—but a deep, distant, ominous threat.

As a medic in the European war, I'd once treated a man who had dislocated his hip, actually had it blown out of its socket in a mortar attack. Manipulating the man's leg and the joint until the hip ball slid back into its socket produced the same kind of deep, troublesome sound. The sound brought the same sense of something where it wasn't supposed to be, soon on the move with not a thing to be done about it.

I could already see the sheen of patches of glare ice—or maybe water. For the first time I hesitated. To go ahead more quickly? To go back? *Do I really want to do this? Do I really have a choice? And what if I choose to not do what she told me to. Could it mean* never *waking out of a sound sleep to see her again? Who would take that chance?*

In the end my feet made the decision. I found myself stepping forward quickly, slipping through a slushy patch, ankle deep, just beyond the ice edge and then crunching along, slipping and sliding. All the while I tried not to think about how much more dangerous this quarter mile stretch of walk seemed now that I'd left the riverbank.

And I couldn't escape the nagging feeling that someone followed me. Not more than a hundred feet out, with a patch of good footing ahead, I spun mid-step and began walking backward, feeling pretty sure that if someone *were* following me, they wouldn't be able to tell from my outline which way I faced. Sure enough, the silhouette of a tall man, hatless, wearing a long, dark overcoat and what looked like unbuckled stateside galoshes, came over the crest of the riverbank and started down the slope toward the ice. I saw him stop at the edge. I was pretty sure I knew what he was thinking: *This doesn't look good. Maybe I should turn around.* But he didn't. After a brief hesitation, on he came.

But why follow me?

I began to hear water flowing. Not such an unusual sound but one not heard this far north since last September or October. I stepped over a small flowing rivulet and resisted the urge to break into a trot. This wouldn't be the time to dash carelessly into an open channel. I imagined a conversation between my parishioners. "What happened to Hardy?" "I dunno. He disappeared. Woke up one morning and he was gone."

Nearing the halfway mark, unsafe in either direction, I felt the now rumbling ice actually slip. Like a train, large, solid, powerful, shifting just a bit underfoot. Like the world wobbling. It didn't move much, just enough to really shake me. *Did it really move?* Not more than a couple of inches. *But this ice is still four or five feet thick. It's not supposed to be moving at all.* Says you!

Okay, I threw caution to the wind and began to trot. In the strengthening predawn glow, I caught the reflected wink of light off the windows of my pickup truck on the far shore. I knew—hoped—that in minutes I'd stand on that shore looking back across the frozen expanse wondering what was the big deal. Could the river really be breaking up with me standing on it? Nah. Maybe I even imagined movement. Maybe I'd buy an Ice Pool ticket at Nenana for a date two or three weeks from now. I splashed through a wide shallow puddle, letting its stillness convince me, on the run, that it wasn't really open clear to the bottom of the river.

A glance over my shoulder told me the tall man was also jogging, quickly closing the distance between us. I could feel my heart rate spiking as I began to be truly frightened. It had only been a couple of months previous that one of my parishioners, one of the crazy ones, apparently, brought me and Evie—a woman I had begun to care for—out on the ice to die. That he died instead was only the grace of God and the marksmanship of Andy Silas—native Athabascan World War II sniper and my first friend here in Chandelar. Somehow, I found myself back out on ice again—maybe thin ice!

The tall hill in front of me, a dark, shapeless mass when I'd stepped from the far shore, had been slowly revealing details of itself in the first light. Even as I looked up, a red-gold sliver of sunlight caught and sharply outlined its topmost rim. Digging up my parka sleeve for my wristwatch I read five-oh-three. Official sunrise. I remembered Mary's warning. No more trotting. Now I ran.

Feeling at the same time foolish and yet compelled to get off the ice, I ran like there was someone following me, gaining, as indeed there was. But it wasn't fear of the tall man making me run, though it may have helped. It was the certainty that something bad or dangerous was about to happen, and it did.

Scant feet from shore, my firm foundation, ten or twenty miles of near-arctic ice shivered and roused itself into motion, abruptly sliding under my feet, nearly dumping me. Though it didn't shift much at first—a foot or so—I had the sense of it shaking the arctic winter off its back, freeing itself, sliding heavy and dark between its banks, an unstoppable, unchangeable power. I full-out sprinted the last twenty yards, vaulting a small, clear channel to land solidly on a narrow scuff of exposed sandy shore. *Safe! Thank God.*

"Help!" It was a shout from right behind, from what had become in seconds, an open expanse of maybe thirty feet. It might as well have been a mile. A dull roar rose as the entire, flat, blue-white river slid into motion, fracturing into slabs, shushing and grinding its soft and hard edges. The man stood close enough, even with his back to the sun, for me to see his face, to see his terror. "Help me!" he shouted again, his voice muffled by the rumble.

How could I help him? With the truck near could I throw him a rope? I had no rope. In the summer there would be boats here. People who left cars on this side would motor or paddle across to drive to Fairbanks. But this early in the season, there were no boats, no rope, no life preservers—not that any of those could save this man's life.

15

"Help!" he shouted again, and reaching into his overcoat pocket, pulled out a handgun, aiming it at me.

My compulsion to get out of the way of that pistol was nearly as great as my recent need to get off the ice. How to help him? Ultimately I did the only thing I *could* do, crossing myself, dropping to one wet knee in the slush. I asked God to save him, to not make him one of those lost persons who came to Alaska, made a foolish mistake, and was never seen or heard from again. I asked God to get him safely to shore, although downriver just a bit so that I would have time to jump in my truck and drive away.

It seemed a reasonable request under the circumstances. When I stood back up and opened my eyes, he was already nearly fifty yards distant and certainly out of range. He had put the gun back in his pocket and now stood motionless on a large, stable-looking floe, his stance wide. Our eyes met and he held his arms out at his sides and shrugged. We stood like that for a few long moments, me being with him, as though he were not all alone in this and likely to soon die. Then he turned away to look down the river and didn't turn back.

After a few minutes I walked to my pickup and opened the door. No one locked a vehicle in Chandelar, either. Someone had left a package for me to mail in Fairbanks, wrapped in a cut-up brown grocery bag and tied with twine. It was addressed to someone stateside—probably a relative—with a dollar bill tucked under the string. The note said I could keep the change.

16

I pushed the package aside, slid up onto the seat and turned the key in the ignition. The vision of Mary waggling her finger at me was suddenly very present. "Before dawn, Hardy," she had said.

Backing out, my shaking hands could hardly grip the steering wheel. And they kept shaking most of the way to Fairbanks.

CHAPTER 3

*M*ary wasn't the only one who wanted me out of town. Two days earlier, breakfast found me at the Coffee Cup Café, at a smallish table topped with red and white checkered oilcloth, studying a faded, finger-marked menu I knew by heart. In early May, with daytime temperatures at last balmy in the thirties, four-and-five-foot dripping icicles hung in front of the restaurant's big, moisture-fogged plate glass windows.

We were doing what most people did in central Alaska this time of year: speculating on the nearby Nenana Ice Pool. No matter the exact date—sometime between April 20 and May 20—breakup signaled the official end to the long, subarctic winter. With more than a two-hundred-thousand-dollar payout, it was a chance for an ordinary person with a dollar to strike it rich by betting on the day, hour, and minute the river ice would slide into motion. In a village where people still had to hunt to survive, that kind of cash was a fortune beyond imagination. Any job for cash, like working for the Ice Pool, or the railroad, or on a riverboat was nearly a miracle.

Here in Chandelar—especially in the absence of Evie and Andy—I found fellowship in the early morning crush and din of breakfast at the steamy, smoky Coffee Cup. On this Tuesday morning, Guy Mitchell was 'Singing the Blues'—his new hit—from the pulsing Rock-Ola, while our waitress, Rosie Jimmy, effortlessly negotiated her way through

18

the too-close tables, elbows, shoulders and broad gestures of the capacity crowd of about twenty. Somehow she managed to make it point to point, refilling piping hot coffee without spilling on anyone. In her pink waitress uniform, popping pink gum bubbles, she had perfected the art of pouring on the run, and she made it look like fun.

This morning she wore her fashionable white swept-wing eyeglasses, accentuating her dark skin, high Athabascan cheekbones and shiny black hair. A Chandelar fashion maven, she also had similar frames in black and turquoise. With spring coming on, she had swapped out her trademark waffle long johns and mukluks she typically wore with the pink dress, for a pair of shiny, black rubber knee-high boots, the perfect fashion accessory for sloppy, melting snow.

I knew Rosie missed Andy too, with what she saw as his smooth cosmopolitan ways. Rosie subscribed to *Life* magazine, and more than just reading it, she studied it for fashion tips and life secrets. A recent photo spread on the delights of the Italian Riviera had her stashing tips in a mayonnaise jar under her bed. She told me this. I hadn't seen it for myself. Andy had already been to Italy, fighting the Nazis as a U.S. Army sniper, and in her mind this made the two of them kindred spirits, a match made in heaven: he had been there and she wanted desperately to go.

I think Rosie thought that she and Andy might have a future together, which surprised me a little. Before he left, Andy had confided something, his 'dark secret,' that he wasn't interested in Rosie or in women generally, that he was homosexual—

what he called 'gay'—though it seemed an odd term. If he thought it would make a difference with me, it didn't. As his friend, his priest, and someone whose life he had saved at considerable personal risk, he could have been born purple for all I cared. I had since learned that his secret was somewhat known in the village but never mentioned.

Somehow the information had missed Rosie, leaving her a little hurt when Andy went back to Italy a couple of months ago without even thinking of taking her along. He claimed it was "just for a visit," but I had my doubts. Somehow the kind of life he could live there had gotten inside of him. "Ciao bella!" he would call out to Rosie's considerable delight. The Italian phrase somehow worked charmingly on his Athabascan tongue, and she would come on the run with another round of coffee 'from the red can that means good taste.' "This stuff is swill," Andy always said of any coffee that wasn't Italian, and I continued to be hopeful that if and when he did come home, he would come home with coffee.

My feelings about my other missing tablemate, Evangeline Williams—Evie—were more complicated. She left, almost without warning in January, just a couple of weeks after her cousin Andy left. She had decided to try attending the University of Washington in Seattle and had been accepted for the following autumn term. But a winter term last-minute opening in their Teacher Ed program took her away about eight months earlier than either of us had expected. Eight months we thought we had to figure out who we were to each other, or who we might be.

I missed her quick knock, cheery 'good morning' and light, easy laugh. And I missed the comfortable evenings we spent together, reading the *Saturday Evening Post*, taking turns napping on the sofa, drinking coffee, chatting about almost nothing—like old friends or a comfortable couple might. Maybe we had been becoming that comfortable couple. Maybe that possibility was what I missed as much as anything. Now I wouldn't know, or wouldn't know for a while. "I'll be back," she had said, and she kissed me.

"Two eggs easy, bacon—crispy—and hash browns," I said to Rosie, snapping back into the present. She smiled a genuine smile, popped her gum and searched in an apron pocket for a stub of tooth-marked pencil.

"Where's my breakfast, Rosie," someone called.

She raised both eyebrows at me, as though our moment had been intruded upon. "It's cookin'," she called over one shoulder, smiled at me apologetically and whirled away.

"I am here ... bring coffee," said William Stolz, custodian at the school, just arriving, nodding, greeting, and waving to Rosie for a pour. Unlike Andy, William always enjoyed and celebrated the coffee here. Like almost everybody in the place, William was a World War II veteran, except that he had served in the Russian army. There, he said, it was always a race to see whether the Germans could kill him before he froze to death or starved. He had learned about real coffee from his American allies, instead of some kind of terrible grain drink the Russians only called coffee and he'd been surviving on until liberation. Once he tasted genuine U.S. military coffee there was no turning back. He was bound for America! He drank it *clear*, as he called it, no sugar, no cream to dull the taste, and as hot as he could get it. Or not. Come to think of it I'd seen him just as happy over a cold cup.

Even though still a Russian citizen, he said he spent his evenings studying for American citizenship and, unlike a lot of natural-born Americans, truly loved this country and considered every day here a blessing—especially if coffee were served.

William displayed a hand fan of his ice pool tickets while sliding one arm out of his parka. More than six feet tall, he stood at least half a head taller than me and most of the villagers. He wore his steely-gray hair slicked back, and rimless glasses. William had seen so many truly horrific things in the war yet had somehow emerged the most positive person I knew. "I have a very good chance to win," he said, "in fact I have six very good chances." Pulling off his knit toque, hanging it on his chair back, he simultaneously pocketed his tickets while extending his mug for a fast Rosie pass with the coffee pot.

"You?" he asked.

I shook my head. "No tickets for me." Thinking of Mary I said, "I already won the lottery of life." William gave a little snort and wiped his drippy nose on his sleeve.

"But Father, you have God on your side." He sniffed then smiled slyly. "Or at least you *think* you do. Not to worry. If I will win, I will share."

And I knew he would.

"Singing the Blues" ended, exposing the room's various conversations in the unaccustomed silence, available to all. When nobody jumped up with a fresh quarter for three spins on the jukebox, Rosie pulled the plug and switched on the bright red plastic Philco. Fairbanks station KFAR swelled in on a wave of static, warming tubes, and Elvis Presley.

Presley had been a low-paid truck driver from Mississippi who somehow struck gold by selling a million copies of this tune, "Heartbreak Hotel." Some people said he would be bigger than Frank Sinatra or Perry Como. It was hard to imagine, though I liked his music. Maybe because I had lived much of my life in the South and the music sounded southern to the bone. Like the race tunes I used to pick up on the Philco late at night. Thumping up-tempo Negro tunes with heavy bass and drums. Tunes that stuck in your head or feet and made you want to break out whistling, dancing, or singing a chorus days later. But, bigger than Sinatra?

As if following my thoughts William said, "One *million* copies. Amazing!" He went back to studying his menu, which he also knew by heart, and when Rosie appeared with her pencil stub and notebook, ordered what he always did, biscuits and gravy with a side of the local moose meat sausage. Handing Rosie the menu he came back to the conversation. "You know, it is said he only went into that studio to record hymns for his mother. Now look what has happened!"

"What *has* happened?" I asked.

He has sold *this,* one million times, instead of selling hymns.

"I don't know what's wrong with that," I said, "except that when the hit parade ride ends it will be difficult to go back to driving truck. How many times can one person sell that many records?"

"Ha!" exclaimed William, as he often did. "The President—your President—Eisenhower, says this is godless, Communist music." He ducked his head confidentially. "Although Communists would hate it." And he summed it up. "An automatic ticket to the Gulag."

Just then Rosie arrived with plates of steaming breakfast and we set ourselves in silence to applying napkins, salting and peppering—and ketchup—William covered everything with ketchup.

Doris Day started up after an ad for the Northern Commercial Company. The smooth announcer voice assured us that round bear-paw snowshoes were now in stock—just as winter ended—and the new SureHold beaver traps, just in, were nearly a steal at two dollars each. But supplies were limited.

"A big one from Doris Day," the announcer said, "entitled *Que Sera Sera*, from a new Hitchcock film. Translated as 'Whatever will be, will be.'"

"Oooh," said William, entranced. "Doris Day, she is ... what are the words ... *my dream girl*. All pink and blond."

She certainly was pink and blond, and thinking about pink and blond soon brought me around to thinking about Mary. But from there, I went back to thinking about the metaphysics of "Whatever will be, will be." Could that be true? Was it all fate? What does 'what will be will be' say about prayer? Does it say *anything* about prayer? Does it say something about free will or fate? Was John Calvin right? *Are* some people predestined and damned in advance by God? Was my wife *always* supposed to die and was I always supposed to be sitting at this breakfast table without her?

I admit to not liking the notion and felt that *thing* tightening up inside me that always tightened up when I started wondering about her death. My day began to darken and even my hunger to fade. William, who knew me at least that well, gave me a look. *On the other hand,* I thought, trying to shake it off, *should I even consider moral implications in popular music, especially at breakfast?* Probably not. So from there my mental train ran completely off the track until Doris Day had long finished and half my breakfast was gone. I startled back into the room hearing my name spoken on the radio, on the *Tundra Topics* radio show, a kind of Alaskan Bush telegraph and the only way to communicate with remote villages and scattered settlers.

"... and to Father Hardy in Chandelar," said the voice, "meet Simon Nicolai at Chatanika on Thursday. Ask for directions at the Chatanika Trading Post. To Esther Charlie in Tanacross, your daughter Elsie had a six-pound baby girl. Mother and daughter are fine and will be home on next Wednesday."

"How *is* old Simon," said William, breaking what had become an extended silence.

-"The fact that he's sent for me makes me think he's not doing well, which surprises me. Last time I saw him, about a month ago, he seemed good."

25

"He's old though," said William. "Up in his seventies. But I had been thinking he was still in pretty good shape." He trailed off then said, "Want company?"

"No, I'm okay. It's not that far. About an hour beyond Fairbanks, unless the road washes out again."

William took a long slurp of coffee, sighed happily, and blotted his lips neatly on his napkin. "Lucky you moved your truck across the river."

That startled me. I hadn't told him about moving the truck. But then nobody had to tell William much. When something happened, he knew about it. And sometimes he knew about it even before it happened.

The small brass bell above the restaurant door jingled as the door opened and a flow of cool air shouldered aside the warm, moist, heavy food smells and cigarette smoke. I saw a few of the diners lift their heads and stretch their necks to get a look at the fresh arrival. I'd been living among Athabascans—people whose faces didn't show you much—long enough that I could tell when they deliberately weren't showing much. This was one of those times so I had to turn to look, too.

Since Chandelar is much too small to have a police force, and since the Alaska Territorial Police don't venture far from the highways, law enforcement in the small towns and in the Bush fell to the U.S. deputy marshals and this was one of them.

Because my line of work often has something to do with the dead or dying, whether by accident or by design, I already knew Marshal Frank Jacobs well enough to turn in my chair and wave him to the empty seat at our table.

He stood about five foot eight and appeared perpetually fit, cutting a snappy figure in official olive-drab and leather. Clean-shaven but neatly mustached, his steely blue eyes surveyed the room from behind military-issue, amber-framed spectacles, probably not missing much. He wore a service forty-five automatic in a flapped holster on his belt, which he had to twist out of his way a bit when he slid into his chair and accepted a cup of fresh-poured coffee from Rosie.

"I am certain you did not drive in," said William, nodding and lifting his heavy restaurant mug in salute.

"Flew," said the Marshal, who piloted his own Cessna to save the Territory the cost of an extra man. His parsimony famously extended to syllables as well. He ventured a cautious sip. "Called to Clear," he said, "Air Force problem." And then he offered wheels as his explanation as to how he was able to get here without landing on the river. He had exchanged the skis on the Cessna for fat rubber tires, and landed at the Chandelar airstrip, likely hitching a ride into town with one of the CAA people.

"Eggs. Easy," he said, turning to Rosie. "Bacon. Crisp." She smiled warmly, he nodded—but just once.

At Clear, Alaska, about twenty miles south of Chandelar, construction of a giant radar station was underway—part of the DEW Line early warning system. The Distant Early Warning Line, huge radar stations from Greenland and Iceland, all the way across arctic Canada and Alaska to the Aleutian Islands. It had been envisioned as the last line of defense, or maybe the first line, in what people were now calling our "cold" war with Soviet Russia.

Ironically, here in Alaska—right next to Russia—thinking about being attacked wasn't so much a part of the daily routine. But south of here, in the "states," fallout shelters were popular. School children practiced so-called 'duck-and-cover' drills for the day that blips on the DEW line radar screens turned out to be nuclear bombers inbound from the Soviet Union instead of Canada geese.

Marshal Jacobs shook his head, clearly frustrated.

"Calling a *marshal* for Air Force problems? That doesn't look good," I said.

"For spies," said Jacobs. "Called out to Clear about spies."

"Did they catch one?" William asked mildly, pushing his plate away. He hadn't finished, in fact had pushed his food away without even touching one of his moose-meat sausages. Not like him.

Jacobs looked both ways before speaking and then lowered his voice. "Damn fools think there are Russian spies here."

"In Chandelar?" I asked.

Jacobs gave me a look. "As though a damn Russian spy wouldn't stand out around here like a frost-bit thumb." I marveled. It was one of his longer sentences. He made eye contact. "Seen anything suspicious? Strangers?"

"I have personally seen them moving in," said William. Jacobs straightened, looked at him. "They arrive with spare trench coats and footlockers of disguises."

"Funny," said the marshal, relaxing. "That's what I told them. Just arrest newcomers. Who thinks of this stuff?" His look softened as Rosie slid his plate in front of him. He buttered his toast, salted and peppered his eggs and picked up his knife and fork, fork in the left hand for maximum feeding efficiency as he cut with the right.

"So," he said, "Ice Pool? Two more weeks?"

"The three of us agreed it would likely be two more weeks until breakup. As the moment slid by and the marshal devoted himself to breakfast, I watched William relax—so much that his appetite came back and he managed to reclaim his moose sausage just before Rosie might have swooped in to make it disappear forever.

Chewing, William's eyes met mine. I could imagine his thoughts. He'd moved here soon after the war, nine or ten years ago. He had a good job as custodian at the public school, was well known and much appreciated by kids for continuing to ring the bell until the last tardy student made it across the snowy playfield and into class. His bravery and marksmanship had saved my life earlier this winter.

Politics aside, I believed him to be a good man even though I knew him to be a Russian spy.

CHAPTER 4

Simon Nicolai's Chatanika cabin looked abandoned under an overcast gray sky. Mostly surrounded by skimpy birch and cottonwood trees, its bit of view consisted of mounds of old dredge tailings stretching off into the distance. "Simon?" I called out. No one answered.

This cabin had been something special in its day, more than just found logs quickly stacked and notched before the short summer ended. This one had been artfully constructed from larger, straight logs ripped to about six inches square and skillfully notched as tightly as toy Lincoln Logs at the corners. It stood about twenty-foot square with a corrugated metal roof, now mostly rusted. Wide overhangs all around allowed for plenty of dry firewood storage although snow here would likely drift this cabin all the way to its eaves. A door and window on the north side told me that wind and weather blew in from the south or southeast here, off the distant Bering Straits.

I called again, with no expectation of an answer. It felt beyond empty—desolate. Walking in, my year of woodcraft instruction from Andy had led me to notice the single line of human tracks headed out. My guess—the tracks had been made maybe as much as a week ago. I could guess the age of the tracks by noticing how the snow had time to melt to dirt in the middle of the footprint. The warmth of extra sunlight absorbed by the dark earth had rimmed each track with a clear ice outline. Newer tracks would show less melting.

So was this Simon's track? It seemed unlikely since I couldn't find the period-dot track of his walking stick alongside.

Someone had kicked open the door, a solid door made to resist anything from arctic blasts to marauding black bear. Whoever kicked it wasn't from around here, since no one from around here locked anything when they left. Every old-timer has a tale of being lost. Near frozen and desperate, he would happen on a cabin and stagger up to find it open, with some kind of basic food ready—like a tin of beans—with a fire laid in the woodstove and dry matches in a jar. No, this door-kicker hailed from elsewhere.

Kicking the door had only broken the sliding wood latch, leaving the door to shift and creak in the breeze. Once inside they turned the place upside down, even prying up random floor planks. It couldn't have been a long search. There was little furniture: a metal bed with flat springs and meager cotton mattress, now torn to ribbons and fluffs. There was also a table, the remains of two straight-back chairs and a stacked-up shelf of wooden Blazo boxes that originally contained pairs of five-gallon fuel cans. It was likely every cabin in central Alaska used a Blazo box for some kind of furniture.

Even the honeybucket, normally sequestered behind a drape in the corner, had been kicked over and kicked around—fortunately empty.

The intruder dumped contents of the Blazo shelves, mostly books and magazines, along with odd bits of busted furniture and other debris into a wide pile at the center of the room, as if for burning. I kicked through them with the toe of my Bean boot. There were vintage *National Geo-graphics*, an array of *Alaska Sportsman* magazines from the 1930s and '40s, old *Life* and *Look* magazines, and a few *Popular Mechanics*. Books included a pretty good collection of Dashiell Hammett thrillers with lurid pulp-style covers. I picked up one on top, gloving away its fine felt of dust to reveal book cover colors of vibrant yellow, blue, green, and especially blood red. One book lay open revealing a story called *Dead Yellow Women*, now crossed with an old trail of dry, seed-like mouse pellets. Other volumes included a well-worn King James Bible, a copy of Drieser's *The Financier* and a well-thumbed volume entitled *Stock Market Investing to Build Your Future*. I could see how stock market investment related to Dreiser's tale of a street railway tycoon, but how it related to Hammett's street-savvy shamus was less clear.

"Where are you Simon?" I asked the empty room. In spite of all the damage, I wasn't alarmed yet. After my first quick look for human remains or signs of a struggle, my heart rate slowed and my sense ebbed that something tragic occurred.

In fact, my more calculated guess, after another quick survey, was that he had left on his own. For one thing his guns weren't on the rack. It's true, someone could have stolen them, but his underwear and socks were gone too. Not that there wasn't anybody around who needed underwear or socks but not that many who would break into an unlocked cabin to make off with them. No. I was convinced Simon packed and left under his own power. But when? And why? Since he specifically asked me to meet him here now.

I drove up expecting to find a corpse. It happens to me a good deal on this job. Someone like Simon sends for me because he feels the clock of his life slowly ticking down. Many of my parishioners attended the mission school and expect last rites when they reach the end of the trail. Because of the nature of communication in the Bush, they send for me and I sometimes arrive after they've gone on. They get last rites anyway. Finding them like that is not such a terrible thing, especially in the cooler part of the year. I served as a medic in the European Theater, mostly in France, and have seen how really bad a body can get as a result of such variables as explosives or hot weather. But even though these Alaska corpses tended to be in better condition than those in wartime, I hadn't gotten used to how it left me feeling, in spite of my firm belief that each has gone to be with God and is in a better place.

I don't think it will ever be easy for me to encounter a physical body that's been shut down and abandoned—the lights off, the store-case of memories closed down and swept out—the laughter and tears all finished and everything so terribly quiet. It's especially true with people I've become close to, like Simon. I'm not sure I will ever get used to finding them so not at home.

Our first meeting began as many of mine do, with a soft tap on the inner door of the rectory at Chandelar. After a marginally productive hour spent on the next Sunday's sermon, I was looking for a break and couldn't have found a better diversion than Simon.

He came in the door leaning on a cane, moving slowly. I aimed him for the office guest chair, a Morris chair so old it appeared in turn-of-the-century photos of the young Bishop Rowe. About five foot seven, he didn't look like anybody so much as an Athabascan version of the dancer, Fred Astaire. Slim and almost dapper, he wore his hair in an uncharacteristic—for a man his age in the village—waxed crew cut, now gone to gray, and it was only up close that his parchment-smooth face revealed a weathered landscape of fine wrinkles.

"I was eighteen years," said Simon, "when Captain Rufus Edmonton hired me to go out on the river. A job for cash money. Weren't many of those then."

The old man pulled what turned out to be a surprisingly upscale cigar from the pocket of his blue plaid flannel shirt and fired it up. He had perfected the fine art of working the cigar from one side of his mouth to the other without actually putting his fingers on it. He did it by working his lips and the muscles in his face until the cigar deftly made its way across his mouth. He inhaled with great satisfaction, drawing acrid smoke deeply into lungs that must have been as hard as horsehide, then blew a series of smoke rings as big—or bigger than—New York bagels filling my small office with a thick cumulus of cigar smoke that, no matter how good the cigar, would make my whole cabin smell like an ashtray the next morning.

He nodded emphatically. "Eighteen ninety-eight," he said. "Worked for nearly fifty years on

34

steamboats on the Tanana and the Yukon. I been all the way from the Klondike to the Bering Straits, many times."

"Were you a deck hand?" I asked. Simon shook his head.

"Worked inside, started as a cabin boy for the Captain, worked up to purser. The old man said when he got to the gold field his whole crew came down with gold fever. Couldn't run the boat without them. When he couldn't keep a white crew, said he'd hire natives. Turned out to be mostly Athabascan. That's how I started out." He smiled, inhaling cigar smoke through his nostrils as if he couldn't get enough.

"Pretty soon, I did everything but steer." He thought about that a minute. "Did some steering, too. 'Specially if the old man had been drinking. Done pretty good for an Indian. That's what the old man said."

So we had agreed that I would come out here, to his cabin, near the end. He would get word to me, as he had. So now here I am at his cabin but where is he? And I wasn't the only one looking. About two weeks after our conversation, someone called.

"Looking for Simon Nicolai," the voice said.

"He's not here," I told him. "Have you tried his cabin in Chatanika?"

"Yeah," said the voice. "Know any way to get a message to him?"

"Only the Tundra Times."

"You sure?"

"That's all I know," I told him. I admit the 'You sure?' gnawed at me a little. Back to thinking about that, I closed Simon's door and tied it shut with a length of found leather boot lace, to keep out wild animals. Then I walked a slow circle around the cabin looking for the rest of the tracks. I quickly found tracks of three large, most likely white men—judging by the size of their feet in large rubber boots—the pebbled imprint of a distinctive rubber sole still frozen and clear. Meaning they had arrived and departed from the south more recently than the footprints I'd followed in from the east. Could it really be a coincidence that Simon gets a visit yesterday or last night, and I have a tall man in rubber boots tailing me across the ice very early this morning? Or maybe not so coincidental since nearly everybody in Alaska with a radio knew I'd be headed this way.

So, I'm wondering, can these two creepy events possibly be related? Last fall, when I found the body of a murdered local thug—frozen, spread-eagled in a snow-drift—I experienced for the first time in my life the nearly overwhelming sense of a bull's-eye gradually appearing on my back. As though someone crouching like a sniper, just out beyond the tree line, might slowly be sighting me in. Now I felt like that again and found myself looking back over first one shoulder and then the other. No snipers to be seen. But I didn't know who might want to do all this and I didn't know why. Yes, I might be paranoid, but as they say, even paranoids have enemies.

Satisfied I'd seen everything there was to see, I started back up the trail toward my truck. Ahead on my right, from a clump of stunted black swamp spruce, a ptarmigan exploded into flight, wings beating noisily away. I didn't have long to wonder what spooked the bird. A tall man stepped out onto the trail, not the man who tailed me across the river, but it looked like they might do their shopping together. He wore a long, dark coat, a stateside brimmed hat and rubber overshoes. He smiled a greeting but it was a smile that didn't get anywhere near his eyes. And even his simple act of stepping out onto the trail, standing at the center to block it completely, radiated menace.

"I'm looking for my friend, Simon Nicolai," the man said, "have you seen him?"

"I'm looking for him, too. Looks like we both missed him."

He shook his head sadly. "Why do I think you're lying to me?" He pulled a nasty-looking sap out of his pocket, a small leather sack, likely filled with sand or birdshot, and he smacked it in a slow, meaningful rhythm against his leather-gloved hand."

Since I'd seen three sets of tracks I wondered where the others were. One thug I might be able to manage, but not three. I appreciated that he hadn't pulled a gun, like the last one, but maybe the gun would still appear.

"If I were lying to you, and I'm not, why would I come out to this empty, trashed cabin and walk around calling Simon's name?" The question seemed to confuse him.

He took a step toward me. "I'm not going to ask you again. Don't think I won't cold-cock a priest."

Since I hadn't said I was a priest, and wearing my parka it would be impossible to see the white collar and black shirt, I now knew for sure our meeting wasn't accidental. He knew I'd be coming out here and knew when, so he came out to wait for me.

He carried the sap confidently, like the two of them were accustomed to confronting people who weren't carrying saps and having their way.

It rubbed me wrong. I had been a boxer through seminary, in fact it's how I met Mary. Late one night in the third round of a Chattanooga smoker, a fighter named Lefty Grizzard, from Soddy Daisy, Tennessee—really—put me down hard on my back.

Lying there with a severe case of the whirlies, I rolled my head over to see a pale, angelic presence just a few feet away at ringside. Her lovely face floated above spatters of my blood on the stained canvas and I saw her lips move. She said get up. The funny thing is, even through the racket I've always thought I actually heard her voice, so much so, that later in the evening, when she came back to the dressing room, I already knew how she sounded. But she never believed me. 'Get up,' she said, and I did, walloping Lefty, winning a fat seventy-five-dollar purse for the evening, and meeting the future love of my life. Does it get any better!

I know people who think it strange that I worked my way through divinity school boxing. Though only about five foot eight, to this fellow's— I'm guessing six foot two—I had carried away some very good prize cash from tall, overconfident, somewhat slow-witted opponents.

This guy? Slow-witted maybe, but not slow. Cat quick he took a step forward in the rhythm of his hand slapping and nearly caught me hard on my right shoulder. That would be bad, though I had a pretty good left when I was training. I stepped back, which surprised him. His quick swing missed me completely and he had to fight to keep his balance on the slippery trail surface. I saw something flicker in his eyes. He wasn't used to missing. I easily imagined his fresh resolve to not miss again.

"You got lucky," he hissed. I let that one go, and decided to try jabbing back.

"Too bad about your friend on the ice," I said to him. "Ex-friend."

"My ex-friend? You talkin' 'bout Dave? He's the one went to Chandelar to pick up your trail. What about him?"

"Gone," I said. "Tough break. The ice went out with him standing on it, holding that pistol of his. He's probably feeding the wolves downriver somewhere. Not that he cares anymore if they tear him to pieces."

For all his tough-guy demeanor, this thug couldn't help wincing at the thought of the other guy—Dave—being torn apart by wild animals. Not from around here, I guessed. He went back to slapping his hand with the blackjack, but seemed to have lost a bit of his cockiness.

"I don't want to hurt you," he said, but I didn't believe him. He had something about him that made me think he *did* want to hurt me, and planned to start soon. I saw him try to set his feet on the slippery trail then give it up and go into a kind of crouch. "Last chance," he said.

Instead of coming straight for me, he reared up to his full height, blackjack arm extended tall so that he could bring it crashing down on the top of one of my shoulders, putting me down and out of commission. I'm sure the move terrorized widows and orphans, but anyone with boxing experience saw an open, unprotected gut. Which is where I landed a couple of hard right and left jabs that drove the wind out of him, and folded him over so far and so fast that his blackjack completely missed me and thudded on frozen ground. Trying to stay out of his downstroke lost me the chance at an uppercut, but I was able to put a forearm on the back of his neck, driving his face all the way into trail ice while his feet shot out behind him. I put my foot on the back of his neck making it hard for him to breathe in the trench his nose had plowed.

"You're gudda be berry sorry for this," he mumbled, the ice and mud playing heck with his enunciation. "I'm gudda tear ya to bieces. Yu'll be wishing for wolves. Ya know you godda led me up somedime."

"What makes you think that?" I asked him. The question startled him, especially all spread-eagled on his face on a lonely snowy trail miles from anywhere, with my boot on the back of his neck. I could have a gun or a knife at his back for all he knew. He suddenly went very still.

"You know I was just toggin'," he said. "Just tryin' to scare a little info oudda ya. C'mon now. A guy's got a job to do. I'm just tryin' to find my friend. You startled me. Wudden expectin' ya."

"Sure you were," I said. "You heard on the radio I'd be coming up here. You were waiting."

"Wull, yeah," he protested. "Yeah, bud I thought you wudden 'ere yet. Hey, man, I can't breed! C'mon, lemme up."

"Just tell me," I said, "why you tore the place apart? What were you looking for?"

"We din't do that," he mumbled, "it was like thad." I noticed he said 'we.'

"So where are the others?"

"Whad others? There wadden any others. Jus' me. C'mon man, led me up."

He was such a bad liar and sounded so pathetic I took pity on him and took my foot off the back of his neck. Not surprisingly he came off the ground like a coiled spring, fists rising and ready to strike, when I turned his head with my right cross and flattened his nose with the left. He went down and stayed down, lights out.

I can't deny it felt good to be fighting—and winning—again, but knocking him out severely limited any chance of getting more information. I rolled him on his side to keep him from choking on his nose blood and headed off up the trail.

I quickly found his car, an Army-styled Willys Jeep, parked a few hundred feet farther along the road, out of sight around a bend. Unlatching the hood I yanked his coil wire and gave it a toss into a grove of stunted spruce, stamping out an arrow in the snow so he'd know which direction to start looking. Worst case if he didn't find it would be a mile hike back down the highway toward Fairbanks to the Chatanika Trading Post. He wouldn't have any trouble knowing the place as he had surely stopped there to ask for directions on his way out.

I gave my pickup truck a quick once-over to make sure no one had left any surprises for me, and finding none, turned the Ford for Fairbanks.

In just a couple of hours, melt on the gravel road seemed to have lifted it from a glaze of packed snow and ice. I was able to push my speed as high as forty-five on a couple of straight stretches. So I'm driving, playing the whole thing back and forth like a tennis ball in my brain.

I now knew these guys weren't looking for me, they were looking for Simon. Why? Why would a stateside-type guy with a blackjack have any reason to know Simon existed, an old man who spent his entire working life on Alaskan steamboats? Talk about the twain never meeting. And to make matters even odder, the big dumb guy back at the cabin was pretty sure I knew where Simon was and would tell him. Wrong on both counts, but no less perplexing.

Okay, so next step. These bad guys are already looking for Simon. Then when they and everyone else within broadcast range hear on the radio that Simon is sending for me, they get the bright idea to follow me, expecting I'll lead them right to him.

On the other hand, maybe they rigged this whole thing: they somehow knew he was going to send for me and when they couldn't find him, sent for me themselves. That made sense. Except how could these guys know what we had privately discussed?

And then there's the cabin itself. The cabin bothered me, too. Even a quick look around made it clear Simon hadn't been there for quite a while. There was a layer of thick dust on everything, old trails of dried mouse pellets, and even rust in the cast iron skillets. Mr. Blackjack denied he and his buddies trashed the cabin. If they were telling the truth, then somebody tossed it before they got there. And if Simon wasn't at the cabin where he said he'd be, where was he?

I slowed to miss a moose crossing the highway, nearly stopping the Ford, ready to jam it into reverse and evade. He turned his head to squint at me as he passed but didn't change course and didn't lower his rack. A full five feet, tip to tip, big bulls like this had been known to total mere vehicles and walk away.

Another minute or two, with the moose safely out of sight in the willows, I had shifted up, accelerating away as it all fell into place. If Simon knew these guys were after him, and he wasn't here but sent for me anyway, then he sent for me knowing these guys would do what they did. In the end that's what bothered me most.

Had Simon set me up?

CHAPTER 5

*T*he bishop met me at his door before I could knock, a thin man in a gray suit, black shirt, and clerical collar, with a fringe of graying hair framing a pinkish bald top.

"We need to talk," he said, "before..." And that's when the telephone started ringing.

"It's for you," he said—nearly snarled—startling me. "Evangeline Williams calling again, long distance from Seattle. She's already called four times," he looked at his wristwatch, "in the last three hours. She says she's in Seattle and she's in *trouble!*" He put a curious emphasis on the word 'trouble.'

I stared at him for a long minute, not quite processing his message to me, and the pointedly unpleasant way he delivered it. The bishop had liked me, hired me, had been consistently quite congenial and nearly charming every time I'd seen him—until now. All this I juggled while the phone jangled harshly in the background.

"Well?" he said. "Delay won't help now. You must talk to her."

"She's in trouble?"

"That's what I've been saying." He pointed to the phone. So I picked up the handset.

"Hello?"

Distantly I heard the tinny, unnaturally nasal voice of the long distance operator. "Person–to-person-call for Father Hardy from Evangeline Williams. Will you accept the charges?"

"Yes of course, operator," I said, making a mental note to reimburse the charges.

It's hard to describe how good hearing her voice felt. It had only been about four months since we'd said goodbye and I put her on the Pan Am Clipper bound for Seattle and the University. Something settled in me, hearing her, like a missing piece dropping into place. I flashed on the first time I'd ever seen her, knocking softly, stepping into my office, studying book titles on my shelves—she turned out to be a voracious reader—unusual for the village. I remembered her shiny, softly curly black hair, dark skin, warm brown eyes, and not so much a smile as a luminous glow. And of course there's nothing like nearly being murdered together to help forge a bond.

"I'm in trouble, Hardy," she said, and I could hear the underlying stress in her voice. "Don't talk. I'm supposed to read this to you. It says, 'get on the plane this afternoon or the girl dies.' That's me, Hardy" she said. "I'm the girl. Just like in the movies." I could hear her voice quiver and she did her best to suppress a sob. "I'm babbling."

"It's okay," I said. "I get it. Is there more?"

She took a breath and continued reading. "'You're to bring Simon Nicolai, or know where he is *or*'—this part is smeared—'the girl gets it.' That's still me," she added. "Hardy?"

"Yes?"

"I'm a little scared."

"Yeah, I know, me too. But it's good to hear your voice. How serious does this seem?"

"Very," she said. "I have a gun stuck in my..." she gave a little sort of grunt. "He says get on the plane, and when you get to Seattle, go to the water-front and get on the the Ka-*lack*-a-lah ... the ferry to Bainbridge Island, and when you get there ask for Lizzie Ann, and..."

"Lizzie Ann who?" I said. But that was it. I heard a sharp metallic click and the line went dead. I'd lost her. Slowly, deep in thought, I settled the handset back in its cradle.

"She *is* in trouble," I said.

"And I must say," said the bishop indignantly, bringing me up sharply, "I don't appreciate being the last to know. And you of all people, a priest with the honor and good name of yourself, of the village, the mission and of the church—and now you've gone and gotten yourself in a mess like this." He turned on me with wrath. "What have you to say for yourself?" The top of his head flushed bright red.

That's when I realized that he and I were trains on totally different tracks.

"Not in *trouble*," I snapped back, my tone a bit loud and sharp, considering this was not just my employer I was talking to, but my bishop. "Not *trouble* trouble, not pregnant—in danger. Kidnapped! Held at gunpoint." And I repeated the gist of the call with all its scary details.

"Oh my," said the bishop, much more quietly, visibly deflating, his scalp slowly fading back to pink. "And to think, I was concerned about her being pregnant. This is much worse. I see that now. He tilted his head thoughtfully, wrinkling his forehead. "I remember baptizing Evangeline at the Old Mission, confirming her, too." More headshaking. "I suppose we had better figure it all out then, hadn't we. And make sure to get you on that airplane." He looked out the window as if help might be on the way. "If only Andy were here," he said, as though reading my mind.

Hours later, installed in a window seat on the Super Constellation, I watched drifting silvery cigarette smoke thread rays of piercing sunlight. Beneath us, the Alaska Range fell away, distant and blue through the high atmosphere, as the bishop's parting words played again in my ear. In spite of the roar of those four huge propeller engines I could hear him clearly. "I know you are not without talents and abilities," he said. "I have my sources and have heard about that nasty business in Chandelar earlier this winter. I am aware that you made it right. You saved your friends and protected your parishioners. That's a big part of why we're here." Then he looked at me directly and set his jaw. "Go with God." "Do what you have to do."

Do what you have to do, I thought again. Why did that sound so ominous? If only Andy *were* here. What would he do? What Andy *could* do, an ex-sniper and the best marksman I'd ever seen, was to shoot the buttons off a wrong-doer from so far away that they still thought they were doing fine until they weren't. But as a priest, in the business I'm in, I still prefer to think, or to hope that alternatives to shooting people exist. Possibilities like appealing to innate goodness, considering examples from the teachings of Jesus, Mohammad or Ghandi, or at the extreme, maybe an instructive punch in the nose just to get someone's attention and to put them in the proper frame of mind for self-improvement.

From there I went back to thinking about Andy, which got me to wondering where he would look for Simon. For there could be little doubt that all of this tracked back to something involving Simon. But what? Clearly someone had been trying to find the old man and failing that, had switched to finding me, with the notion that I knew where he was. So they tried following me, tried asking me directly then threatening me. Now that I'd proved 'uncooperative,' They'd found Evie instead, trying to leverage her to get me to tell them about Simon—information I might possibly have given them anyway if I'd known. Well, maybe not.

What to do first? Obviously fly to Seattle. Next step of course would be to find this Lizzie Ann and if nothing else, attempt to reason with her. Whatever was going on shouldn't involve or endanger Evie.

So what about Evie? Was it love between us? Could I really be in love with two women, one living and one dead? Mary had warned me about the possibility. "I'm dead, Hardy, move on," she said. For a while I thought I couldn't. Then meeting Evie, getting to know her, and nearly dying with her on the ice, I began to believe I might. It's a fact that hearing Evie say my name after these months apart changed my heart rate. What does it mean that I had to be near to dying before I could allow myself the possibility of being in love with the living?

It's for the best, I told myself when she went off to Seattle to the University. And now, suddenly just when I might have been getting used to life without her, even the idea of her in danger again gave me a sick feeling. Maybe I'd been crazy to let her get away. But maybe where she went wasn't a bit of my business.

The irony? There was a time, not so long ago, when I never imagined I'd find even one woman to be in love with. I had seminary—boxing—I even thought of joining a monastery. Well, not a lot.

Andy had warned me about getting involved with an Indian girl. Making the point, at least one too many times, that a Caucasian priest would never get the 'big parish' in the lower forty-eight with an Indian wife. Not that I ever said or even thought that I wanted such a parish. I never chose how to feel about her. When I thought I might lose her forever it's just how I felt.

I thought back—again—to our brief telephone conversation, and remembered the quiver in her tone. She wasn't a person who quivered easily. I kept hearing her say "... or the girl gets it. That's me, Hardy, I'm the girl."

So I fidgeted as the flight took forever, landing in Anchorage, then Juneau, then refueling at Annette Island in Southeast Alaska. Though I knew we were traveling at several hundred miles an hour, I didn't feel like we were moving at all. I hadn't brought a book, didn't smoke, couldn't sleep more than fitfully, and with the seat next to me empty, couldn't pass the time making small talk with a complete stranger.

Finally, just after midnight, the big airplane set smoothly down on the runway at the Seattle Tacoma International Airport. I could feel my heart rate quicken as the tires bit into the tarmac, let out a high-pitched chirp, and we settled smoothly back to earth. Now I could get out and do something instead of just sitting. I clicked out of my seat belt as soon as the plane came to a halt, stood up quickly and lined up in the aisle with everybody else who was in a hurry to get off the plane and get out and do something. Not that there likely would be much to do in a small northwestern city in the middle of the night.

In spite of the pretentious name, Seattle Tacoma *International* Airport, it was a pleasant enough place to land airplanes. Unsealing the airtight door simul-taneously released the cigarette-smoke-saturated stale air while allowing entry of fresh, cool, moist air that carried in just a tinge of saltwater and the shore. And one more thing that I'd forgotten after most of a year in Alaska: the scent of summer. Even from within the belly of this beast I smelled flowers and cottonwood trees and the nearly forgotten scent of pavement-warmed air, and just a hint of aviation fuel.

"Stewardess, can we light up?" came the pathetic voice of a cigarette addict who had been forced to extinguish his smoke most of fifteen minutes ago.

"Good grief no!" said the stewardess in an instant of candor. Our eyes met and she smiled a brief, it's-after-midnight-and-I've-been-on-my-feet-all-day' warm, genuine smile, the first of the trip. Blond, fair-skinned and blue-eyed, all done up in sleek Pan Am blue, she switched on the microphone in her hand and, in her well-modulated airplane voice, reminded the fifty-some of us to please keep all cigarettes and cigars unlit until we had passed safely through the terminal doors. She smoothly recited the piece from memory, her eyes never leaving mine—until the requisite benediction: "And thank you for flying Pan Am." And then with a small shrug she turned to move beyond my view into the galley.

"Bitch," said the would-be smoker, and laughed too loudly. His friends looked uncomfortable. It was clear now that he'd been drinking on the flight while I was stewing. I thought briefly and uncharitably about knocking him down the stairs but then gave it up when I imagined myself in the Seattle jail for assault, phoning the bishop for bail, and the mug shot of the man in the clerical collar who went berserk on the midnight plane from Fairbanks. Probably a drinker. And all of that while I should have been on my way to Bainbridge Island—wherever that might be—to save Evie.

Still, when you're a priest, you're supposed to at least aim for the higher moral ground. Not just be safe and still. Of course that's why a goodly number of us have lived shorter lives and died badly, returning to our heavenly home on the express bus. I thought of the line from the hymn: *And one was slain by a fierce wild beast*, though probably not by a drunken smoker on an airplane.

"Don't be a jerk," I said, as I pulled abreast. He tried an unsteady spin but ended up just staggering in place. He was too far gone to cause real trouble, large, unshaven, reeking of cigarettes, sweat, and booze. He launched into a line of aggressive mumbling but couldn't even sustain that, grinding down at last to the obligatory, "Sorry Father. Jus' needed a smoke."

Sure he did. He looked like a vet. Most of us did. And during the war, the tobacco companies gave out cigarettes for free. Now I know why. A whole generation of American soldiers came home unable to *not* smoke. What I had mistaken in wartime for an act of benevolent patriotism turned out to be an amazingly effective ad campaign. What had started out free in Europe now cost the ex-G.I. a full quarter at the machine. A quarter! There were places you could still get a whole sandwich for a quarter. Shaking off my tobacco rant I gave the man a pat on the back and started down the rolling airstairs. Although he'd behaved poorly it was me who had been unkind: I knew better. It's my job to know better. The jerk was me.

I'd been through the Seattle terminal just the one time, headed north nearly a year ago to assume my Chandelar mission post. Still adrift after Mary's death, I can now admit to traveling the whole twenty-five hundred miles from Chattanooga in a personal haze of grief. So I remembered very little of the trip and nothing of the Seattle terminal.

After nearly a year of living in and being around one-story log cabins and tarpaper shacks, the expansive, modern Seattle-Tacoma Airport building glistened and gleamed whitely in moonlight. Shaped like a massive bird, the tall control tower stood at center where the bird's head might have been, and two brightly-lit glassy concourses extended on either side like squared-off wings. I couldn't help but stop and stare up, remembering only to close my mouth so I didn't look like a total rube. And that's when she came up behind me and lightly took my arm.

"Been in the Bush awhile, Father?" asked the stewardess.

"Oh no," I said. "It's that obvious?"

"It's the looking up," she said. "All you Alaskans come Outside and stare up at the tall buildings. We stood alone together on the expanse of tarmac in half light and gathering silence as the other passengers and attendants flowed by us and on into the terminal. You seem a bit..." she chose her word, "lost. Someone picking you up?"

I wasn't sure what to say. "I'm..." I said. "It's complicated. I suppose I am lost. Never been here before and not entirely sure where I'm going. Can you point me to a cab?"

She hesitated, drew a breath in and then out slowly through her nose, considering. "I'll be your cab," she said. "I'm headed into the city. I think you'd wait a long time for a cab out here this time of night. I'm Ellen," she said, though I knew it from her brass name badge, "and you're Father Hardy." Her eyes flicked downward just a beat. "I noticed it on the manifest. Thanks for that back there."

"He was just drunk and being stupid."

"I know," she said. She gave my arm a gentle pull. "C'mon."

Instead of entering the main terminal, she led me through a side entrance, across the concourse, out an 'employee-only' door and across a restricted parking area, at this hour only about a quarter filled.

"Here she is!" she said with audible pride and made a sweeping gesture, all the more gracious with her white-gloved hand, at a brand-new 1956 Chevy Bel Air Hardtop, the extra-sleek model Chevy calls the Sports Sedan. The car was white over sky blue, just a shade lighter, but not a lot different than the Pan Am blue of her uniform. *Not an accident*, I thought.

"It's wonderful," I said. And it was, especially the new-car smell. And in the face of her obvious joy and pride of ownership, what else *could* you say? She keyed on the ignition and the car started so quickly I didn't even hear it turn over. Then it rumbled quietly—obviously the V8 option—while true to form, Ellen directed me to fasten my seat belt. Another of the car's new features.

Switching on the headlights, she shifted into drive and gently pushed the accelerator. She blew an airy kiss to the security guard at the employee gate and we eased out past the taxi stand and into the exit lane.

Ellen had been right. No cabs waited after midnight, only a man loitering near the main terminal door, face mostly buried in the *Seattle Post-Intelligencer*.

The dazzle of the Chevy's headlights kept him from seeing our faces, but he carefully eyed the car before returning to his newspaper.

People often ask me about prayer and particularly about whether God answers our prayers and how we can know for sure. I knew for sure when I saw the lone man waiting at the taxi stand. Back in Chandelar, with the Tanana River breaking up and massive sheets of ice grinding, gnashing and roaring into motion, it had been his life I prayed to save.

CHAPTER 6

*W*ith the windows rolled down and the night air warm and fragrant, the Chevy purred effortlessly down Route 99 at a steady fifty-five miles per hour. Ahead of us, about twenty miles distant, city lights rose into the darkened sky until they met stars. One building stood taller than any of the rest, the Smith Tower. Ellen, in tour-guide mode, enjoyed pointing it out, telling me it had been the tallest building west of the Mississippi since 1914. After my year in Chandelar, they all looked tall.

Leaving the airport Ellen turned the radio on, the night deejay nattering about baseball. "I need music," Ellen said, and started pushing the chromed select buttons on the radio face. We came in on the end of Perry Como's "Hot Diggity," and after a word about Colgate Dental Cream, Dean Martin's "Memories Are Made of This" came oozing from the speakers. My wife had liked Dean but I was always a sucker for his annoying, nutty partner, Jerry.

I'm such a long way from home, I found myself thinking. Chandelar as 'home' took me by surprise. I thought of being there now, sleeping in my squeaky bed in my chilly log cabin. Then unexpected, came the memory of Evie curled up beside me, properly outside the covers, to be sure. She had stayed over one night last winter, after someone had broken in and trashed the place. I admit the break-in had been a shock and I must have looked as exhausted—and as depressed—as I felt.

"Look," Evie had said, "I usually stay up most of the night. Why don't you crawl into bed—you look bushed—and let me just clean up here until I do get tired. Okay?"

In the morning I woke up to the warm lump of her next to me and the soft scent of her hair. A funny thing to think about now. We had never talked about it and I think we had both been careful to make sure the moment never repeated itself. Gossip spread like wildfire in the village.

"It's so summery," I murmured to Ellen, who just smiled, intent on her driving. I had shed my jacket. After Alaska, riding at night in an open car, in shirt sleeves seemed unreal. I couldn't help remembering that yesterday morning's temperature in Fairbanks had been thirty-three degrees. It had to be mid-seventies here now.

I must have been smiling—until I thought of Evie, what she must be going through—and the smile slipped away from my face. Ellen noticed. Even with her careful driving she had managed to keep a close eye on me. "You thought of something," she said. "Something serious?"

"Yes, serious. A friend in trouble."

"Bad?"

"I think so."

"And that's why you're here."

I nodded. "Yes."

"Can I help?"

I looked at her and couldn't help smiling. She seemed so young and fresh, and at that moment very serious. "You are helping."

She sat up a little straighter, gripping the wheel with both hands. She had taken off her white gloves, and her Pan Am jacket, revealing a long-sleeved white blouse, its sleeves dancing and shifting in the breeze. She drove deliberately and would occasionally chance a glance or a comment, but her focus was on driving.

"So," she said after another song, "how long have you been a priest?"

I told her about my ordination a year and a half earlier, about my trip from Tennessee to Alaska, and a little about life in Chandelar. I avoided mentioning the murder I'd been forced to solve, and attempts on my life related to it. Instead, I talked about the people and the weather, about getting used to extreme cold and going without some of the comforts of stateside living.

"Do you have a hotel reservation?" she asked.

"No. I didn't know I would be heading this way until just before I got on the airplane. But I'm sure I can find something."

"Here's an idea. Why don't you overnight at my place? Quick, easy—comfortable—and the price is right." She laughed, maybe a little nervously, as if she wasn't used to bringing priests home.

"That's very kind of you," I said, "if you're sure."

"I am sure," she replied, in a way that made it all sound settled.

"Look at that!" I pointed at a gas station built under a huge cowboy hat, right next to an outbuilding constructed to look like a cowboy boot. "Nothing like that in Chandelar." She smiled.

"What's it like," she asked, taking a breath as though diving, "to never marry and to know you never will?"

"I don't know," I said, and might have felt the car swerve a little.

"But you're a priest!"

"An Episcopal priest. We marry. I *was* married but my wife died before I left seminary."

"Oh," she said. We drove in silence as Gogi Grant sang "The Wayward Wind" and an ad for Vitalis Hair Crème came on. "Who says men don't care about their hair?" said the announcer.

"I was thinking ..." she said, then paused.

"That giving a ride to a priest—a Catholic priest—seemed pretty safe? Now you're not sure." She smiled apologetically.

"My wife would tell you I'm harmless," I said, "but of course she's not here. Look, I don't want you to feel uncomfortable. You've already helped me more than you know. You can just let me out downtown and I'm sure I can find a hotel."

She turned and stared at me hard for several seconds. It was the longest I'd seen her take her eyes off the road and it made me wish I had a spare steering wheel, like an airplane co-pilot. Finally she let out her breath like she'd made her decision. "I assume you'll be okay on my couch?"

"I'll be fine," I said. "It sounds wonderful." I was settling back, relaxing a bit when she nailed me.

"Does this have something to do with the man waiting at the taxi stand?" I must have startled. "I thought so," she said. "Tell me."

So I did tell her. What could it matter? Okay, I left out the part about Mary waking me up. But I told her about crossing the ice, being followed, and the ice breakup. And I told her about Simon's wrecked cabin and the blackjack thug, and finally about the bishop, and about having to get on a ferry and go to some island to rescue Evie.

"Holy cow."

"How did you know about the man at the airport," I asked.

"You ducked as we drove by. Not a lot but I noticed it. I watch people for a living. They think I'm serving their food and pouring their drinks and lighting up their smokes. But I'm actually watching them. I know who's not with his wife and who is leaving Alaska for good. I know who's happy, who's sad, who's sick." She shrugged. "I notice."

By now we had passed through the downtown area of Seattle. I saw a tall building in the middle of it topped with red neon, the Roosevelt Hotel, and wondered if there was a city in America that didn't have a Roosevelt. I got a sudden fresh breath of salty air and in almost the same instant heard a big boat whistle close by.

"Elliot Bay," she said. "Puget Sound is just a couple of blocks down. That's where you'll find your Bainbridge Ferry. I'll take you there tomorrow."

Another ten minutes brought us to a turnoff by a darkened restaurant constructed to look like two Indian teepees—fittingly called the Twin Teepees. We turned off the highway by a sign that pointed to Green Lake, not that we needed a sign, it was right there, ringed by a boulevard lined with small, well-built houses. Frogs called from the lakeshore, just across the street from the early 1930s bungalow that Ellen called home.

"It feels like I'm back in America," I said to Ellen, but she had gone around the back of the house to let us in. Except for being maybe a bit cooler, it felt like nights that Mary and I had spent on a small lake at a little rented cabin in eastern Kentucky, back when we had a life. Lights flicked on and the front door opened. "Well, come on in," said Ellen, seemingly relaxed and more expansive now that she was off duty and already unbuttoning her blouse. She headed for the privacy of her bedroom, calling out over her shoulder, "there's a beer for you in the refrigerator, open one for me, too, please."

I looked at my watch. Close to 2:00 a.m. Way after my bedtime, but probably just unwinding time for someone who worked a late shift. Stifling a yawn I made my way down a short hall leading toward the back of the house and in just a few steps found the kitchen. I pushed the light button, illuminating a bright yellow kitchen that looked like something in a magazine. The refrigerator was a GE, large and nearly new. This model had a freezer on top with its own door, rather than having to open the whole door and then get into the freezer. It looked good to me. But then I keep anything I want frozen on my back porch where the winter temperature averages minus thirty-five.

The labels on the short stubby brown bottles of *Olympia* beer boasted of being brewed right here in the Seattle area. I discovered the drawer containing the opener on my second try. It might have been all kind of pleasant except for feeling anxious about Evie and it being the middle of the night after a very long, trying day.

"Let's sit in here," Ellen called from the living room. It was another room fit for a magazine. She indicated a seat next to her on a fashionably gray sofa with a short, bristly fabric. She had changed out of her work uniform to a gray, loose-fitting cotton sweater worn long, and a pair of blue denim jeans, the kind Mary used to call 'girl jeans' with the zipper on the hip, tapered to a pedal pusher length and worn with low gold slippers. She stretched her legs out on the coffee table, crossed a trim, elegant pair of ankles, sipped her beer and sighed. "Does anything feel as good as just coming home?"

She wanted to know about the man at the airport taxi stand, and how could I be sure it was really him on the ice?

"I saw his face clearly," I said. "A moment like that is not one you forget."

"I wouldn't," she said dramatically, then laughed, drained her beer and went for more.

"So what I don't get," she said later, "is why you don't just tell these people where this Simon is, and then they'll just let Evelyn go."

"Evie," I said. "Evangeline."

"Yeah, her," said Ellen.

"Because I have no idea where he is."

"And you don't know why they're looking for him?"

"Haven't a clue."

"But he told you to meet him."

"Yes, but he wasn't there."

"So what are you going to do?"

"I don't *know* what to do. I hope I'm going to find Evie and convince whoever is holding her that I don't know what they want to know and that they should let us both go."

"But they said they'd kill her," she said, the beer beginning to make her very serious.

"Yes, they did. That's what troubles me."

It took a while but I finally managed to steer the conversation away from Evie and Simon and what I could possibly do tomorrow. Right now I didn't have a lot of confidence I'd be able to do anything.

So we began to talk about her job and her house. She didn't have a boyfriend, she said, had never had a real one. She had been a stewardess for five years and saved every penny to buy, first the house and then the brand-new car. She described herself as a 'career gal,' a new breed. She was in no hurry to marry or have a family—"Oh, there'll be plenty of time for a husband and children later"—she wanted to experience life.

She wanted to know more about Mary, a story I now felt I had told too many times. Mary lived, she was wonderful, we made plans, she died quickly and I have come on alone. Women are always sympathetic to it. Men are uncomfortable, as they often are with emotions. Strangely, it often seemed to make women desire sex, just as it made men want to talk about baseball or cars or look for a men's room.

And although we didn't start out sitting closely together, as time wore on, and one beer turned into more, I noticed we kept getting closer. I would inch away and she would follow. I could feel the warmth of her along my side, smell her perfume and her hair, more than a little aware of elbows and arms brushing and the general intimacy of the late hour with a beautiful young woman and more alcohol than I was used to.

At about four she turned to me. Our faces were suddenly way too close and her eyes very wide and blue. I felt the way a late evening commuter must feel, standing on the platform after the last train has left the station. Like it had suddenly grown too late. It had. "Do you want to kiss me?" she whispered. It's a silly question to ask a man, any man, any time. The answer is always 'yes,' but I wasn't foolish enough to say it.

It didn't matter. She quickly began kissing me before I had a chance to explain why we shouldn't. It was interesting to note she had come to grips with her discomfort about me being a priest.

I managed to get my arms between us and gently disengage. She looked dazed. "I thought guys liked kissing?" she said.

"Kissing *is* nice, but..."

"You mean you want to make love now?" she asked, looking around, pulling herself together as if to get up."

"No, I don't," I said. "I mean you're very lovely, but I'm in love with someone else."

"Oh," she said in a small voice, hanging her head and clasping her hands in her lap. I had begun to relax a bit when she looked up. "You know, it's okay with me if we're not in love." She reached into her jeans pocket. "I have a condom," she murmured reassuringly. Then she startled a little. "Condoms aren't against your religion, are they?"

"No," I said, "Condoms are okay. It's just that..."

"It could be our secret. She doesn't have to know."

"Well," I said, "she does. She would. She would expect me to tell her the truth ... and," I found myself shaking my head, "I would want to be able to tell the truth. So..."

"It's okay," she said.

"I'm glad."

"You're not gay, are you?"

"No."

"The last man I brought home turned out to be gay. I had never heard of gay, actually, but it turned out he was. Very handsome, too. A pilot. What a waste."

'Handsome' came out 'handthom,' and I knew it was my last chance to get a couple of hours of sleep before setting off to try to find Evie. I kept imagining Evie tied to a chair somewhere, alone, afraid, and uncomfortable, while I'm here with a very young-seeming blond, kissing, drinking beers and yes, becoming aroused.

"It's time for bed," I told her.

"You mean us together?" she said, her eyes bright.

"No, I'm afraid I mean you in your bedroom and me on this couch."

"Oh," she said dejectedly. "That's what I thought you meant." She couldn't seem to get her legs to stay under her and I couldn't seem to snatch her into the cradle of my arms—I had seen Clark Gable do it—so I sort of clutched her under her breasts from behind and dragged her along on her heels into her bedroom.

I didn't bother undressing her. I was too near that male edge. People talk about the little devil sitting on your shoulder, whispering in your ear. Mine was bellowing by now. I covered her with a crocheted sort of spread and tiptoed out to find the bathroom and a blanket for my couch.

I undressed quickly, stretching out on Ellen's sofa, covering myself with a lightweight, terribly pink cotton blanket. *Keep Evie safe*, I prayed, and wondered briefly about just staying up; it was already so late—or early. But when I closed my eyes it was all over, and I must have been asleep instantly. Except that—teetering on the edge of my dream—I heard a ferry whistle, very close, and Ellen saying, "Puget Sound. It's just a couple of blocks down. That's where you'll find your Bainbridge Island Ferry."

Then I heard another voice, I think it was mine, saying "I never told her *which* island."

CHAPTER 7

*I*n one more second Ellen was shaking me. I startled awake, nearly blurting Evie's name, fresh on my lips from a fragment of dream. The sense of it quickly scattered around and away from me like blown snow. Gaining my bearings, I found the sun risen and the steepled Seth Thomas on the oak mantel chiming eight o'clock. Outside, cars swished by at a steady rate carrying city-bound commuters. A yard-or-so over I could hear the rhythmic push-and-pull clickety sound of a rotary push mower, a sound I certainly never heard in Chandelar.

"Up and at 'em, sleepy head," Ellen chirped, all brightness and cheer. "Coffee?"

"Please," I said. Taking advantage of her coffee run back to the kitchen, I kicked aside the pink blanket, yanked on my khakis and fumbled into my black clerical shirt. I hadn't felt this woolly since three days and nights of village potlatch.

"Cream? Sugar?" she called.

"Both." The quick tinkle of a stirring spoon, and she came back carrying two brimming Pan Am mugs.

"Here you go," she said, my mug gripped in her hand so as to offer me the handle. I took it, thanked her and sipped. As I suspected, not the coffee from the 'red can that says good taste,' but actually pretty good coffee.

Her eyes were bright, her golden hair brushed and lipstick already applied although she left quite a bit of it on her coffee mug. The soft, somewhat needy girl with too much to drink and a condom in her pocket had been replaced by a young professional woman, apparently none the worse for wear after maybe three hours of sleep and way too much to drink.

In addition to the jeans, she wore a close-fitting, white, short-sleeved sweater. She had a plaid scarf knotted fashionably around her neck and several round, gold bracelets on her wrist, jangling musically each time she raised her arm to sip.

She saw me seeing her and made a gesture, arms wide. "Day off," she said. "No SeaTac, no airplane ... no *passengers*. I'm a free woman today. I intend to make the most of it. I'm going shopping. But first," she said, all business, "we need to get you to the boat."

A fifteen-minute drive found us back to downtown Seattle, a smallish tightly-clustered city center rising from a curve of fresh gray-green bay. Just offshore the sunny day gave way to a looming bank of sulky fog, tendrils blowing ashore and mewing seagulls chasing wisps of it up Cherry Street.

"This will burn off," Ellen assured me. "Sunshine by noon." Somewhere out there, a foghorn sounded, deep and slow and foreboding, feeding my anxiety about Evie and making the fog feel like it had come to stay.

In front of Pier 48, Ellen swooped the blue Chevy to the curb. "Your boat." She nodded to a sign that read 'Bainbridge Island.' I grabbed my bag, found the chrome door handle and got out, turning to thank her."

"You're welcome," she said. There must have been something in my expression that passed for regret. "Don't worry," she assured, "I'll see you again on the airplane." And that was it. She blew me an exaggerated kiss with her too-red lips, "Safe travels," she called out, waved, shifted into drive and was gone, the rear white-walls actually chirping as she blasted away into traffic.

"That was interesting," I said aloud, shivering slightly in the cool, damp, salty air. Slipping into my jacket I started up the long, two-story ramp to the Washington State Ferry terminal. *Is she a twin?* I wondered. *One last night who couldn't keep her hands off me and the other one this morning who couldn't wait to get rid of me?* I guessed not. But no other explanation made a bit of sense.

I saw him as soon as I got to the top of the ramp, tucked behind the same edition of *The Seattle Post-Intelligencer* he'd been reading late last night, staked out at the airport. I thought about it for a moment, whether he might be tempted to aim that automatic at me here in the ferry terminal. When I decided he probably wouldn't, I settled into the chair next to him.

As he pretended to keep reading, I studied the terminal, a long, narrow room with lots of windows, and a high, arched, echoing ceiling. Rows of green Naugahyde chairs with chrome arms ran the length of the room, punctuated by freestanding ashtrays, also chrome, on a checkerboard of light and dark gray linoleum tiles. Next to vending machines for cigarettes, candy and knickknacks, a café counter blended fresh smells of coffee and bacon into the stale mix of old grease, cigarettes, beer, some kind of pine-scented disinfectant, and faintly, urine.

Settling back, I said, "I think you'd just about have that issue memorized." He tucked the paper down slightly to look at me, and started to raise it again like he was going to say he had no idea what I was talking about. Then he grinned, folded the paper, and tossed it into a nearby waste bin.

"Just about," he agreed. He looked me over. "How'd you get around me at the airport?"

"Caught a ride with a friend," I said. He nodded.

"Thought so." He was quiet for a moment, as if considering, then stuck out his hand. "Forsythe," he said, Dave Forsythe, and you're Father Hardy."

I agreed that I was. "I guess I'm surprised to see you in one piece." He appeared a good deal less sinister in daylight, with a blondish crew cut, blue eyes, and considerable tan, suggesting he wasn't from around Seattle with its reputation for raining nearly half the year. In the broad light of day, smiling, relaxed, he looked about as threatening as a young dentist.

"Owe it all to you. Your ... connections." He jerked a thumb skyward. Didn't know how much trouble I was in 'til I saw you drop to your knee to pray right there on the riverbank." Forsythe was a gum chewer, spearmint Chiclets by the scent of it. He would chew it in one corner of his mouth and talk out of the other. He spoke in clumps of sentences punctuated by noisy spasms of gum chewing.

"Sorry about the gun back there. Not sure what I thought I was doing. Just desperate, I guess. Anyway I dropped it in my pocket and thought if you were praying then things must be pretty bad and I'd better start praying, myself. I like to be with the side that's winning. So I'm praying away, a little rusty—hadn't prayed since Sunday School—and just about the time I'm ready to die, I mean, really expecting to die, my ice floe kind of twirls around a big curve then drives completely up on the shore. I step off without even getting water in my boots! A few minutes later, Indians come walking along a little trail there and guide me to railroad tracks. Five more hours, I'm in Anchorage. Of course I've lost *you*."

"The question is," I smiled at him, "why you were following me in the first place?"

"Fair question." He smiled back and chewed more on his gum. "But I don't know the answer. It's a job. I'm just supposed to follow you. I *can* tell you it has something to do with finding an old man named Simon Nicolai. Here's his photo."

The photo was an old one, a black and white of Simon, much younger, in his riverboat uniform, a business photo not a snapshot. "And you have no idea why you're hired to find Simon?"

"Well," he said, "it has something to do with gold."

"Gold?" As I pondered, an almost completely unintelligible voice came over the public address system, advising something about Bainbridge Island. Other people waiting climbed out of their chairs and headed for the gangway so we did too.

70

Standing, Forsythe stood half a head taller than me, thinnish but muscular and fit.

"Let me get that bag," insisted Dave taking it out of my hand, but then instead of walking on, stopped at the top of the ramp and set the bag down, forcing other passengers to spill past us. He didn't seem to mind or notice. He gave me an earnest look. "We don't really know each other, and you have no reason to do anything I tell you, but I'm gonna try it

anyway. Don't get on this boat. Go home. Go back to Chandelar while you can."

I looked at him and he looked at me. I didn't like the way 'while you can' sounded, but knew there wasn't anything I could do at this point but walk on down the gangway. "I have to get on this boat," I said.

"One reason?"

"They have my friend, Evie. And, in a way this is my job."

"I get that," he said, "but is she worth dying for?"

"Dying for? That's crazy."

"Yeah, it is. But you didn't answer the question. Is she worth dying for? I've seen her. Pretty, but ..." He snapped his gum.

"She's one of my parishioners."

"You fly twenty-five hundred miles for all your parishioners? I don't think so."

"She called. She asked me to come and I told her I would."

"And you just jumped on the plane," he said.

I nodded. "I love her." I hadn't intended to say it. Hadn't said it to anybody else and certainly not

71

to Evie. There it was out in the open to a stranger. "But I would have come anyway," I added.

"Ahh," he said, as if it now all made sense. He let his breath out forcefully through his nose, picked up my bag and turned to the ramp. That seemed to be the end of it. "Better be sure we're on this boat then."

By the time we made it aboard the Kalakala and forward to the bow to find seats, the whistle had blown, lines cast off and the boat surged ahead. I'd never seen a boat like this one, skinned with shining stainless steel, curved and rounded into an aerodynamic, dolphin-like figure. Cars drove into one end and out the other while passengers walked on, then ordered coffee, smoked cigarettes, and sat at tables watching seabirds or water traffic. Elliot Bay and the Seattle waterfront gave way to the larger Puget Sound and an array of islands, now only slightly visible in low-lying fog.

And while the Kalakala may have been an art deco treasure, there couldn't have been more than a panel or two on the entire interior that didn't rattle as though the surface of the Sound was corrugated. We had to raise our voices to hear each other.

"I don't get how you're involved in this," I said. "Are you a ..." I admit I hesitated, "a gangster?"

"Nah. But I can see why you'd think so." He indicated the automatic in his suit jacket pocket. "My brother is. Half-brother. That's the guy you beat up at the cabin. Clyde. Claimed you ambushed him, hit him with an axe handle. That true? You don't look like the type."

I didn't answer but must have made my famous 'that's-ridiculous' face. It was one that my wife frequently commented on.

"He lied! My brother lied to me." But Dave didn't look surprised. "So how *did* you get him?"

"Dodged the blackjack, punched him in the gut. He folded like a cheap chair."

He grinned and nodded. "That's him, all over."

"So if you're not a gangster, what are you?"

"What am I?" he said thoughtfully, stalling a beat. Again I had the feeling of him making up his mind about something.

"I'm a government agent."

I must have appeared doubtful. "Which government?"

He looked surprised at the question. "Ours."

"Agent?"

"I know it sounds weird. I'm with the CIA." That stopped me.

"I never heard of the CIA."

He laughed. "Central Intelligence Agency. It's an oxymoron. There's not a thing intelligent about it. We were OSS in the war, when it all meant something."

"I can't keep up with all the initials," I said. "And I can't figure out what the CIA wants with Simon Nicholai."

"Nah. That's my brother's gig. I've been on assignment overseas, just got home, agreed to help my brother out for a few weeks on the Q.T. because, frankly, they offered me too much money."

"I noticed your tan," I said. "Overseas? Africa? Certainly not Korea?"

"Nah." He chewed. "Viet Nam. Ever heard of it?"

"Viet Nam? No, never."

"Well," he said, "I hope you never do. It's a little shit-hole country—sorry Father—in Southeast Asia. I've been over there for most of a year with what's called the United States Military Assistance Advisory Group. We've been telling the French how to not get their clocks cleaned by small brown people who call themselves freedom fighters."

"Why that?"

"They have some crazy idea it's their country."

"It was only *noble* when *we* did it," I said. "But we had George Washington. So what's that got to do with the U.S.?"

"Stoppin' Commies, of course. It's crap. You don't know that the U.S. spent more than three hundred million dollars last year to save Viet Nam from the Vietnamese. For the French.

"For the French? Three hundred million dollars? That can't be true. I've never even heard of the place."

He shook his head. "It's true."

One of the natural consequences of working in the 'priest' trade is that an amount of money the government wastes on political brinksmanship—in this case three hundred million dollars—starts to appear in my imagination as piles of food, brand new diapers, medicines, and little kids marching off to clean, warm schools.

"And so now you're home," I said, "and you're more than a little outraged at having to subjugate people on their own land, and to atone, you've helped capture, and are holding, a person who is completely innocent and uninvolved."

"Not me," he said, and had the decency to look a little uncomfortable. "I'm just helping out."

"I don't get it," I said. "I was in the army in France. We were the good guys. You're supposed to be one of the good guys." He sighed and turned to stare out over the water.

"I think those days may be past, Father."

"This Viet Nam thing can't last," I said. But he didn't answer. So we stood there, watching a misty evergreen-treed point slide to center in the forward porthole and gradually emerge from fog and enlarge as we approached.

"I need your help," I said to him.

"I can't help you."

"Why not?"

"Because before it's over I would end up shooting my brother."

"Hard to explain to Mom?"

"Sarcasm from a priest. Interesting. Nah," he said, "I can handle Mom. But I only get to shoot people *out of the country* without a big hassle." He reached into his pocket. "I'll give you my gun ... unregistered, untraceable."

I held up my hand, shaking my head.

"You're gonna need it," he said.

"If I take it, I will. I've figured out the quickest way to need a gun is to be carrying one. I'm somewhat confident I can talk them into releasing her. So the two of us can get on the airplane and go back to Chandelar where we belong. I don't know anything. She doesn't know anything. I think I can convince whoever this is to let us go home."

Forsythe looked doubtful. "Must be a special girl and a special place."

75

"I think so." Unbidden, a twisting kaleidoscope exploded a thousand image fragments behind my eyes, of Evie and Andy and my year in Chandelar. Unexpectedly it hurt like a sucker punch of deep loss.

"Bainbridge Island," said a mechanical-sounding voice on the P.A. "Winslow."

"We're here," said Forsythe. "You sure about the gun?" I nodded.

Nearing the slip, the *Kalakala* shifted into reverse, bow propellers abruptly slowing the approach, causing anybody standing to shift their stance or reach out for something to hold onto. Not Forsythe. Solid as a rock, he extended his hand. "Bainbridge Island," he said. "I'm out of here, Father. Leave's over in a couple of days and I'm back to Saigon. Glad we met." He stepped back as if to leave, though the boat hadn't landed and he really had no place to go. "Look," he said, "what makes these guys so dangerous is not just that they're greedy but, for whatever reason they feel so entitled. It's a deadly combination and you and this Evie are in the way. They *will* kill you."

"Okay," I said. "I consider myself warned. How do I find them? Who is this 'Lizzie Ann?'"

He allowed himself a brief flicker of smile. "Not *who*," he said, "*what.*" *Lizzie Ann* is a boat. A ship, actually. An old sailing ship. You won't have any trouble finding her. Ask anyone."

The *Kalakala's* whistle sounded, a long quavering wail that continued to echo around a small, evergreen-lined harbor long after the actual whistle quit sounding. And although it wasn't nearly noon, a knife blade of sunbeam pierced the fog and washed the frothing ferry wake to a rich, warm green. When I turned from looking at the water, Forsythe, or whoever he really was, had disappeared.

CHAPTER 8

*W*hat to do? Who to call? Nobody, of course. But as the *Kalakala* eased up to the Bainbridge Island ferry slip and deckhands looped heavy hawsers around dock cleats, I made myself nearly frantic trying to figure out the smart thing to do to get Evie and me safely out of here. Forsythe's attempt to give me his gun and his blunt assertion, "They will kill you," was not a confidence booster.

Even a tiny town on an island has to have some kind of law, I reasoned, although of course there was none in Chandelar. But a civilized town out here in the lower forty-eight must have a sheriff, someone to call, but who? And calling the law wasn't quite the same as coming by myself, as Evie had directed. No one would be more at risk than Evie if a posse showed up. Again I wished for Andy.

Deckhands held back the small crowd of us who had walked on at the Seattle side while two cars and three older pickup trucks casually off-loaded. They could have pushed them off faster by hand. The last of these was an old Ford Model A that revved up its engine and ground its old, straight-cut gears to somehow propel it up the ramp now made steep by the lowering tide. Then we walked the two hundred-some feet of single-lane pier to dry land. Most of the way, the greenish water was shallow enough to see barnacled rocks on the bottom.

I strolled in a loose cluster of people who all knew each other. As a stranger with a traveling bag, and as a priest, I'm sure I stood out like a sore thumb, but no one struck up a conversation. Instead, they talked about shopping in the city, hopes for the strawberry harvest—kids about to come home from college. In that moment I envied them their uncomplicated, safe lives while I felt like I might be walking, not just to my own grave but to Evie's, if I screwed up.

On up the grade from the pier, an intersection revealed a hand-painted sign: "Winslow," with an arrow pointing left. A short, timbered bridge carried me over a deep ravine, an unseen creek murmuring up from cool shadows. The bridge led me to the wide, nearly deserted main street—one of few, by the look of it—basking in the morning sun and the last of shifting tendrils of fog. Compared to Chandelar, Winslow was a small city.

I passed a grocery, a Woolworths, a hardware store, an auto parts/garage—still featuring the large blue and yellow enameled REO sign—a tavern with its door already open—I could smell cigarettes and stale beer at a distance. The main street with its wide sidewalks, some wooden planked, and a scattering of false-front buildings extended just about three blocks, finally giving up at the white clapboard Eagle Harbor Congregational Church. I thought about going in to pray, something like topping off my tank. By now my sense of needing help to find Evie was palpable. But a glance back down the hill toward the cove showed me a marina. "Boats," I said aloud, feeling that the first of my prayers—where to look for her—had been answered already, and I started for them.

Emerging from the tall trees at the bottom of the grade, from the vantage of the marina ramp, I could look back across the small harbor, now with a flattened look on the low tide, toward the ferry dock. As I watched, the *Kalakala* gave another of those long, quavering whistles, backing out slowly for the return trip to Seattle.

The marina dock stretched out before me with fingers of five long floats like an outstretched hand. I saw boats of all color and description, almost evenly divided between well-kept, masted sailing boats and scruffier work-a-day craft outfitted with nets, hydraulic lifting apparatus and stacks of chicken-wire crab pots, all of it bathed in the heavy scent of old sea life.

I saw only one man working this morning, about halfway down the far-left float. He was scrubbing out galvanized metal pails and washing down what looked like fish-cutting benches on the stern of a large gray-and-white cruiser. It had *Kingfisher* scripted in blue along the bow. Half a head taller than me he wore rubber boots and dark green rubberized bib overalls over a sleeveless white undershirt. He looked up as I approached, backing off the force of spray from his nozzle drift to avoid wetting down my pant legs. "Father," he nodded, straightening, "you're not from around here."

"Because you know everybody that lives on this island?"

"Yeah."

"That's good, because I think I'm looking for strangers. And a boat. The ..."

"*Lizzie Ann*," he said. And rotating from the hip he swung a long arm at shoulder height to point, semaphore-like, not toward the marina but out to the center of the small harbor. "Out there," he said, "the third one."

Anchored out and rafted together, floated three ancient wooden sailing ships. Flagless and mastless with massive deck cleats, their anchor chains hung deeply rusted and flaked.

"Old," I said.

"Left here to die."

"And there are strangers aboard?"

"Yeah." He waited a minute before asking. "Friends of yours?"

"No," I said. "But I think they may be holding a friend of mine. One of my parishioners. I'm from Alaska," I explained.

"I know," he said.

"You do?"

"I read my Sherlock Holmes." He grinned. "Not a bit of suntan on that face." He pointed at my bag. "The luggage tag helps." He shifted his body around to stare at the boats. "You said *holding* your friend."

"Yes."

"Maybe I should go out with you." It wasn't a question.

"Tempting, but I was told to come alone."

"That doesn't sound good, either. You sure?"

"Sure." I said, feeling anything but. "Can you rent me a rowboat?"

"No rent," he said. "Help yourself." He looked at me for a long minute and then back out midharbor toward the *Lizzie Ann*. "How long you gonna be out there, Father, if you don't mind me asking?"

"I don't know," I said. "I hope not long."

"Well, you watch yourself. I seen those guys going back and forth, four of 'em, three white guys and an Indian. Hard lookin'. Nobody goes out there anymore for any *good* reason. Used to be eight of those old girls rafted up out there. Somebody—a squatter, I think—built a fire aboard and burned the rest of 'em to the waterline. Don't look like much now but some of 'em, like the *Lizzie Ann*, were gold rush ships, way back fifty years ago. They carried groceries and miners to Nome, and gold dust home. Used to be a story there was gold dust in the bilge, but it never," he hesitated, "panned out."

"So look," he said, as if making up his mind. "I'll be out there in four hours. If everything's okay, you just say so. If it's not okay, then ..."

"Thanks," I said, "I really appreciate that," and we shook hands. It felt better having backup. I dropped my bag into the skiff and clambered in after it, settling myself on the center seat, grasping the oars, the leather soles of my boots slippery with an accumulation of old motor oil and fish guts. My benefactor eased the loop of line from a silver cleat."

"Nels. Nels Nelson. If you need me, you can ask for me at the town tavern. My office," he said with a small smile. "They always know where I am." He dropped the line into the bow and gave the skiff a shove.

"Here goes nothing." I waved at Nels, who gave me a quick wave back and returned to hosing down the *Kingfisher*. I had everything I could do to not call out to him and turn the skiff back to pick him up. But there *is* something worse than getting yourself killed. It's getting someone else killed too.

I once learned to row a boat backward, on a lake in Tennessee. That is to face the direction you want to go, rather than rowing with your back to your destination, pulling on the oars. With water this glassy, nearly as flat as a lake, I could push the oars and not have to take my eyes off the ships as I approached. "Seth loves Lucy," read hand-painted graffiti at the waterline of the first hull. "I like Ike," was popular, and "Gunnar + Akiko," the logical result of an island populated by Norwegians and Japanese.

As I pushed my skiff past the forlorn remains of the *Empress of the North* and the *Sophie Christianson*, and out of sight of my new friend Nels, back on the float, I saw a man wearing a suit but no tie, seated low, smoking on the stern of the *Lizzie Ann*. He looked about as natural in this setting as a wedding cake.

"You Hardy?" he asked, and I had to wonder how many other priests they were expecting. I nodded and he pulled out a .45 automatic. "About time," he said. "Get your ass up here ... Father," and he laughed.

I struggled up the shifting rope ladder with my bag. *Aren't we having fun,* I thought.

He shoved me hard through a solid-looking windowless door below decks, into darkness, and I crashed into something soft, Evie. We hit the wall together, already in each other's arms. "Oh Hardy," she said, starting to cry, and she held me and kissed me and wept. And I admit that I held and kissed her and, in spite of whatever predicament we were in, felt only joy in being able to do so.

The room's available light, little more than a glow, eased in through a tiny opening, probably a vent and it seemed likely we were being held in something that used to be a storeroom. I smelled the honeybucket before I saw it, with a roll of toilet paper on the floor beside it. Another bucket with a dipper hung from its side, held water for drinking. The entire rest of the furnishings consisted of a wooden chair with its back broken off and a rack-like bunk with no mattress. Evie's three days here had been quite a few sandwiches short of a picnic. I shifted some kind of gear from being unsure and a bit fearful, to being angry, and wanting to make someone pay. In a little more than three hours I knew that Nels would be showing up, maybe with a few friends, and I began to like the possibilities.

Evie interrupted my daydreams of vengeance. "They want to know about Simon Nicolai," she whispered, "and they want to know something about gold. But I'm not sure how much they know themselves. They seem to be working for someone. They go into Winslow to make phone calls and come back with information. One of them went in just a little while ago, and when I heard your skiff clunking against the hull, I thought you were him, back already. Do you know where Simon is?"

"No clue," I said. "I got a *Tundra Times* message to meet him at his cabin at Chatanika, but he wasn't there, hadn't been there for a long time and the place had been trashed."

"Trashed? Who would do this? What's going on?"

"I don't know. I'm hoping we can talk some sense into these guys and get them to let us go."

"I'm hoping you have a backup plan," she said, her voice small. "I don't think these are talk-sense guys."

"How did they grab you?"

"Walking to the grocery near my apartment, I saw a guy from the Mission School, Jimmy Lucas. Hardy, I was glad to see him. It had been years. He always had a terrible crush on me, followed me around. And he was always a really terrible practical joker. Toothpaste on doorknobs, and he once sent away for a joy buzzer that he saw in an ad at the back of a comic book. So when he grabbed me and began to stuff me into the back of a car, I first thought he was still goofing around. I told him to knock it off—just like always. But he wasn't goofing around, and that's when I saw the others. By then, they had me."

It was another fifteen or twenty minutes before we heard the telltale skiff clunk, and within minutes found our storeroom cell door thrown wide and heard an invitation to come out, which we did.

"Clyde," I said, recognizing the big thug from the cabin. Startled I knew his name, he bent his face into something like a mean smile, and raised a hand to stroke his still-scabbed nose and chin.

"Nice to see you again," he said. "Nice for me, anyway." He turned to another guy, who looked

Athabascan. "Get 'em up to the stern," he muttered. "You got those anchors?"

"Got 'em," said the Indian, and he and another guy, answering to Ted, each grabbed an elbow and led us back up the ship's ladder to the main deck, blinking and squinting but happy to be back in fresh air and daylight.

Out of the corner of my eye I saw the Indian nudge Evie and do a head bob in my direction. "Hardy," she said, "This is Jimmy Lucas. He went to the Mission school with Andy and..."

"Pleased to meet you, Father," said Lucas, extending his hand, which I was shaking when Clyde came bustling back along the side deck to where we were standing.

"Tie 'em," he said to Lucas, who was surprisingly quick with a pair of short lengths of stout cord. Whatever Sam Spade move I thought I might make went completely over the side when Ted jammed something gun-like into my kidney.

"You want to know about Simon Nicolai," I said. "I can tell you."

"No," said Clyde, "you missed that chance."

"And you want to know about gold." He blinked.

"You been busy, but I already know you don't *know* anything about Nicolai or the gold. Too bad." He did a head bob in the direction of a couple of anchors arranged on the deck near a section of missing rail. The hairs on my neck stood up. When Nels got out here, he wouldn't be doing us any good.

"Yeah," I said, "I know about the gold."

Clyde gave me a sharp look. "No," he snarled, "you don't. Or you don't know enough for me to keep you alive."

"Look," I said, feeling nauseous with fear, "let her go. You never wanted her, never needed her. You only took her to get me. Now I'm here, you've got what you want. Just put her in my skiff and let her row away."

Clyde laughed. "Nobody rows away." To Lucas he said, "You know what to do." Lucas nodded.

He finished tying Evie's hands. "I need you to sit down now, Eve," he said, calling her by her childhood school name. He looked at me. "You too."

That's when I used my tied up hands to club Ted at the back of his neck, knocking him down and nearly out, his pistol clattering across the wooden deck, over the side and into the water. Lucas saw Ted hit the deck and saw me coming for him and jumped up from working with Evie to scrabble in his back pocket for something—a gun or a blackjack.

"Hardy," Evie shouted, and I only half turned before something heavy caught me at the base of my neck, driving me to my knees. Stars came out suddenly and I went flat on the deck, hard. I managed to land on one shoulder rather than breaking my fall with my face, not out but not really reviving until Lucas had us both knotted to our chains and the anchors dragged over to the deck edge.

"Make sure he's awake," said Clyde, "I want him to know he's dying. I want him to know he's holding his breath a long time, and what's going to happen when he can't hold it anymore. He grabbed me by the hair to lift my head and stare into my eyes. "Not so tough now, are you!" He let go and my head bounced on the deck, I was still so dopey.

"Sorry Father," said Lucas, when Clyde had gone. "Eve, I need to tell you something." She looked at him, saying nothing, tears streaming out the sides of her eyes and down her cheeks. "And I want you to remember this," he said, cupping her cheeks in his hands and kissing her gently. "I've always loved you. I always will love you."

"I know," she said with difficulty. "Can't you let us go?"

"For chrissake," shouted Clyde from below, and I heard oars splashing, "do it!" Then bring that other skiff back across so they waste some time looking for 'em in town." I lay on the deck, slowly coming back into myself and trying to think of what to do. And coming up dry.

"I could pay you," I said, "fifty thousand dollars to let us go."

"Can't do it," Father. "Mighty generous, though. I heard how you got that money."

"Fifty thousand," I said, "just to let Evie go. You say you love her. Prove it, and make yourself rich at the same time."

"Can't do it. These guys are the most vicious guys I ever seen. And right now you can bet some-one's watching me with binoculars. If I don't push you over, one of 'em will push *me* over and shoot me for complaining 'cause the water's cold. So," he concluded, pushing my anchor off the deck, "over you go." I was still seeing Evie's eyes, deep and brown and lovely, filled with tears, until the water closed over me and the anchor dragged me down.

I closed my eyes, but opened them when I heard Evie's anchor hit the water, and then her. I watched her sinking and she could see me, the water first clear and green, but soon stirred up with silt until we lost sight of each other and of the sky. I didn't feel like we sunk that far and sure enough, could see the surface as light above me and the hulking mass of the *Lizzie Ann's hull*, encrusted with barnacles, her heavy-planked bottom a waving garden of sea grass—never to sail again. I felt a metal bar under my feet, had landed on my anchor in the seaweeds. Dimly, I could make out a landscape of seashells and occasional trash. I had landed near a small nest of automobile tires.

Thanks to the buoyancy of the water I was able to lift the heavy anchor, even tossing it a few feet up the slight grade toward shore and the possibility of deep breaths of clear fresh air. But then, starting to feel the desperate need for air, remembered that it didn't have to be deep water for us to drown. One thing led to another and that's when I realized I'd done it again.

One other time, near death, I forgot to pray. Forgot to pray for myself and for Evie. Then as now, I wondered what it says about a priest, on his way to meet his maker, who doesn't pray. "Dear God," I prayed, "deliver us, or at least deliver Evie. Amen."

And I settled into silt and tall sea grass at the bottom.

CHAPTER 9

*W*hen I boxed and got knocked down, I had the good fortune to always be able to climb back up. I was known for always getting up. I admit that getting up to be pounded again wasn't always what I wanted to do, but seemed like the right thing.

Encouragement helped. In fact, that's how I met Mary. Boxing, in a smoky club in Chattanooga, knocked flat on the canvas, staring up into spinning lights and a shifting gauze of bluish smoke, I saw her, blond and angelic, and she smiled at me. Then I saw her lips moving and even with the roar of the crowd I knew exactly what she said. "Get up."

And I swear I heard her again now. Kneeling in sand and weeds at the bottom of Eagle Harbor, wrestling with my anchor, lungs screaming for a good breath. "Get up!" Well, why not. So I bent my knees, lifted my bound hands straight above me, and drove for the surface in what I already knew would be a vain attempt to catch a breath of air.

Except that Lucas, the love-starved practical joker had dropped us into shallow water tied to our anchors by long-enough ropes to make breathing not only possible, but easy. So I came blasting out of the water like a breaching whale, snatching my lungs full of air and trying, in that quick rise and fall, to see who might be seeing me. But a quick glance showed us to be in the far-side shadow of the *Lizzie Ann*, out of view of anybody on the town shore, with or without binoculars. Moreover, we were only about forty or fifty feet from dry land on the other side of what I now knew to be a quite shallow cove—at least at low tide.

Another second and Evie burst forth in her own whale-like breach in search of air, also looking sur-prised at its relative proximity to the beach.

"That Lucas!" she spluttered, blinking saltwater and shaking wet hair from her eyes like a spaniel.

"He saved our lives," I told her and she nodded, saving her breath for treading water with her hands and feet bound.

"I'm going to move our anchors," I told her, seeing her nod as I dove, managing to find my anchor and then hers in not more than eight feet of water. With my ankles bound I hopped two or three paces toward shore before giving each the biggest toss I could muster and—completely out of oxygen—blast for the surface, gasping.

"God, Hardy," she exclaimed, shivering in the chill water, her chin quivering. "You scared the crap out of me, you were down there so long. Don't *do* that."

"Sorry," I said, and did it again and again. By the fifth or sixth time—I lost count—I could breathe standing on my tiptoes with my head tilted back, and then one more time moving Evie's anchor had her chin clear out of water and her panic level beginning to subside. Hopping toward her but tripping on a rock and going completely underwater, I finally managed to get close enough to work on the knots at her wrists, which weren't easy in the frigid Puget Sound waters with wet rope and well-numbed fingers. But eventually I felt the ropes fall away and her arms open and rise, immediately folding me close. She held me tight and kissed me long and hard there in the cold saltwater. "I thought we'd lost us," she said, weeping freely now, finally letting me go and fumbling with my knots until she freed my hands too, and we dragged each other up out of the water to stand and shiver on the shore. There, large black birds with an S-curve in their necks—birds we later found out were cormorants—stood on rocks, logs and old pilings with their wings held up and open, drying their feathers in the breeze.

Finally untying our feet, we staggered out of the shadows to begin drying ourselves on sun-warmed rocks. In the sunshine and warmth, with hands and feet free and plenty of air to breath, the icy fingers of the terror of it began to slide away from us, back under rocks and into shadows where they belonged.

"What can this possibly have to do with Simon?" said Evie, wringing saltwater out of her jacket. Whatever makeup she'd been wearing was long gone and her hair hung limp and flat to her head.

"Gold. Something about gold. They think he has it and they want it. No, more than that, they feel entitled to it. That's the part I particularly can't figure."

"Wring out your jacket," she said. "And stop staring at me. I feel like a nearly-drowned rodent." She lapsed into thoughtful silence. "But Simon isn't a gold miner. I've known him, or known of him, most of my life. He was a ... purser ... I think, on the riverboats, on the old *Nenana*. He made a wage when many didn't, but it wasn't gold."

"Somebody thinks he has gold," I said, "several somebodys. The good news is we've seen a couple of them. We know them and can see them coming."

"And the bad news?" she said, hanging her damp jacket across her shoulders, shivering.

"The bad news is that they'll kill for it. This proves it. They'll kill anybody who gets in their way."

The echoing rattle of oarlocks tipped us that someone was coming, but too late. We had no more than enough time to wonder if we should hide, if we *could* hide, before a skiff with a single rower rounded the stern of the *Lizzie Ann*. At the oars, Nels Nelson who—also rowing face forward—quickly caught sight and made for us on the beach.

"Four hours up?" I said to him.

"Yeah," he answered, "saw everybody but you and the lady get out of here fast. Thought I better have a look. Gave me a bad feeling." He looked us both up and down. "I'm guessing it wasn't your idea to go swimming." He saw the line we'd un-knotted from around our ankles. "Damn!" he said. "C'mon, we can call the sheriff. He can greet 'em proper when they walk down the gangway on Seattle side."

He stepped out of the skiff in his high rubber boots, extending a gentleman's hand to help Evie aboard. He sat her in the stern while directing me to push off and step aboard, which I did. He sank the oars deep and pulled them hard. The skiff, even with the three of us, fairly flew. "Makes my blood boil," he muttered, and judging by the wake we left, I believed him.

Though Nels called the Kitsap County Sheriff, who alerted Seattle Police to meet the inbound Bainbridge Island Ferry, nobody matching the descriptions of Clyde, Lucas or Ted walked or drove off. The three had probably just made it onto the earlier boat. That was it, as far as Seattle police were concerned, though we were welcomed to come back into the city to file a complaint, just in case.

Later that evening, dried out and fed up, with Norwegian bachelor cooking that is, Nels drove us to the evening's last Seattle sailing in his 1937 pickup truck that somehow still looked, and even smelled new.

"It's been a real pleasure meeting you folks," he said, eyes on Evie but flicking to me as he shook my hand goodbye. "Come back anytime—and we won't make you swim!"

I still had my bag. I'd rowed myself back out to the *Lizzie Ann* not expecting much, but found the bag and the few items of clothing and personal effects tossed around. In fact it all looked like nothing so much as the travel bag exploding, spreading my stuff around the deck.

We found the downtown Olympic Hotel, about six blocks up the grade from the ferry landing. Nels had called ahead to reserve two rooms, with a door between, we discovered. "Gotta bathe," sighed Evie who took herself off for a long hot soak while I caught the elevator back to the first floor lobby and the battery of public telephones I had noticed as we checked in. Sliding into a chair at the back I lifted the handset.

"Hotel operator," said a voice, a young woman.

"Long distance, please." I could hear the mysterious ticks and clicks of the system, and the line opening, which always gave me a tremendous sense of distance, like listening down a pipe for thousands of miles. When the long-distance operator came on I gave her the number for the call and when I heard the phone pick up far in the distance, and a cautious hello, I almost spoke before the operator set in.

"I have a person-to-person call for William Stolz from a Father Hardy?" She had a way of saying my name like she knew it couldn't possibly be the real one. "Will you accept?"

"Oh yes, operator," he said, "most definitely." He gave the operator a second to clear the line.

"Father," said William. "I have been concerned. The bishop called. Did you find her ... did you find Evie?"

"Yes, we're safe for the moment, but we need your help. Can you meet our flight in Fairbanks around noon ... and bring your..." I hesitated to say *gun* on a telephone where someone could be listening. I already knew William's views on telephone security; there isn't any. Governments of all kinds can listen in on telephone calls.

"You can give me all the details when we meet. Yes, of course," he added. I will bring my ... car." We both knew he had no car, but he would get one and he would bring the weapon. "I wonder," he said, "how ... serious?"

95

"I met a man from the government, working in a country called Viet Nam ..."

"Ah," he said. "Say no more. A lovely country. I vacationed there shortly after the war. French culture and cooking, marvelous white-sand beaches, small beautiful women ... a paradise. I understand completely. The airport at noon ... tomorrow?"

"Yes, perfect." I hung up feeling a bit safer for the first time since this whole business began.

Rooms at the Olympic Hotel were large enough, well outfitted, and at twenty-five dollars each per night—in what for me had previously been a Motel 6 world—certainly not cheap. Done up in tones of pink, what Evie calls 'mauve,' and in charcoal—what I call gray—they radiated 'upper crust hotel' good taste, which for me, and I suspect for Evie, couldn't have been more sterile and depressing.

Although sanitized and deodorized, decades of old cigarette smoke now seeped back out of the very bones of the place to create an airless impression that all the oxygen in the room had already been used. Searching for a breath of the cool, fresh, salty air I knew to be just outside, I went window to window yanking but found them all screwed shut.

"Why would they do that? Seal all the windows?" I muttered to Evie.

"To keep us from jumping?"

"After paying twenty-five dollars a night, why would I jump?"

"How about lack of oxygen?"

She had come through the common door after her bath, wrapped in one of the hotel's over-sized

96

terry cloth robes with her hair done up in a towel like a turban. Wearing no makeup and after several days of being held captive and then nearly killed, she still looked lovely. Now as I sat on the bed she folded herself into the soft guest chair and regarded me with brown eyes that appeared bottomless.

"We need to talk," I said.

"About the blond?"

I must have looked as surprised as I felt. "Yes… among other things."

She smiled her soft smile. "I guess she's really something. Did you sleep with her?"

"No… but the opportunity was offered."

"Did you tell her where Simon is?"

"No, but it was just dumb luck. I didn't know I was being played until she turned out to know something I was sure I hadn't mentioned. I thought I had met someone nice, and we were talking. But how did you know about her?"

She made a face. "Locked on that ship I had nothing to do but use the honey bucket and listen at the door. They went on about her being 'really something' and you being a gullible chump who would 'spill' for sure. I should tell you that each of them mentioned wanting to be you."

"And that's when they talked about the gold?" I asked.

"Yep." She hugged her smooth brown shins and stared at toenails painted pink. "They said if you knew where the gold was, she'd know soon. So," she said, looking up, "why *didn't* you sleep with her if she was so terrific?"

"Something she lacked," I said.

"Didn't sound like she lacked anything." She raised her eyes to mine.

"She wasn't you."

"Oh Hardy," she said, and climbed out of her chair and padded across the room, hips gently swaying, to crawl up on my bed. "Feel like holding me for awhile? It's been a rough couple of days and I just need to feel your arms around me."

Silly question.

In the morning we made it to SeaTac and onto the airplane without seeing anyone who wanted to kill us. It wasn't that we were so tricky we got by them. They simply had no reason to stake out the place, believing we were dead.

We found William waiting in Fairbanks, parked in front of the main airport doors in an Oldsmobile he claimed he had borrowed, a car I'd never noticed in Chandelar. He climbed out the driver's side and came around, first to shake my hand and then to tenderly greet Evie who walked into his outstretched arms, allowing herself to be patted gently and kissed on the top of her head.

"We will find who has done this," he said, "and make it right." I had never heard words spoken so softly sound so deadly.

CHAPTER 10

*N*ot knowing a single other thing to do we decided to make a return trip to Simon's cabin. We offered to leave Evie with the bishop, and of course she refused. "I'm going," she said and sat resolutely in front between William and me.

The gravel road west out of Fairbanks undulates through a mix of low rolling hills at times thickly treed with small, dark evergreens, alternating with low birch or cottonwood, and intersected with stacked-up gravel tailings from old gold dredges.

"Tell me about the man from Viet Nam," said William, and I did. "And he claimed to be just helping his brother out?"

"That's what he said."

William leaned forward to look at me past Evie. "Did you believe him?"

"I did at first," I said. "Now I think Ellen called him that morning—told him what she'd learned— and he took another run at me on the boat. Offering me a gun to build trust, then when neither he nor Ellen could learn anything, delivered me to the *Lizzie Ann* for disposal."

"That would be my conclusion," said William softly. "You both were extremely lucky in this. You will not be this lucky a second time."

"But why do you suppose he claimed to be a government agent?" I asked.

"Does that seem unbelievable to you?"

"Well… yes!"

"Moose!" said William, braking and swerving to miss the huge creature. After we passed it he said, "I not only believe it, I think it may be the only part of anything he told you that is true."

"But that's crazy," I said. "We know they're looking for gold, willing to kill for it. Would a government be that hungry for gold?"

"Well," said William, "it is still possible that he is looking for it for himself and his friends—and lying about it—but do you really think governments are not interested in gold? Who spends more than a government? Let us say, just for the sake of argument, that a government could get their hands on a large quantity of unaccounted-for gold. If you did not have to say where you got the gold, how could you spend it?"

"Any darn way you wanted," said Evie.

"Exactly!"

On the inside of Simon's Chatanika cabin nothing had changed. The few floorboards pulled free were still free. The stack of old magazines and books in the center of the room, arranged with scraps of kindling as if for a blaze, still awaited the match.

"This is just such a lonely place," said Evie, "and shabby. This is *years* of dust. It's not a bit like the Simon I know—neat and … dapper. If he ever *did* live here," she said, standing next to the sacrificial pile, revolving slowly, "he's been gone a long time."

Outside though, someone with a spade had turned the entire clearing, all the way around the cabin, into a Swiss cheese. They got extra points for neatness. Stake marks in the ground showed where strings had been stretched for accurate hole digging, row by row.

"Whatever it is," said William, "they did not find it. These are all exploration holes and none are *discovery*. None has been expanded to facilitate removal."

"But ..." said Evie. She looked puzzled.

"But what?" I said. And I noticed that William stopped what he was doing to listen, too.

"What if whatever it was they were looking for was tiny? Not any bigger than hole-sized. What if it was a key or a map? A treasure map!"

"So they found it, you think?" William considered the possibility. "Maybe they are long gone, and we are left to be wandering around this lonely place peering into holes as if for rabbits?" He stood pondering a few minutes more. "No," he said, "I am not thinking so. They dug *all* the holes, the full grid. So I am *not* supposing they found what they were looking for." That's when he looked up, over my shoulder. "Ahhh," he said, and raised his hands shoulder high. "You would be the man from Viet Nam."

I turned, raising my hands also, not much surprised to once again meet Dave Forsythe, though he looked more than a little surprised to see me. Hatless in the cool clear air, he looked smooth and dapper in his long, dark overcoat and stateside galoshes. The gun he had previously offered me while riding the *Kalakala* across the Sound, he now aimed at all three of us, sweeping it back and forth. I knew that gun, that model, a service-issue Colt

.45 automatic like one I carried as a med-tech in France during the war.

"Father Hardy and," he said, his gaze shifting, "the lovely Evie, alive again. Is it Easter already?"

There didn't seem to be much to say so I didn't say it. He looked from one of us to the next as though inviting someone to tell him something. When no one did he started again.

"I don't want to have to kill you," he said, lying easily. I found myself wondering if he lied easily because he worked for the government, or if he worked for the government because he was such a smooth liar. Or if it even mattered. Either way, he and the government were a match made ... probably not in heaven.

"We have no beef with you," he went on, "just tell me what I need to know and you can be on your way."

So they hadn't found what they were looking for! "Let me see if I have this right," I said. "You want the gold, or something that leads you to the gold, or you want us to hand over a friend so you can torture him until he tells you where to find the gold."

"Very good. You've been listening." He looked at me expectantly. "Which is it to be?"

"None of the above," I said. "As far as you're concerned we're all dead already, just still walking around."

"A fact that perplexes me," he said.

He spun the .45 on Evie. "Then say goodbye to Miss Evie."

"Goodbye Evie," I said, without taking my eyes off the muzzle. I crossed myself, bowed my head and began to pray silently.

"That's it?" said Forsythe "You have nothing else to say to save the woman you told me you love?" I looked up. That won a definite side look at me from Evie and a tiny grim smile.

Exasperated, Forsythe spun the weapon on me and this time cocked back the hammer. "I guess you're the goner then, unless Evie has something she wants to say."

"I do," said Evie.

"That's better." Forsythe softly lowered the hammer and turned his face to her expectantly. "Let's hear it."

"Hardy," she said, still facing forward, "the best moments of my life started when I met you. I feel the same. I love you." She also made the sign of the cross and began to pray.

"Damn you both," said Forsythe. Pulling back the hammer again he raised the pistol up to his shoulder level, sighted carefully on the center mass of my chest and began squeezing the trigger.

"Are you sure you're a government agent?" I asked. He looked startled but stopped squeezing the trigger.

"Of course I'm sure." He actually lowered the gun for a heartbeat. "Why would you even ask a question like that?"

"Because you seem determined to kill the people who could be your best link to finding Simon."

The pistol came back up. "But I know that you *don't* know anything about where he is or where the gold is."

103

"We could be lying."

"But you're not, are you?"

"Well," I said, "we could be partners. Find the gold together. After all, this is Alaska. We know it and you don't."

He laughed. "Already got partners, Father. And right now, you'd say just about anything to keep you and your friends alive. Right?"

"Sure," I said, "wouldn't you? But it doesn't mean I'm wrong. You'd have a better chance with us than without us."

"Say your prayers," he said, "quickly, as if that will help you." And although nothing was funny, he suddenly laughed. "I saw," he said, "in a Saigon market place, a Christian pilgrim, begging, doing quite well because he had contrived to bleed from both palms, as if his hands were Christ's hands from the so-called crucifixion. As if a bleeding hole in each of my palms proves the existence of a God, of some

benevolent being greater than ourselves."

He laughed again and then he thumbed back the hammer, aimed the pistol at a spot I imagined in the middle of my chest and again began to squeeze the trigger.

A thousand scenes, or a hundred thousand scenes from my life, flashed in front of me. Too many to even begin to remember. I thought Mary, of seeing her again soon, thought of my dad, thought of a beloved Collie I had as a boy back in Kentucky—a dog I hadn't thought of in years. Thought of my ordination and the beginning of this new life, now apparently ending. Mostly I thought of Evie, with great sorrow that we wouldn't have more time together, and reaching out for her hand found hers reaching for mine. I had to force myself not to look away from the gun. That's why I saw it.

Soundlessly a small hole appeared in the back of his gun hand, driving the gun sideways out of his grip, followed by a fine spray of blood and tissue and a grinding shriek of shock and pain. I didn't hear the sound of the shot, though Evie claims she did. I bet I've seen guns shot out of hands a hundred times, but always for a dime in the Saturday afternoon matinee. In the army they cautioned us about headshots and extremity shots. "Aim for the big parts," they told us. So I'd come to believe that hand shots were just for Roy Rogers, the Lone Ranger, Hopalong Cassidy, or the Cisco Kid. Of course that was all before I met Andy.

At the same time, the unmistakable metallic sound of a weapon cocking drew my eyes to William. Like an old Mississippi River gambler, some kind of mechanism up his sleeve had produced a small-caliber two-shot Derringer. I had somehow forgotten William in the equation.

So had Forsythe. It had never occurred to me or Forsythe that the only one dying today could be him. Grabbing the whimpering Forsythe by the arm, William turned to Evie. "This one?" he asked, his meaning clear.

"Yes," said Evie, "this is one of them. Maybe the leader."

The no-nonsense question, the answer, and the none-too-gentle grip on his shoulder finally cut through Forsythe's fog of pain. "Wait a minute," he protested, "wait a minute ... what are you doing?" He held his bleeding hand out from his body like something fragile and not actually connected to his arm. "I'm an agent of the U.S. government. Anything that happens to me ..."

"Shut up," said William, giving Forsythe a push toward a brushy area. "I know something about being a government agent and this is one of the logical outcomes." His eyes met mine. "You two go and greet Andy ... I am certain that most excellent shot was his. I will not be a moment."

"No!" blustered Forsythe. "If I go missing ..." Somehow he'd lost his man-of-the-world veneer, the difference made more dramatic by his sniveling.

Evie caught up with the two and put her hand over William's left hand, the one propelling Forsythe into the brush for his rendezvous with a small-caliber slug. Clearly payment owing for his attempt on Evie's and my life. Frankly, in the heat of the moment, it didn't seem like such a bad idea.

"William," she said softly. "No, I don't want this."

I saw William's jaw clench and unclench and he smiled at Evie, though a little grimly. "This man has tried to kill you, to kill both of you, for nothing but money. If he were a dog and bit you, we would none of us question putting him down. Worse than the dog who is a simple creature and does not know better, is this bit of excrement who has known exactly what he was doing. Payment is now due."

"But William," said Evie, so softly I almost couldn't hear her. "I don't want it on your conscience or on mine. He's not worth it. Please don't kill him!"

William's eyes met mine. "And you, Father," he said, "he did his best to kill you, too."

I shook my head. "If we shoot him, what's the difference between him and us?"

"That is easy," said William. "He is moldering in a shallow hole, and we are enjoying a cup of the good coffee, and the air is moving in and out of our lungs. Sometimes we are laughing. Sometimes we are enjoying Andy's excellent Italian food. So," he concluded, "I will kill him now."

Forsythe's knees buckled. Seems he dealt death more confidently than he received it.

"Don't kill him." Andy called as he approached. "Not worth it. That's why the hand shot. I vote we let him walk back to Fairbanks. He'll be leaving a blood scent all the way. If a bear eats him ... so is that our problem?" He shrugged. "When he wakes up in the morning, he still has to be him. Leave him alive."

"Oh," said William, straightening, the derringer snapping back into his sleeve, "if I must." All the same, he quickly frisked Forsythe on the ground, coming up with only a pocketknife. He pocketed it and Forsythe's .45.

"Do not get up," he warned Forsythe, "or I may change my mind about shooting you. I may anyway." Then he turned with the others to greet Andy. A small caliber rifle with a big scope hung from his shoulder, having made his impossible shot from only God knew how far away.

Evie ran into his arms, actually knocking him back a step, then stood alongside her cousin as William stepped up to solemnly shake his hand. I held out my hand but Andy brushed it aside, and we embraced—which in any other situation would have made me a bit uncomfortable—but now, thumping each other on the back just made me happy.

Standing back to look at him I could only shake my head and smile. The small-town Andy we knew and loved—all-Athabascan in plaids and jeans or old army khakis, and a little shaggy—had come home cosmopolitan Ligurian Andy! A narrow mustache and precisely clipped and groomed sideburns, wide brimmed elegant fedora and long chocolatey wool overcoat—a suntan—even a new way of standing and speaking, made the conversion complete.

"*Ciao, Padre,*" he said. "*Ciao, bella,*" to Evie, and digging in his overcoat pocket produced what he had promised on the morning he went away ... one pound, whole beans, Italian roast ... and not a red can in sight. Coffee!

CHAPTER 11

I knew," said the bishop, pausing to sip from his coffee mug and sigh happily, "that we needed help; we needed Andy."

"How did you find me?"

It turned out the bishop's boyhood friend was now a Roman Catholic priest who knew a bishop who knew a monsignor who was friends with someone at the Vatican. From there Andy took up the tale.

"Imagine the Mediterranean," he said, looking around the table, "if you can. It's early, fishermen are hauling their dories down from the town square into the little harbor. They sing as they carry the boats to the water. It's a village called Vernazza. A thousand years ago Romans terraced the steep hillsides and grew grapes. Most of the streets are too narrow for cars, so they use bicycles, or just walk. A little way up the hill the train comes out of its tunnel, unloads passengers, blows its whistle and hurries away into the next tunnel in a cloud of steam and ash. So I'm sitting there with my second cup of espresso, and I look up the main street and see a priest coming down. Long black robe, flat-brimmed hat, and I think, 'He looks like a man with a mission.' And then I think it looks like he's heading straight for me. But I don't know any Italian priest, so I go back to watching the fishermen, but when I look back, the priest still seems aimed right for me.

Then I realize he's probably hungry, headed down to breakfast just like me, mouth set for the fresh-ground coffee, the breakfast sausage with fennel, croissants the French way, and he stops right in front of me."

"That's a little spooky," said Evie.

"It gets spookier," said Andy.

"How?" I asked.

"He looks at me for a long moment then calls me by name! 'Signor An-dee,' he says. He doesn't even ask. He knows it's me. But it was what he said next that really got me." Andy put his mug down and looked around at us, obviously for effect.

"What?" I prompted, now intrigued.

"The priest said, 'You are needed at home!'"

CHAPTER 12

*I*t was lucky you found us when you did," I said to Andy later.

"Lucky heck," said Andy. "The bishop told me where you were going and lent me your truck. I borrowed the rifle from my cousin. Freddy," he said to Evie, before she could ask which one, and to me, "my mother's sister's oldest son. He moved to Fairbanks when he came back from the war."

We three were back around the kitchen table in my rectory cabin in Chandelar where we belonged, seated on the uncomfortable tippy stools, drinking Italian coffee, hand-ground in our presence by Andy. He didn't much like putting the coffee in a coffee pot strainer to perk, but didn't have whatever it was the Italians used to make theirs, so he made do.

"Catch me up," he said, and we did. Although less than a week since I'd crossed the ice in the dark and then gone searching for Evie, it felt like months so much had happened. With the river running clear of ice, we'd brought ourselves and the pickup truck back across the river on the Chandelar summer ferry, a ramped barge made fast to a small sternwheeler riverboat. With daytime temperatures balmy—in the midforties and lots of sunshine—only piled snow remained unmelted and I had the sense of brown earth and grass not so much being revealed as flowing back. Though I welcomed spring, I was less enthusiastic about mud everywhere and streets filled with standing water, some of it too deep to drive through.

Three days ago, in Seattle, driving in a classy Chevy with the windows rolled down, now seemed like a summertime dream. We drove the sixty miles home from Fairbanks with none of us tempted to roll down the windows.

"Home sweet home," said Andy, surveying the sog. "I left Italy for this?" Evie half turned on the seat and punched her cousin in the arm.

"Ow! Okay, maybe I had better reasons ..."

Back at my cabin we made coffee and talked and then made more coffee and kept talking, not just about gold and people trying to kill us.

"So how was it," asked Evie, tilting her head and smiling at her clearly favorite cousin.

"It was," he actually kissed his fingertips and exclaimed, "*Fantastico!*"

"It's not just gold," said Andy, still later, with Evie camped on my phone trying to salvage her University semester by long-distance. "I mean not just gold for the finding, like 'Where is the gold dust along the creek bed so we can go pan?' These guys are looking for a supply of gold in bars all stacked up and waiting for them to torture or kill someone so they can haul it off. Who has that much gold? Nobody! Well, Fort Knox. But far as I know, Fort Knox is still heavily guarded and still in Kentucky. And how Simon, a life-long deckhand fits into this pile-of-gold notion... Any luck?" he said to Evie as she returned to the table.

"Big phone bill," she said to me. "I'll pay you back!" "Yeah," she said to Andy, "they have a thing called an incomplete. I have six months to finish up. I was almost finished with the semester anyway. So it's cool."

"Cool?" I asked.

She blushed a bit. "What they say on campus. *Cool* means it's okay or good. And saying cool means I'm hip," she added with a grin.

"Hip?"

"Never mind," she said, clutching my arm fondly. To Andy she said, "He's old but dear."

Andy shrugged. "Didn't know what 'cool' was, either."

She dropped my arm and reached for her jacket. "You're old but dear, too—or maybe just *old*."

They went out my door arm-in-arm, laughing, leaving me with the feeling that things had gotten right again after having shifted a bit out of kilter for too long. I admit I allowed myself to forget that nothing ever shifts all the way back.

On the next day, Saturday, much of the town turned out for the church's spring rummage sale, held in our steel war surplus Quonset hut. Our rummage sales were what passed for fashion events in greater Chandelar. Churches in the South 48—that distant place we called The States—boxed up their used clothing and sent it north to missions that served native Alaskans. They did it completely without thought for what native Alaskans might possibly want or need to wear.

Many of the items were what didn't sell in those far-distant estate sales, after the death of their former wearers. Whoever closed out the estate simply folded the rack of the 'unchosen' into a box—sometimes hangars and all—and sent it north. So we had a great supply of wire coat hangers, even though few in Chandelar had closets or even clothing that needed to be hung. We had a great supply of pre-war 'zooty,' wide shouldered suits and sport jackets for Chandelar men whose only possible need for such a garment might be their own funeral. And for women, an array of summer dresses—dating all the way back to the mid-nineteen thirties and sometimes off the shoulder in incredibly sheer fabrics. The young women would model these things, shyly with so much dark shoulder exposed, with all of us laughing uproariously. Pleated seersucker Bermuda shorts in impossibly large sizes nearly crippled us with laugher, some of the older ladies excusing themselves to walk across the street to the rectory toilet, probably to avoid peeing themselves.

In a far-northern culture of people who hunted and worked the land, who wore jeans or surplus khakis and flannel shirts and always kept as much skin as possible away from the mosquitoes, these clothes might have been from another planet.

One unintended blessing of used clothing from the states had always been the cash left undiscovered in the pockets. Ones and fives, sometimes even a twenty or fifty became like treasure in a treasure hunt and a core group of us got together to search every garment in every carton that arrived from the states. The money went for brand new things, usually for children and babies, like diapers, new-born-size clothing and jars of Vaseline or Vitamin A&D ointment.

I hadn't yet been able to escape the fact that nearly all of the people whose clothing we were selling and wearing were dead. An afternoon spent in the Quonset hut with the smell of old clothing and the pervading sense of all those people gone— and their clothing here without them—often left me low. As the last happy shopper straggled away, having traded nickels and dimes—or nothing—for good quality but largely inappropriate clothing they'd wear for years, I snapped the padlock. Then wading back across the street, I thought of the man or woman in Boston, Chicago, Chattanooga or Miami who spent part of a day and a chunk of change shopping for some particular item of clothing. They tried it on, fingered the fabric, maybe hesitated at the price, but ultimately took it home and probably wore it.

Now, the item they had been so very particular about was several thousand miles away, used clothing folded on an old wood table, waiting to be purchased for pocket change and worn to cut wood or feed huskies. Yes, it seemed right that rich people's clothing ended up on poor people in a faraway place like this. Jesus would approve—I believe—but in some not very definable way, it also seemed sad.

I had almost reached my cabin door when I heard something unmistakable and wonderful, something not heard around here for a few years—a steam whistle—long and low, powerful, thrilling, each blast ending just a bit mournfully on a flatted note. I admit I stood watching the railroad tracks just across the street, expecting a steam locomotive to come rolling through, though I'd never seen one on the Alaska Railroad. They went over to diesels several years before my arrival. I finally realized I wasn't hearing a train whistle, but a boat whistle from the river, just another hundred yards beyond the tracks. I couldn't *not* start walking, following the sound.

Even in the somewhat backward Territory of Alaska, most of the riverboats had long gone to steel hulls and superstructure, propeller driven. The great wooden boats, steam powered, with their huge red-orange paddle wheels, had long been pushed aside, dynamited, burned, sunk, or beached, rotting by the Tanana, Chena, or Yukon rivers, sun shining through gaps in old planked hulls. Save one, apparently, and I was seeing her now.

Last of Alaska's great river steamers, the old *Nenana* pulled up to the dock. I'd seen her before, of course, moored around the bend from the town of Nenana on a quiet backwater, locked in ice and covered deeply with snow. I'd been out hunting with Andy and his goofy cousin Jerry—in better days before Jerry did his best to murder the two of us and Evie. In a time of no moose to be found, we'd been hunting rabbits—arctic hares gone to white in winter—hard to see and shoot in the snow. But we needed the meat. Neither Andy, nor Jerry missed much when pulling a trigger, and lucky that! Rabbit was our only meat for a while.

So, I had seen the *Nenana*, mournful, alone, seemingly forgotten, nothing at all like today. The huge paddle wheel revolved slowly, steam chuffing—and the triumphant blast of that steam whistle! Deckhands and dockhands lined up to cast and receive lines, making the old girl fast to the dock that she and boats like her had once owned. I admit I was thrilled.

"I'll be dipped," said Andy, over my shoulder. In just a few minutes more, at least fifty people gathered to watch. Evie arrived and stood between us, careful not to touch me or stand too close. Though villagers already knew we were fond of one-another, Evie was careful not to give them too much to chew over or write to the bishop about.

The *Nenana* looked bigger than I remembered, probably some of that due to the absence of drifted snow. She appeared to be well over two hundred feet, with maybe a forty-foot beam, and four decks plus a pilothouse deck.

"Never thought I'd see this again," said Evie. "The *Nenana* used to stop at the Mission for wood when I was little. Cutting wood was one of the jobs for the big boys. And sometimes the purser— Simon, as a matter of fact— would come out on the upper deck and throw us penny candies. Jerry and Frankie used to grab up as many as they could and sell them to us later for two pennies, or three, or trade for whatever treasures we had, which wasn't much. Those were the days," she said, a bit wistfully, and I risked an arm pat.

"She burned more than a cord of wood an hour," said Andy. "Except for the war, hardest job I ever had. We whipsawed it all by hand. Boats like this one ate wood almost faster than we could cut it. They converted to oil, but looks like somebody took the tanks out, 'cause they're burning wood today. Sure wonder what she's doin' here."

"She has been pressed into service," said William, strolling up, knowing something none of the rest of us knew, as he frequently did. He smiled at Evie. "The *Nenana* is about to set off on her old route west, pushing a barge to the Yukon and then on to the Bering Sea.

"You know all this?" said Andy.

"I do."

"How?"

William looked around a bit before he answered. "Because it is my business to know things. I am a professional knower.

"So," said Andy, "ya know any more?"

"Oh yes," said the taller man, bending slightly, "and this would be the time to discuss it, but would not be the place."

I wondered if I thought he sounded secretive because I knew him to be a spy, or did he actually sound like that because he had secrets? Pulling my eyes from the spectacle of the old riverboat, I looked at him and he, raising both eyebrows, tipped his head in the direction of the rectory.

"Better get back," I said to the others. "Want to walk me?"

"Sure," said Andy, who had been following the exchange with William. The move caught Evie off-guard and she looked from one face to the next.

"What a minute," she said, "what did I miss?"

"Time to go, dear," said Andy, and clutched her by the elbow, bringing her along.

"That old boat is so much a part of my memory," she said, walking back across the railroad tracks. "You know I've never ridden on her! Guess I missed my chance."

With coffee set to perk and the three of us assembled and orderly, William regarded us over the top of his silver wire-rims before speaking. "You do not know any of this," he said, and we nodded. He seemed far too serious to be talking about what was probably the final voyage of an old steamboat.

"None of this is about the boat," he said.

Andy made his doubting face. "Then what's it about?" he asked.

"It is about oil," said William. "I have learned of a discovery of vast oil reserves in the Arctic, possibly one of the biggest oil and gas strikes in the history of the world."

"Really?" I said, expressing a good bit of doubt. "It hasn't been in the news. What you're talking about would be a banner headline. But why the hush-hush? There've been oil strikes in Alaska since the late 1800s. Some oil company will make a big profit and life will go on."

"There has never been an oil strike in Alaska this big," insisted William. He hesitated. "My sources tell me there has never been a strike so big in the U.S. or in all of North America. And there has never been, not just an oil strike, but a bonanza of wealth so deeply rooted in the American political dynasty. Life as you know it— political life—will be changed forever."

"Huh?" said Evie.

"William," I said, "that sounds pretty far-fetched."

"Yes, it does. But let me tell you..." He hesitated. "Some things I know and some things I am guessing. You can decide for yourselves if I am wrong or right. But not now, not immediate. Some of this may play out over time."

"Nah," said Andy. "Too much."

"Oh, that is for certain," said William. "But here it is." He looked around the table. "Even now there exists a cabal at the highest reaches of the American government. It exists to profit from participation in the energy future, not just of this country, but of the world."

"That's just crazy," I said. "You're saying President Eisenhower is in on this?"

"Possibly, but I don't think so."

"Well then who?" demanded Andy. "If it isn't Eisenhower, who could it be?"

"Come on, William," said Evie, "just spill." He smiled at her fondly.

"Okay," he said, "now I am spilling. Take notes."

"The *Nenana* has been brought out of mothballs because it is the only riverboat of its size—available on short notice—to move barges of heavy oil equipment to the Bering Sea. That is the fact. Now here are my predictions. Alaska will be a state—soon—and without any mention of this oil strike. But make no mistake, it will be oil that greases the skids of statehood."

"Okay," I said. "I think statehood will happen anyway. Though I wasn't expecting it quite so quickly."

"As a major oil producer," William continued, "the United States will go head to head with oil producers in the Middle East and elsewhere. There will be oil diplomacy, maybe even wars fought over petroleum."

"Okay," I said, "so statehood and possible international conflict. I can see that."

"But maybe," William continued, "the strangest occurrence of all..."

"I'm ready," said Andy. "Hit me."

William gave a little snort. "We are talking about nothing less than the presidency."

"Of the United States?" I asked.

"At least," he said.

"So you do think Eisenhower is complicit!"

"Not Eisenhower," he said. "It will be Nixon. An entire dynasty founded on profits of oil. He will ascend to the presidency, and it will change the world."

The room fell silent as we stared at him.

"Nixon?" said Andy. "Nah. *Vice President* Nixon? The guy who makes speeches about his dog and his wife's coat? Never happen! That's just too weird."

CHAPTER 13

I went over all of William's prognostications again on Monday morning, standing in my flannel bathrobe on the furnace grate in my forty-degree cabin. While basking in the warm updraft, I waited for coffee to perk—coffee "from the red can"—and not from my Italian stash. Ironically, I now kept my Italian beans wrapped tightly in their waxed bag, secure in a spare red coffee can on my chilly back porch.

Having real Italian coffee beans put by, made me feel oddly wealthy in a way that real cash had failed to do. Last winter I had the great good fortune to not only *not* die at the hands of Jerry, my demented parishioner, but to inherit more than fifty-thousand dollars cash and a brand-new 1956 Ford pickup truck. It's a complicated tale, but the salient point is that I found myself suddenly, if not wealthy, very comfortable with more money than I'd ever had, ever wanted, or even dreamed of. A distinctly odd situation for a mission priest.

Although the money and the truck were bequeathed to me, I chose to believe they were intended for the church. Certainly the money in question had been squeezed out of the people of the Tanana Valley, many of them my parishioners, and it needed to go back to them, to benefit them. So I would be the custodian. Which led to my Monday morning dilemma: the chance to buy something I'd wanted for the rectory and for myself.

With the school year ending and some of the teachers leaving for good, heading back to the States, I had been offered a really good deal on an Amana refrigerator. I admit to being tempted though it's the size of a black bear and would have to stand around in my cabin somewhere.

I heard a quick knock on my front door and then a tentative, "Hello?"

"Coffee's on, Andy," I called out. "Just getting dressed."

The short hallway between the front room and the kitchen passes right by my bedroom door, just about where I stood on the grate. He looked in.

"That's not getting dressed," he said, "that's standing by the heater. On the heater!" He went on into the kitchen and I could hear him rattling around getting coffee, opening the sugar, getting a spoon from the drawer and the canned milk from the back porch. "Your milk's right on the edge," he called out. "Back porch is getting too warm. Least it's not frozen."

"All I got," I answered.

"Lucky I like it edgy," he called back, ever the realist. "So whatcha doin'?"

"I'm pondering." I pulled on my khakis.

I heard him pause. "Pondering? Priest business? Somebody in trouble?"

"No," I said, buttoning my shirt, deciding to wait on the collar. "Everyone's okay so far as I know."

"That's good." I could hear the sugar spoon clink the side of the mug as he stirred.

"Well what then?"

"Trying to figure where, in this house, I could stand a black bear."

That brought him. He came back to my bedroom door, shaking his head "They don't make good pets."

❖

We were at the table, sipping coffee, not talking about much, and me still trying to figure out where to put my new refrigerator when we heard one quick knock.

"Are ya decent?" Evie called, Then William's voice. "I smell coffee. Good!" We had a quorum, which is why on most Monday mornings I made the full pot.

Evie came down the hall into the kitchen, kissed Andy on the top of his head and patted me on the top of mine. "No kiss?" I said. She managed to also kiss me on the top of my head without much slowing her advance to the mug rack.

"Evie and I have just come from the river," announced William, grabbing his mug, pouring and sipping his 'clear' coffee, but not saying more.

"A-a-a-nd?" said Andy, rising to the bait.

"The barge is here," said Evie. "They brought it down empty from Fairbanks overnight.

"Empty?" I asked. "There goes *that* theory."

She gave me a look. "It would have to be empty."

"Have to be?"

"*Yes,* to load all the heavy machinery they're pulling off the rail cars." She leaned across the table. "Right. This. Minute. William was right!"

"And you can tell it's oil rig stuff?" said Andy.

"Can't tell anything. It's all wrapped in canvas tarps. Just big gray shapes."

"Did you ask?" She gave Andy one of her that's-a-stupid-question looks. I hated those.

"I asked a couple of the longshoremen. Terry Evan said it was road gear, highway equipment. And Ronnie Charlie said it was gold dredge stuff."

"There you go," said Andy.

"There I go?"

William blew on the edge of his coffee mug, took a sip and made an 'aah' happy sound. "It is oil drilling equipment," he said, "bound for the Arctic."

"We'll have to get a look at it," said Andy. "Maybe just go down there at night, dodge the watchman and peek under the tarps." His idea brought back images of him and me letting ourselves into the home of the dead man, Frankie Slick, sneaking around at night trying to find some clue about who wanted to kill him, and why. Though truthfully, it might have been a smaller job to figure out who *didn't* want to kill him.

"I *hate* sneaking around," I said. "And I'm not good at it."

"Probably skipped that class in seminary," said Andy. And the three enjoyed a laugh at my expense.

"And they've got—whatever it is—wrapped completely around, like Christmas presents," said Evie. "You'd have to cut the canvas, which would be hard to cover up. And, the barge sails tomorrow."

"All we must do," said William, "is get onto the *Nenana* and ask—or get a look at the manifest."

"Oh," I said, *"that's* all?"

125

"Maybe we could just get on as passengers," Evie suggested, "like in *Murder on the Orient Express*. If we just ride along on the river until they land the barge, we can easily tell if it is or isn't oil gear."

"Passengers?" I said. "Does the *Nenana* carry passengers? I thought it was just a freight boat."

"No," said Andy. "I've been all over her, back when I was cutting wood. She's what they call a *packet* boat on the river. Means she carries both freight and passengers, which in her day—back in the 1930s—would have been the only summertime way to get up and down the Tanana and Yukon rivers. Seventeen or eighteen double passenger cabins, plus crew bunk space below."

"Like we could get on," I said doubtfully.

"We don't have a prayer, do we?" said Andy looking my way, laughing at his—by now really old—priest joke.

"Dear God," I said, setting down my coffee mug and steepling my hands, "please get us on the *Nenana* for a voyage all the way down the Yukon. There," I said to Andy, "we do have a prayer. Now if I could just justify buying my new refrigerator and figure out where to put it..."

"You don't have room for one of those *and* a black bear," said Andy. "You're gonna have to choose."

"Black bear?" said Evie.

"Wants a pet, I guess."

Evie gave Andy another of her looks then turned a softer expression to me.

"Just trying to figure out if I can justify buying a refrigerator with church money, and then if I do, where to put it? Jens Holland is moving south and offered me his for nearly nothing. Can't decide."

"The Amana," she said, apparently up-to-date on local refrigerators. "That's a really good one. Take it now, and put it right ... there!" She pointed to a spot next to my propane range, currently occupied by Blazo-box shelves holding—not that much. "It'll fit." She made a face and pointed at the canned milk. "It'll keep your milk from turning."

"And you can use it to keep church potluck stuff and the Bible school Kool-Aid in," added Andy. "So see, problem—problems—solved."

Distantly, from the office at the front of my cabin, I heard the telephone start up. Since almost none of my parishioners had telephones, a call often came from somewhere else and frequently meant trouble for someone. So I never walked down my hallway and into my office to answer without reviewing a whole range of the possible tragedies this call could reveal.

Lifting the heavy black handset I said, "Hardy," and recognized the bishop's voice. A call from Fairbanks.

"Nothing's wrong," he said. He had once confided feeling the same anxiety about phone calls. "In fact, I have news. Good news. An opportunity."

I must have looked as stunned as I felt, walking back into the kitchen. "Uh-oh," said Andy.

"What's wrong, Hardy," asked Evie.

"Gotta pack," I said. "You too, if you want," nodding at both Evie and Andy.

"Is this more Forsythe?" asked William. "I should have shot him when I had the chance."

"No, no," I muttered, "not Forsythe. Far from it."

"Well what is it?" demanded Andy. "Where are we packing for?"

"We leave tomorrow morning—early—on the *Nenana*. An anonymous benefactor has given the bishop three full fares on the *Nenana*, for me and two guests. We're to visit and take the communion service all down the Tanana and Yukon, sailing clear out to Marshall, nearly to the Bering Sea. They've reserved a couple of staterooms for us."

I looked at Andy. I must have spooked him.

"What?" he said.

"I guess we *do* have a prayer."

CHAPTER 14

*L*ater in the day I heard 'the knock' and Evie came into my office and sat in the guest chair. We first met here in this office, although only about six months ago, it now seemed like years. To me we seemed like old dear friends, at least.

She didn't say anything for a time, just sat looking at me while I looked back at her. It was clear she had come to say something, and sitting in that chair, my 'priest-business chair' meant she got to go first.

"Coming back to the village is harder than I thought," she said. "It's very small here. I had managed to forget that. In Seattle, living in the University District, I could go out to the library almost anytime I wanted—even on Sunday! I could go out for pizza or coffee alone or with friends and nobody thought a thing about it. Here I can't even go into the Coffee Cup without Rosie peering around behind me to see who I'm with, or muttering about me taking up a whole table by myself, just to drink coffee. And then actually drinking that terrible excuse for coffee isn't easy either."

There didn't seem to be anything to say, so I didn't say it, just nodded. She didn't seem to mind.

"And then there's you," she said.

"When I worked for Frankie—with Frankie—people thought he paid me—well, he did pay me, of course—but not for sex. As you know, we never had sex. We were never *connected*," she hesitated, "that way. But some people thought we were and most people accepted that it was our story. He kind of talked it around that I was a prostitute—his prostitute—because it made him feel like a big shot. Part of what he paid me for was to let him feel like that, if you know what I mean. And he paid me really well. I'm ..." she hesitated again, "really comfortable. Except that it's all money extorted from—everybody. But that's a different problem."

"So along comes you," she said. "You're my first adult boyfriend, really, or you would be if I didn't always walk around knowing that you're a priest and much of the village thinks that I've been a prostitute. Hardly a matched set. Not to even mention you being white and me being Indian. Another unmatched set. You're my first ..." she really hesitated a long time on this one, "you're my first love, even though I'm in my early thirties. Most of the girls I went to the Mission with had four or five boyfriends and have been married for at least ten years."

I nodded some more.

"Did you really tell Forsythe you love me?"

"Yes."

"Why?"

"Because he wanted to know what was so important about you that I would come all that way and be willing to risk my life. I didn't mean to say that I love you, because it isn't really any of his business, or anyone's. I said that you were my parishioner and my friend, and that I had told you I would come, and just kept giving him reasons until suddenly that one popped out. When I heard myself say it, I knew it was true. Even Forsythe knew it was true."

"But here's the rub," she said. "Sometimes single priests out in the villages, even the Catholics, find girlfriends, or boyfriends—lovers, people to have sex with—and over time everybody knows it. Then the girl gets pregnant and the priest leaves. End of tale.

Okay, sometimes they really do love each other, or feel obligated, and they get married. But then the priest can never leave. He can't take a church in Omaha or Poughkeepsie—or Chattanooga—and show up with a 'colored' wife. Do you know what I mean?

"Of course," I said.

She looked at me hard. "And you agree?"

"I know it happens."

"So you realize we can't go on like this?"

"How can I answer that?

She pressed her lips together. It's possible she had never looked lovelier.

"With a yes or a no," she said.

"It's not a yes or a no question." "Either way, I'm doomed. It's like asking, 'Are you still beating your wife?' She smiled a little.

"Or you're too kind to answer. Or you won't give me the right answer because you do love me and don't want to hurt me. Or ... I don't know. But I think that you think the answer is yes. And I love you back," she said, "but too much to sneak into your bed at night, and too much to go around pretending we don't have sex when I really want to. That's funny." She gave a kind of snort. "I used to pretend that I *was* having sex and really didn't want to. Which is why we need to put some space between us and I need to get back to Seattle as soon as possible. I'm pretty sure I don't belong around here anymore. Just right now I'm not sure I belong anywhere. And you," she added. "you're about to share a cabin on a riverboat, either with a man most people here know is gay, or a woman many people believe is a prostitute." She laughed and shook her head, ruefully. "If I stay home at least you'll have your own stateroom."

"But..." I said.

"So *bon voyage*," she said, rising. Then she gave me that soft Evie smile, the one that breaks my heart.

"I'm glad we could have this little talk," she said, and went out.

CHAPTER 15

*B*y evening, they had the barge loaded, all the huge canvas-wrapped parcels shifted from flatcars. It could have been oil-field equipment they were loading, or logging, dredging, road building, bridge building—just about any kind of heavy construction.

At about ten o'clock William and I walked down to the river, still in daylight. The sun wouldn't actually set until after midnight, and rise until about three, so the night would never really get much darker than twilight.

We waved at the watchman and he waved back. There were several boats tied up along the earthen wharf: the steel-hulled *Tanana*, a tiny wooden river tug called the *Taku Chief,* and the *Nenana* with a long, flat barge made fast to her bow. I had heard she could only manage pushing one barge on the curvy Tanana but would push as many as four when they joined up with the wider Yukon River.

Andy's observation about the old steamboat's oil tanks had been accurate; they'd apparently gone into one of the newer boats. So all the way down the Tanana and the Yukon, we'd be stopping to take on the wood she required, more than a cord an hour. Even now, agents were going village to village buying seasoned wood, in effect paying villagers to get out and cut more. It would be a welcome transfusion of cash into villages that didn't see much of it.

A massive stack of cordwood had already accumulated here. About half of it was in four-foot sections, unsplit, just four feet of tree trunk, ten to twelve inches through. The other half was clearly firewood, cut for home fuel, and now purchased—probably at a pretty steep price—to fill in as steamer fuel. It hadn't occurred to me to wonder how they'd get enough fuel for a trip like this."

"You're not saying much," I said to William.

"Nor you," he said. He was right. All afternoon I'd been unable to get Evie out of my head, even more than usual.

"We have not seen the last of the man Forsythe," he said, taking off his glasses to polish them on a fresh hanky he pulled from a back pocket.

"William, that hanky looks ironed," I marveled. "Who do you find to iron your hankies?"

"I iron them myself," he said firmly. "What do you do with yours?"

"I use Kleenex. Sanitary paper hankies as God intended."

"Bosh!" said William, carefully refolding the hanky and sliding it back into his pocket. He sighted through the polished spectacles before sliding them on and hooking the bows over his ears. "Bosh," he said again, and as we paused at the river edge, William stepped over one of the *Nenana's* mooring lines to rest his rump on a steel bollard. "I wish I still smoked," he said.

I watched the muddy surface of the Tanana, all whirl and swirl, sliding swiftly beneath the hulls. Just for a moment I imagined trying to swim there, being surely sucked under. *A metaphor for my life?* I wondered. Being drawn along in something I

134

have no power to do anything about, but I just think I do? Then I came to the same conclusion I always come to when I realize my powerlessness: that's why I pray.

"He will try again," said William. "It is personal now that he has a hole in his hand. For the rest of his life, every time he tries to pick up something and winces, every time one of his friends asks him about the scar, he will think of you and this will become more your fault. Never mind that he was in the act of trying to shoot you when it happened. You may think that you or that Evie saved him. You didn't. One of us, or if we're lucky, someone else he has wronged, will be shooting him. Now it has become messy. We do not know where, we do not know when. Taking this trip, getting out of town, maybe out of reach, seems like a very good thing to me. Watch yourself." While talking he absentmindedly searched his pockets, his jacket, his shirt, hunting for cigarettes I knew he hadn't carried in years.

"You watch yourself," I told him. "The marshal told you himself that he's looking for spies."

"Which is perplexing," said William, slapping at a mosquito on his neck, a big one. "I am not spying on the DEW line. My job is to spy on the spies at the DEW line and thanks to—well—you, the worst of them are dead." I winced inwardly. "Perhaps there are more," he said, mostly to himself. "I need to find a real job, a job that *concludes*." He stood up to move along. "Spying never ends." He looked thoughtful. "Or if it does end, ends badly."

"Priesting never ends," I said, "but I'm okay with that."

He looked at me and smiled. "Perhaps I shall go to seminary," he said. Oddly, I could see it.

I found Evie sitting on my cabin's low front stoop.

"You could have gone in," I said. "You know the way."

"Yeah, I do. But then if someone came, they'd wonder why I was there and you weren't, kind of like I was living there or something. So I thought I'd just sit out here and wait. It's nice tonight, anyway, not many mosquitoes yet."

I sat down next to her. "William and I were checking out the *Nenana*. The barge is loaded and firewood's being delivered—from somewhere. I'm not sure where you get that much seasoned wood, cut to four foot lengths, on short notice."

"I brought you cookies," she said, not seeming very interested in news about firewood, and handed me a small brown grocery bag tied up with a green ribbon.

"You bake?"

She laughed, a soft musical, lovely sound. "I have skills you know not of." I slipped the ribbon off and pulled one from the bag. "Chocolate chip!" I bit into one and sighed. I hadn't seen many cookies lately. "Wants coffee," I told her. "Want to come in?"

She looked at the ground. "Don't know if I should. What would people think? Yes, I know I've been coming in for coffee for months, but maybe it's time to be more careful. I don't want you—or you and me—to be what they gossip about at the Coffee Cup. I don't want to damage your life, your career, to cut off your chances. You might think it can't happen. But it can and it does, and this is how." She stood.

"The thing is," I said, "I didn't become a priest to advance my career. I'm not in it for promotions. I don't want a big church. I don't want to be bishop. I became a priest to be a priest. I never dream about moving to a bigger parish in a bigger town, about having a fancy church car to drive around in—I was thrilled to get the pickup—and before that, okay with walking."

"So what *do* you dream about?"

"You," I admitted. "Pretty much just you."

"Oh Hardy," she said, and kissed me on the cheek before she went away."

CHAPTER 16

*Y*ou know," said Andy, "if ... or when ... the FBI comes to arrest William, they're gonna arrest all of us. He's a Russian spy, our Cold War enemy and I don't know about you, but I ain't reported him yet."

He'd showed up early, at six, so we'd have time for coffee before reporting to the *Nenana*. They were casting off at seven. Andy had doubts about that.

"Still loading wood over there," he said. "Think they might have been at it most of the night. Glad I don't have to do that kind of work anymore. I still have bad dreams about me on one end of a whipsaw."

He ground up some of his Italian roast while I spooned out powered milk instead of opening a can of Carnation that would likely spoil in our absence. "You know," said Andy, "speaking of crimes, putting this stuff in real coffee and drinking it is probably against the law somewhere. Even canned milk should be a misdemeanor. In Italy, there's a small pitcher of real cream—fresh—on the table. That's what we need. Maybe we should buy a cow! No?" He chose a mug while looking around at my small kitchen. "Definitely a refrigerator, then."

"But I'm serious about William," he said. "Have you thought about treason? That's what it is when you make friends with an enemy. And don't report them.

Andy was right, as usual. And the matter of the spy in our midst was a constant presence in my thoughts and prayers. What to do? He'd saved both our lives. And he'd also told us that he wasn't here to steal American secrets. Of course that's exactly the kind of thing a spy would tell you. As far as we knew, he'd been assigned to keep track of who else stole American secrets at the Distant Early Warning base, still under construction. Earlier this winter we'd broken up an East German spy cell, not intentionally. We didn't know they were East German spies until we were in the thick of it and they started shooting at us. So, I still had no idea what to do. I hoped we wouldn't end up explaining all this in court. I imagined cynical laughter, and words like 'gullible' followed by a lengthy prison term.

"What's my job on this trip?" asked Andy. "Or am I like Tonto, just your faithful Indian companion?"

I led him into my office and showed him the communion case, containing wine, wafers, holy oil, a Bible, and my copy of the Book of Common Prayer.

"If you don't mind," I said, "would you be in charge of this." It's all the important stuff. According to the bishop, we'll be holding services where there seems to be a desire for a service, baptizing, blessing, possibly last rites, and otherwise just visiting, talking and usually listening. Of course I'll be doing the lifting on those. I'm afraid you'll have a fair amount of hanging around time."

"No problem," he said. "One of my skills."

"Um," I began. He stopped me.

"I know. I'm also the bodyguard."

"Yep," I said, "and I'm glad you are."

For just a moment, I hesitated then opened a desk drawer. Last winter I took a snub-nosed thirty-eight special from a distraught man intent on putting a bullet in his own head. I still need to patch the bullet hole he put in my roof. This time of year I had to keep a coffee can perpetually in place to catch the melt. Every time Andy came into the office he'd say, "We gotta get that roof patched," but we'd managed to avoid it so far.

So now I hesitated over the gun. In my experience, if you brought a gun along, you were likely to end up using it. Somehow if you didn't bring it, some other solution would arise. Like a negotiation or a firm punch in the nose. Or both. On the other hand, if everyone else has a gun and you don't, then what? Probably something not good. In the end I took the gun out of the drawer but instead of packing it, hid it behind books on my bookshelf. The idea of a priest carrying a thirty-eight still seemed wrong. But I went ahead and hid the gun because I'd been burgled before. Like most of the rest of the town, I still didn't bother to lock my doors.

We finished up our coffee, along with toast and a couple of fried eggs, gathered gear, and struck out for the river at about six forty-five.

"Evie's not coming," I said.

"She told me."

"She say why?" He looked at me but said nothing, only smiled.

"Swell," I said then decided to change the subject. "I'm kind of excited about this steamboat ride.

With the old boat out of service, I thought I'd missed my chance."

"Me too," said Andy. "I cut firewood at the Mission for parts of three years and always dreamed of sailing on 'er. Then one day they said she was done. I remember feeling kind of lost and sick about it. Something from being a kid that somebody stole. Glad we get the chance."

Crossing the tracks, I said, "I wonder where Simon is? I haven't seen him and nobody's heard from him, that I know of. I hope he's not dead!"

"If he was dead it would be because the Forsythe gang killed him. But they're still lookin' for him so I don't think he's dead, at least not on account of them. But boy, I sure don't know where you look for an old river rat like Simon. Hope he's okay. Even if he did set you up."

With the river still high after breakup, the gangplank lay nearly level from deck to shore. A deck hand checked our names on the manifest and led us up steps to cabins. While the outside of the boat looked a bit tattered, the inside still gleamed, with cabins trimmed out in lustrous mahogany and brass. Although each cabin held an upper and a lower bunk, we each had a cabin to ourselves. Evie had been right. If she had come along, someone would be sharing. While, on a personal level, I'd have been happy to share with her, I knew my reality would have been sharing with Andy, which was fine, too, of course. With the exception of my late wife, I'd never had a better friend.

Since it only took seconds to drop bags on bunks, we set off together to explore the ship. Most of the boat crew, maybe fifteen or twenty men, still—somewhat feverishly—balanced four-foot tree lengths onto a high pile on two-wheeled, wheelbarrow-like carts that had a kind of outrigger for loading. When they had more wood balanced on the cart than I thought they could possibly get on board—without tipping the whole load into the river—they'd tip the cart back on its two wheels and push hard to get it aimed up and onto the narrow gangway. By then the cart was moving pretty fast and most of the crew would turn and walk back to load or push the next cart. So the two men on the steamship deck had the job of slowing and taming the cart before it ran clear across the deck and off the other side into the river, which it never did but looked like it could with every load.

"Do we know all the stops?" I asked Andy.

"Stops?"

"Ports of call?"

"In the old days, I think they'd stop something like every twelve hours for wood. Haven't heard what they're doin' now." He pointed at the bow, much of it stacked about four feet high with extra firewood. "Maybe planning to skip some stops."

We paused to lean on the shore-side rail. Only one or two cartloads of wood remained ashore and already the bulk of the crew were boarding and stowing the carts. The engine, which had been chuffing very gently in the background, now ticked up slightly and the whistle let go just above our heads. It startled us with a blast of steam and a moan that echoed across the water, over the town and, long after the whistle had actually stopped blowing, echoed back across the river from the far hill. It was wonderful.

Turning, we noticed the brass plate on a white-painted door. "Bet the purser has a list of stops," said Andy. He gave the door a quick rap as he turned the brass knob and we entered. There was only one man in the cramped cabin, just about the size of two of our staterooms, with three polished desks and a gear locker. The man—his head down as he made tick marks on a form—wore a snappy uniform with shoulder epaulets and a white officer's hat with a shiny black brim.

"Help you?" he said, looking up, answering with that simple motion the question 'Where do you look for an old river rat?' You look on the river, of course.

Simon gave us a hearty smile and rose to shake our hands.

CHAPTER 17

*T*hey think I got gold," said Simon. We had agreed to meet, once underway, in the tiny officer's mess for coffee and explanations. He paused to carve the end off a pretty good cigar with a small, very sharp pocket knife. When he fired it up, a tangle of aromatic blue-white smoke wreathed his head, turning sunlight into visible beams.

"Way back about 1937 somebody stole gold bars, a shipment of 'em, right off this boat. Nobody ever seen any of 'em again. Dumped in the river, they said, maybe a marker alongside. Maybe somethin' else.

"And you were purser?" asked Andy.

"Oh no," said Simon, and taking off his officer's cap, he smoothed his crew cut before carefully redonning the hat. "Waiter," he said. "White jacket, no fancy uniform back then."

"And they never figured out who did it?"

"They blamed some guys," said Simon. "Big trial. Had to swear on a Bible. Didn't help. Nobody knew anything. Nobody went to jail. One of those guys, a guy I worked with on the boat, said I did it. Wrote me a letter about it in 1948. Said he knew it was me. Still got the letter."

"I remember that, the robbery," said Andy, "a little. I was about ten. Every hole me and my friends ever dug after that, we thought there might be gold bars hidden in. One time we were down near the river shore, diggin', we heard a 'clink.' I mean, it's a river valley, nothin' but sand in our holes, no rocks even. But this shovel lets out a 'clink.' We were sure we found gold bars."

"Pretty strange hearing a clink, though," said Simon. "Whadya find?"

"Found a brick. A brand new, unchipped, unmortared brick. Buried in a hole in the middle of Alaska where darn near nothin' is made of brick. I never even seen a brick 'til that one. Kept it for a long time. Frankie wanted to sell it to me. Told him, *you can't sell me my own brick.* Boy he was mad."

Anyway, on account of the brick, we dug a hole big enough to drive the Mission's Farmall Tractor into, but no luck. Nothin'. Got in a whole pile of trouble for digging such a deep, wide hole."

"I remember that trip," said Simon, "like it was yesterday. A real bad trip. The purser on that boat called the Indians 'nigger,' treated 'em like that, real bad. Said one of the kitchen boys stole his shoes. Three of 'em tossed the boy into the wheel."

"Killed him?" asked Andy, horrified.

"Never saw him again. Fact, two Indian boys disappeared off that trip. Gold bars on page one, missing Indian boys on page—whups," he said, "they forgot to write that story!" He chuckled about it without actually smiling.

"You know this?" I asked. "Did you tell anybody?"

He smiled at me patiently. "And buy myself a trip to the wheel? No thanks. Never did sleep very well," he went on, "so sitting up top on the stern I saw three of 'em drag him out, right out of his bed in the middle of the night. Gone. Didn't wanna be

145

next. I just sat there while they dumped him. After all these years, I can still walk back on that deck at night, in the thunder of the wheel I can hear his screams. After it was all done, I stood at the rail back there, crying and vowed I'd get even—I'd do that for him—if it took the rest of my life. Darn near has."

"That's nasty," said Andy.

"Thing is," said Simon. "I saw those shoes again; purser fella still had 'em."

"Might as well tell you," he said, "it was those fellas that stole the gold. Planned it while I poured their coffee, lit their smokes, and cleaned up after their meals. They were real careful 'bout whites hearing 'em, but they didn't even see Indians, us *niggers*," he corrected himself.

"There was no safe on the old *Nenana,* then or now, so they locked the bars in one of the forward cabins and posted a guard, day and night."

"How much gold was it?" I asked.

"It was a hundred bars, each 'bout this big." He indicated with his fingers, a bar about the size of a bundle of six cigars, six inches long, maybe three inches across and two inches thick. "Heavy," he said, "but shiny and beautiful. Stamp on 'em read *First National Bank of Nome.*"

"Nome had a First National Bank?" I asked.

"Oh yeah," he said, "Nome was a big city. Big boom town with a fire department, twenty or thirty saloons, couple of banks, churches, whorehouses, everything."

"Sounds like you got a pretty good look at those gold bars," I said.

146

He smiled. "Oh yeah. We all did. After they got 'em stacked in there, they let us file through to look at 'em. They said we'd never see any of our own, so we could tell our kids."

"Were you a guard then," asked Andy.

"Nah. The boy guarding 'em was the brother of the kid who went into the wheel. By the next morning, he'd disappeared too."

"And they never found him, either?"

"Didn't know his name," laughed Simon, a genuine laugh this time. "The company called him Albert, signed him on with an *X*. Robbers paid him a hundred dollars and a pair of shoes to take a walk. Same shoes they killed his brother for. Wing tips, they called 'em. Black shoes with white. Thing is, someone told him they were gonna kill him too, and blame the robbery on him. All he had to do was let 'em in to get the gold. They'd alibi him, they said."

"Who told him," I asked.

He smiled. "Me."

"And nobody ever saw Albert again?"

"I seen him. Just a couple years ago, up the Koyakuk. His real name was . Had a real fine cabin up there, raised a passel of kids, and sent 'em to school. All eight boys attended UCLA."

"Really?" I said. "Albert from the boat has eight boys at UCLA? That's amazing. So they didn't throw him overboard?"

"They woulda. But when they went to get the gold, Albert was already gone. So they cut off the padlock, grabbed the gold and moved it to another cabin. Then they put a padlock back on the first room, and paid another Indian to stand guard."

147

"So he's guarding an empty room," Andy said. Simon just smiled.

"So did you steal the gold after they stole it," I asked.

He smiled again and shook his head. "I'm not a thief. But then is it really stealing to take gold that's already stolen?" He drew a deep lungful of blue smoke then exhaled. It smelled pretty good for a cigar, but I still wanted to jump up and prop the door open.

"Coming upriver, 'bout a day out of Nenana, all hell breaks loose—but real quiet. Turns out somebody stole the gold they already stole. It's not in the first stateroom, not in the second. Not no-where! Who's got the gold? Nobody knows. So we come to Nenana, where the gold is supposed to go on the train. The sheriff comes down with rifles to get the gold. The key doesn't work 'cause them guys changed the lock. So they pop off the lock, and no gold! They arrested the whole crew, everybody, searched the whole boat, even the bilges. There was only one jail cell in the whole town, and too many of us, so they kept us on the boat. Brought in the marshal, soldiers ... everybody. Never found no gold. Finally they arrested some of those guys, threw 'em a trial. But no jail time. No evidence, no witnesses.

Little boys ... and big boys ... been digging holes and listening for 'clinks' ever since."

❖

"He was right about hole diggin'. Bet that's what they were lookin' for at Simon's cabin," said Andy later. "Must have been a hundred holes around that place. Has to be those gold bars they're looking for." He looked at me. "Doesn't it?"

We were back, leaning on the rail, watching the swift current race us along north and west toward the Yukon. Birch and willow trees with fresh new leaves lined the shore. Every now and then a cabin slid into view, a soft plume of smoke rising from the tin chimney. The pilot would always blow the steam whistle and someone would come out to wave us past. Sometimes, just a lone sourdough, usually bearded, hatted and rumpled. Sometimes, a whole family, from little kids to old folks, pouring out of one tiny cabin to see us pass by, the little ones so excited they jumped up and down.

"If the gold bars were buried at the cabin," I said, "seems like Forsythe and his buddies would have found them. But why look there? Why look now? Why suspect Simon? It sounds—like it or not—like the gold went into the river, and if it did it's really gone. Covered with decades of silt in a river you can't even wade in, and know you'll get out alive. You can't dredge a thousand miles of river."

You couldn't dredge *one* mile," said Andy.

"Sounds like a lot of gold fever for nothing."

"Not gold fever exactly," he replied. "I keep thinking that these guys act like it's *their* gold. Like somebody owes it to 'em.

"So far they've been acting like Simon owes it to them," I said. "That's the part I don't really get. Why Simon? You know the other thing," I looked at Andy, "the *Nenana* making a run down the Tanana and Yukon after all these years, is the boat they lost the gold from in the first place. There's no way

149

they don't have somebody on this boat. Of course, there's no way they don't have somebody following us, too."

"Yeah," said Andy, "the thing is, now we've led 'em straight to Simon without even meaning to."

The next morning it was Jimmy Lucas who poured my coffee. I heard his voice first, over my shoulder. "Coffee?"

"Sure." I extended my cup.

"Morning Father." He nodded at Andy. "Morning Andy."

"Jimmy." I said. Andy was more succinct.

"How would you like a bullet in your head? You coulda killed Evie!"

I looked at Andy. "And me," I said. "I was there, too."

"Yeah, and him," agreed Andy, half rising.

Jimmy didn't flinch, didn't change expression, didn't stop pouring. "You're not the first person to make that offer," he said. "Fact, that's why I'm here. 'Get aboard or die,' was my choice, so here I am, pourin' your coffee. I already seen Nicolai. 'Course I can't report in 'til we reach the radio phone at Manley Hot Springs.

"You did save our lives," I said to Jimmy, "Thank you. Though my heart nearly stopped when I hit the water."

"Glad to help," said Jimmy, with a pointed look at Andy, who sat back down. "'Fraid it was the only way out for all three of us." He hesitated. "Just wondering, how *is* Eve? She mad at me ..." He shot a look at Andy. "too?"

"She knows you saved our lives," I told him, "and knows you had to do it. She's grateful." Jimmy smiled, a real smile, took his coffee pot and moved on to the next table.

"You were right," I said to Andy, "they did follow us."

"Swell," he said. "One time I would've rather been wrong."

"At least we spotted him," I said. "We know who he is."

"Yeah," said Andy, taking a sip of coffee and making his bad-coffee face. "Trouble is, we don't know who's watching him."

CHAPTER 18

*I*f we hadn't put in at Manley anyway, our first big port of call, I could have missed it by blinking or turning my head to say something like 'please pass the sugar.'

A cluster of cabins near the river bank, a tiny log church, small store, barge-line office, CAA office—to keep the grass airfield company—and a couple of fuel tanks made up the town.

I had no more stepped ashore than a small Athabascan boy named Clifford homed in on me—the black shirt and white collar gives me away—to tell me I had a radio-telephone call at the CAA office. Jimmy and I walked over together while Andy kept an eye on Simon.

"I'm real sorry about this," Jimmy said.

"I know you are. But I don't get why you keep doing it. These people will kill you."

"Got no choice, Father. One of 'em is some kind of government guy. CIA, whatever that is. Said he'd hunt me down, kill me, kill my mother and rape my two sisters before he kills them. I don't have a mother or sisters, but I got the drift. Turns out I do have family and I'd like to not get them slaughtered."

"I see what you mean," I said, thinking—again—that maybe we shouldn't have been so quick to call William off from killing Forsythe. I 'jokes'. Sort of.

Jimmy went in first. I could hear what he said. It was brief; no 'Hello' or 'How ya doin'?

"The gold miner is on the boat," he said. And that was it.

The radio operator looked up. "That's all?"

"Yep," Jimmie replied then paid, and left the office.

I had expected that my call would be from the bishop. Who else knew to find me here?

"I've got you connected," said the radio operator. "Call from Miss Evangeline Williams."

I pushed the button. "This is Father Hardy."

"Say 'over' then let go of the button," he instructed.

"Over," I said, taking my finger off the microphone button.

Her voice came over the speaker, a familiar and dear sound. The rest was not. "Father," she said, knowing others would be listening, "this is Evangeline Williams calling from Chandelar. I'm afraid I have bad news." Then she said 'over' and released the button. It wasn't a good opening.

"Go ahead," I said. "Over."

"It's about one of your parishioners, Mr. William Stolz. I'm very sorry to tell you that he has been shot and is now missing and ..." I heard her stifle a sob, "missing and feared dead." The button clicked. She forgot to say 'over.'

The problem with radio-telephone is that much of Central Alaska was listening in. Anybody with a receiver could easily hear both sides of our conversation. Last winter, one of the Minto bachelors called St. Paul, Minnesota to ask his girlfriend if she would marry him. Since she knew everybody was listening, she said she'd get a letter right off with her answer, and the rest of us had to wait two weeks to find out what she said. Fortunately, it was yes.

"Evangeline," I said, remembering to press the mic button, "I don't understand what happened. How do you know he was shot if he is missing? Over."

"He was shot and fell into the river," she came back, then belatedly, "over."

"Who shot him?" I asked.

"It was an ambush. No one knows. A witness said he seemed to know his assailant, a man with one hand bandaged, who shot him from a distance of about twenty feet with a handgun. The witness said William ... Mr. Stolz ... clutched the middle of his chest and fell over backward into the river." Another sob. "Over."

A witness? Probably Evie.

"Should I come home?" I asked. "Over."

"Oh yes, please. Over." Then she said, "Marshal Jacobs requests that you return. Over."

"I'll have to round up an airplane, but I'm on my way. Over and out."

"Travel safely, Hardy," she said, forgetting her charade, her voice small and sorrowful. "Over and out."

The operator looked at me as I looked at him. "That's not good," he said. "We've got one plane you can hire, pilot named Len Samuels. He's here now. I'll send Clifford to fetch him. We'll tell him to meet you at the boat."

"Great, thanks."

He looked at me. "This guy was more than your parishioner, wasn't he?"

"Yes, a friend. A very good friend."

"I'm so sorry. You know there's about zip chance of getting him out of the Tanana alive."

"I know," I said dully, thanked him, and went out.

❖

"Shot William!" exclaimed Andy. Neither of us could say anything for a long moment. "How's Evie taking it?"

"She was crying. Said to come home."

"You goin'?"

"I think I should." We were standing in my small stateroom, me trying to think clearly. The shock of losing William made it all but impossible. Seeing him in his chair at the Coffee Cup, his joy obvious about being alive and ordering coffee, flirting shamelessly with Rosie, his careful measured, precise speech that never knew a contraction. "I'm just beginning to figure out all the ways I'll miss him," I said.

"You know they're doin' this to split us up, don't you? The next move, whatever it is, will be here on the boat."

I hadn't thought about that part of it yet, but knew Andy was right. "Should I stay? I could call her back."

"Nah, I think you gotta go." He looked away for an instant, blinking hard. "Wonder if it gave William any satisfaction, in that last second, to know he'd been right about Forsythe. Shoulda shot him when we had the chance. Who knew he'd be able to hit something shooting with his left hand? What were we thinking— that he would just go away? Hah!"

There came a small, knock at my door. Clifford. "Pilot Samuels is ready for you," he said shyly.

"Thanks, Clifford." I dug in my pocket for change, finding a half dollar. The joy on his face was palpable.

"A big one! Thanks, Mister Father!"

"Got to go," I said needlessly to Andy."

Andy, a Mission boy and one of the truest believers I know, said "Go with God."

I grabbed my shaving kit and started out the door.

"That's all you're takin'?"

"I'll be back."

He looked at me. "Say whatever it is you're not saying."

"What I'm not saying is, losing William makes it painfully clear how I'd feel if I lost you, and if I lost Evie." I thought about having lost my wife, which nearly killed me and still hurt daily. "I'm just not sure I can survive it."

"I feel the same about both of you," he said, "but it's part of the deal here on earth. Everything balances. You get joy, you get sadness. It *would* be hard, but you're up to it. One more thing," he added, "I know—I believe—that you're coming to be in love with Evie. In spite of anything—everything I've said. But even though you love her, you don't really know her. Like right now, you might think you need to protect her. You don't.

"Frankie had a two-inch scar at the base of his neck. Back when we were about ten or eleven, he and Jerry ambushed Evie and tied her up in the smokehouse. Then Jerry left and Frankie put his hands all over her. Real deliberate, just to show her he could do it. Figured word would get around, especially to the other girls, about how powerful he was.

"It took her most of the rest of the day to get herself untied. First thing she did was go down to the Mission fish house and got a knife and a whetstone. She never said nothin' to the deaconess, or the priest, or any of the teachers. Just for a week she sharpened that knife.

"Late one night, she sneaked into the boys' wing, tiptoed cot to cot until she found Frankie. She sliced a thin line in the skin on his throat with that fish knife she'd been grinding on. Then she cut his shorts so when he got up all his privates hung out. 'Course he woke up, but it was pretty much all done before he got his eyes open. Frankie didn't mind his throat being nicked, as much as having a knife that sharp so near his privates."

"He told the deaconess he cut himself shaving. Hah! He didn't even shave as an adult. They couldn't shake his story, though everybody knew all about it in about two seconds. It was a small school. The word that got around wasn't 'don't mess with Frankie,' but don't mess with *Evie* ... Eve ... they called her then, after the Bible."

"Just remember," he concluded, "to get out of the way when you see her flip a knife and catch it by the blade. 'Cause then she throws it."

CHAPTER 19

S amuels had been a fighter pilot in World War II and in Korea. We both wore headsets to be able to talk over the engine roar. "Like night and day," he said, his voice tinny in my earphones. "Prop fighters in the big war, jets in Korea."

"Do you miss the heavy hardware?"

"Guns, you mean? Never. I hated every minute of both wars."

"I meant the aircraft."

"Oh sure. Especially the raw power of the jet, the way your heart feels when you shoot off the deck, body pressed back into the seat. Not a lot of body-pressing in this old De Havilland. Great bird though. Manufactured in Canada during the war. U.S. government bought up most of 'em. This one is surplus. Stubby radial-engine nose, nine cylinders, slow as hell ... sorry, Father. But you know, out here there just isn't anyplace to race to, anyway. Which is why I'm here now, why I won't be leaving."

We flew on in mostly companionable silence. Samuels did the bulk of his communicating with one word and a finger point. "The Mountain," he'd say, pointing at a shifting glimpse of Mt. McKinley, wrapped in its own weather. Or, "Moose." When he said, "Grizzly," we peeled off and flew a quick circle to get a closer look at the huge creature, its brown coat thick and silver-tipped. It sat by a stream bit-ing into a still-wriggling salmon. He looked up at us curiously, but didn't stop chewing.

"The radio op said William Stolz got shot?"

"Yeah," I said. Coming back into that moment made me feel tired all over. I saw William at breakfast, just days earlier. Of course, neither of us knowing it was the last time. I think it was Dr. Einstein who said if we can remember the past, there's no good reason why we shouldn't also be able to remember the future. This would be one of those good reasons, one of those things you wouldn't want to remember.

"I think I met him," said Samuels. "Couple of years ago. I got a call to pick up some government guys at the Clear DEW Line construction site and haul them up north to some kind of relay station. Don't know exactly what it was, or what it was about. Government stuff. 'Fraid, by war's end, I'd had enough government stuff to last my whole lifetime."

"Anyway, your friend Stolz flew in with Marshal Jacobs. Sort of hush-hush, I think. Probably shouldn't be talking about it now. They might hunt me down and shoot me, too." He laughed at the notion before realizing what he had just said.

"I didn't mean to ..."

"It's okay." It was funny. You know, I'm not sure William knew Jacobs then. Might be you've got him mixed up with someone else."

"Oh yeah," he said. "I meet a lot of people on this job." Then he described William perfectly.

"But it sure sounds like him," I said. And on we flew.

Although we seemed to be in the air for days, the actual flight time in the slow plane, even with the grizzly detour, couldn't have been more than an hour. "Here we are," said Samuel's voice in my headphones, "Chandelar." He eased in the throttle lever and I could feel the Beaver slip lower. "Gonna lay over here a day or so if you need to get back downstream."

From my perch I could see my pickup parked by the grass strip, Evie leaning on the front fender. Evie's concerns about our personal privacy and public distance were all well and good but where I came from, heartland America and the Mid-South, when a woman showed up driving a man's car, there *was* something going on.

Seeing me started her crying again. I have that effect on women. Truthfully I was only about half a heartbeat from crying myself. The loss seemed insurmountable. But I folded her into my arms and held her and patted her and, felt the heart swell of being together again. I had seen William take her in his arms in much the same way, tenderly, lovingly. Now he had gone so quickly. It seemed wrong, was wrong. Although it runs contrary to everything I believe and stand for, I couldn't help thinking that if Forsythe were here now I'd gladly shoot him. Heck, I'd have to stand in line for that privilege!

"So, Evie, what happened," I asked gently as we climbed into the pickup. Her lip quivered as she began.

"William came by and said he was out for a walk, and would I join him? Of course I would, I said. He was like the father I never had. So we walked down past the church, across the tracks and along the riverbank, along the docks and down toward where that old steamboat is beached, the *Hazel B*. And it was right there that Forsythe stepped out from behind some cable reels and dock junk with a gun—in his left hand—his right arm was still in a sling. There was no cover. Nothing to duck behind, no place to hide. William pushed me aside and just stood there. Didn't put up his hands or anything. Forsythe smiled a terrible smile, like this was really a fun thing, and then shot him! The impact drove him back over the edge and into the river. With the river high, it was only about a three-foot fall. I'm a strong swimmer and I would have gone for him but he went under and never came up."

"I thought Forsythe would shoot me, too, so I tried to make myself stand as still as William had. But he walked up to me and touched his gun barrel to his forehead, like he was tipping his hat. "Miss Evie," he said, "a little present for your boyfriend." Then he turned around and walked away."

"When I couldn't see any sign of William, I ran to your telephone to call Marshal Jacobs and then to get boats out to start the search. We've got to find him. To bless him and bury him properly. I can't bear the thought of his body lying on the riverbank with bears and wolves and eagles ..." she stopped talking but I didn't have any trouble picturing the grizzly I'd just seen.

William had seen some terrible things in the war. Probably had been forced to do some terrible things. I couldn't help thinking that lying on that riverbank, being consumed by wilderness crea-

161

tures—becoming part of them, their muscles, their hearts and brains—was its own kind of peaceful blessing and conclusion to a life. But with Evie snuffling on my shoulder, heart broken, I didn't bother speaking of it.

Both overwhelmed, we drove the rest of the way back to the rectory in silence. When we were nearly there, she lifted her head from my shoulder and slid back to her own side of the truck seat, but reached over to take my hand, holding it until I needed it to turn off the ignition. I admit we sat a moment with the engine running, neither of us wanting to let go.

I thought she might balk at coming in, as she had on her last visit, but she didn't. I pushed the door open for her and she walked into my small sitting room, leading the way down the short hall to my equally small kitchen, soon to be made smaller by the addition of my new refrigerator.

There's an expression, 'wake up and smell the coffee,' that has to do with figuring things out too late. And so we, wrapped and insulated in sadness and loss, made it almost all the way to the kitchen without smelling the aromatic coffee, still steaming on my propane stove top.

There, sitting on one of the uncomfortable stools, was a man—tall, lean, gray hair, squinting a bit without his glasses—turning as we entered.

"Ah," said William, smiling, "the coffee is fresh and, I must say, delicious! You are just in time."

CHAPTER 20

*A*aaaah! Gently, my dear," said William, smiling while wincing at Evie's enthusiastic embrace. He gently, fondly kissed the top of her head.

"Bruised ribs?" I asked.

"Why yes," he said, "as a matter of fact. How did you know?"

"Seeing you here, alive, I'm assuming you were wearing some kind of bullet-proof vest. And since you went out for an evening walk wearing a bulletproof vest, I'm also assuming he was able to ambush you like that because you were expecting him."

His face shifted, rueful for a heartbeat. "I admit to not expecting him at that moment or I would not have taken Evie along. But yes, you are quite right about the vest. It was made in Korea, mostly of layers of silk."

"But William," said Evie, "how did you get out of the river alive? Almost no one does."

"It is a formidable river," agreed William, "extremely muddy, with no visibility, but I have been in worse. My training included being grabbed without warning and thrown through a hole in ice on the river Volga. Those who made it out alive were formally admitted to the program."

"Ice?" said Evie, incredulous. "Like here, like three or four feet thick?

"Nothing so dramatic, my dear. Less than an inch. Not insurmountable."

"How *did* you get out?" I asked him.

"I was young then and I admit, just a bit panicky. I tried punching the ice, with no result. I tried kicking it and got just a bit of cracking, but knew it would take too long."

"So how?" I asked, unconsciously holding my breath.

"I shot it. I pulled out my service revolver, pulled the trigger three times quickly and then punched. I caught the edge of the hole I created before the current could sweep me downstream. Once I had air I hammered out a bigger hole with the gun grip. Of course, pulling myself out was not an easy task. The air temperature of minus ten degrees Fahrenheit almost made staying in the water seem inviting. But only until lapsing into unconsciousness and dying ... a motivation to get quickly out and seek shelter."

"Okay, so how did you get out of the Tanana?" asked Evie, still snuffling a little and accepting a Kleenex from the box I extended to her. "I looked and looked for you."

"I was almost right below you, about twenty feet downstream, in a niche beneath wharf timbers. It looks solid from above but I was fortunate to find a groove I could wedge myself into. I held on for a time, until you had gone and I judged Forsythe had made his, how do you say, *getaway.*

"I ..." he hesitated, "wanted to call out to you, but I could not risk Forsythe hearing me, too."

"Yes, I see, and it's okay." She raised her eyes to his. "But why do all this? Why take the chance of letting him shoot you? What if he'd shot you in the head?"

"He's not a head-shooter," I said, "right?"

"Just so," said William. "Like most of us, he was trained to aim at the widest part of his target. He has not the imagination, skill, or style to do otherwise."

"And you counted on that?" said Evie.

"He did not disappoint me," said William, and he leaned across to pat her on the knee.

"I still don't understand. Why take the chance?"

"Because ..." he hesitated, looking for words. "Every day I am watching for Forsythe. I know he is coming, that he must have his revenge. It interferes with what else I must do to always be wondering when and how he will come. Now that he thinks he has killed me, and ... what is the expression—'The shoe is on the other foot.' Now that he is thinking I am dead, the advantage of sudden reappearance is mine."

Evie blinked.

"The element of surprise," I said.

William smiled. "Exactly!"

Evie stood up slowly, still taking it all in, and walked around William to the coffee pot. Selecting a mug, she filled it and waved one in my direction. When I nodded she filled it as well and added the flat teaspoon of sugar I took. Then she sniffed the canned milk and added a bit to each.

"It just seems impossible to have you back. To have you sitting here, drinking your coffee just like always." A tear rolled down each cheek and she let them as for a moment, we all sipped our coffee and were silent. She was right. It seemed too good to be true.

"If you like surprises," said Evie at length, breaking the silence, "and it seems you do, then I have one for you, too. Mine didn't seem that important with you ..." she looked at William "... dead. After the boat left, I got to wondering about the original gold heist and decided to call Fairbanks. I have a friend at the *Daily News Miner* who dug back through their morgue issues and read the best of it to me over the phone. Most of it was dull trial stuff. But the part that will interest you is the name of the First Officer aboard, Forsythe, who seemed to be the ringleader. Not the Forsythe we know, of course—ours is way too young—must be the father or uncle. Or maybe just a coincidence, I don't know, but there you are."

"Spy school 101," said William, "there is no such thing as a coincidence." He looked at me. "You agree?"

"Seems like a long shot." I said. "But that explains a bunch. No wonder he feels entitled. He already feels like he's been cheated. Good work," I said to Evie.

She tipped her head modestly, smiled and sipped her coffee. "Aw shucks," she said.

I couldn't shake the image of the Athabascan boy Forsythe and his friends tossed into the paddle wheel. That boy was the one cheated. It would be nice to be able to pay some of that back.

❖

I caught them up about Jimmy Lucas being on the boat, and why. And Andy's belief that whatever happened next would happen on the boat, which William supported. "Samuels, the pilot, is still here," I told them. "So I'm going to catch a ride back to Manley—if the *Nenana* is still there—or if she's moved on, then to any refueling spot with a clearing we can land in.

"They are certain," said William, "to have an unknown confederate aboard to watch Jimmy. Now you will have one as well."

I must have made a face. "I will? And who will that be," I asked, though I had a pretty good idea. He smiled.

"And me," said Evie. "This time I'm coming, too."

"Oh," I said, "I ..."

William agreed. "It's too dangerous for you!"

"But not for any of you? That's hooey."

"Well I ..." I said.

She got that determined look on her face. "How about this. I'll come along and I'll stay in my cabin ... hide out. If something happens I'll be there and know about it, maybe even be able to help, instead of here, worrying, wondering. And I'm bunking with my cousin," she announced, "in case you're concerned."

I couldn't help shaking my head. "I don't suppose we can talk you out of this?"

"Not a chance."

I called and left a message for Samuels at the CAA office. He had driven to Nenana to pick up a shipment of aircraft parts, but would call us. In the meantime, Evie drove William back to his cabin to pick up a few things, Mostly guns, she said later, some little thing with a battery—she thought it was a compass—and a pair of glasses to replace the ones he'd lost in the river. Samuels didn't call back until late and we arranged to fly out early the next morning.

"She's still at Manley," said Samuels. "There was a holdup finding seasoned wood, so they're now a day behind schedule. They say it'll get worse. There just isn't a quick way to find wood on short notice that's dry enough to burn, especially at the end of winter. Everybody who might have had some to sell, already sold it or burned it themselves, getting through the winter. And it's going to be like this all the way down the Yukon. That's why even the *Nenana* went over to oil-burning decades ago."

"Do you have room for two more passengers on the Beaver?" I asked him.

"Sure," he said, and then hopeful, "anyone I know?"

"See you in the morning," I told him.

Hanging up the phone, I stood for a moment in the twilight of my quiet office feeling like I hadn't been there much lately. I could smell the old paper of the shelved books, and the last of a cigar one of my parishioners had smoked. The measured gear movements of an ancient Regulator clock I inherited with the place emphasized the silence. *It's very much like home,* I thought, *which is a good thing since this is where I am now.*

I pushed books aside to pull the snub-nosed thirty-eight from its hiding place. A police-issue revolver, it fired a thirty-eight-special round. With the barrel so short it would be impossible to aim, effective at a range of only about three feet. I gripped it, aimed it at a knot on the pine-paneled wall and—double checking the empty cylinder—

dry fired. I liked how solidly it fit my hand, the sturdy click. I had always owned a gun of some kind; had always liked the precision of them—the way all the pieces fit and moved—the challenge of firing accurately, the satisfaction of hitting the target. Still I hesitated over bringing the gun along. The last time I carried it, I had to use it, forced to kill a man or be killed. Would I be dead now if I hadn't brought the gun? Or would there have been some divine intervention to save my life? Although my faith in God is strong, I still believe that God helps those who help themselves. Would Jesus pack a thirty-eight? Seems out of character.

There's an old joke about a flood—not *the* Flood—but a pretty good one where the water is rising and a man prays to be saved. Three times he turns down help: a call to evacuate, a canoe that comes by, and finally a helicopter. Then he drowns. When he gets to heaven he is a bit peeved that God let him down. "I was praying for you to save me," he told the Lord.

"Well, I sent you a message to evacuate, a canoe and a helicopter!"

So with the notion this thirty-eight might be my helicopter, I grabbed a box of shells and stuffed the gun in my jacket.

We met at the Beaver at five o'clock. William confided he had slept *under* his bed, just in case. If Samuels was surprised to see William it didn't show. "Glad you're back," he said, shaking William's hand.

"I know you," Samuels said to Evie, "from the Mission." Evie looked at him and tilted her head.

"Petey," said Samuels, sweeping off his hat, as if the sight of his mostly bald head might make him look like the child he was twenty years ago.

"Petey! Yes, I remember you!" she exclaimed, greeting him warmly. She got to sit in the front.

We buzzed the *Nenana*, wings waggling a greeting, and although we couldn't hear the steamboat whistle over the Beaver roar, appreciated the plume of answering steam as the whistle blew. Samuels set the Beaver down easily on the grass field behind town—it felt like tarmac, the way he did it—and a walk of a few minutes brought us to the gangplank.

William slunk aboard, except for his height, tough to identify in a brown felt hat pulled low with his small duffle shouldered to successfully block any view of his face from the boat.

A quick knuckle rap, and I opened Andy's stateroom door. I knew he'd spent the time thinking about the loss of William—all the irretrievable moments—as I had, and now got to watch his sad expression ratchet to a subdued welcome for his cousin, and then joy and astonishment at the sight of his friend, alive, well, and—here!

"You old Commie," he said affectionately, shaking William's hand in both of his. "I was hoping ..."

It took a few minutes to get gear stowed in the tiny stateroom, to get past all four of us talking at once and to settle, William and I sitting on the lower bunk and Evie and Andy in hard chairs at the tiny table.

"Nothin' changed here," said Andy. "Simon doin' his purser job, Jimmy waitin' tables, workin' in the kitchen. They been loading wood almost since you left. Takes a cord-and-a-half an hour to keep steam up on this old girl. That's ..." he figured in his head, index finger counting the places. "a hundred ninety-two cubic feet of wood an hour! They can't get the four-foot lengths they like, so they're having to settle for two-foot stove wood. That's what's taking so long." His look sobered. "Tell you the truth, I been expecting Forsythe to show." Andy's eyes met mine. "He will show, you know."

"Yeah, I know," I said, "which is why, if we're going to do something, I think we should do it pretty soon."

"Do something?" said Andy, doubt written heavy on his expression. "Do what? What can we do?"

"Well," I said, looking around, meeting each serious set of eyes, "they shot William. Maybe we should shoot someone."

CHAPTER 21

Y ou're back," said Jimmy. Surprise didn't show in the way he poured coffee or served eggs. "'Bout the last place I'd wanna be!"

I looked around. Except for the potential overlay of danger and death, this felt like a wonderful place in the world to be. The deeply varnished, polished mahogany table and heavy, cream-colored dishware gleamed. They added to dancing flecks of river light on walls and ceiling as—on this brilliant Alaskan day—we chuffed our way downstream.

If anyone noticed or cared that Andy and I put a couple of muffins and apples into our pockets, they didn't let on. "So who we gonna shoot," asked Andy, leaning in, "or were you just trying to keep my spirits up?"

I didn't get to answer before Simon slid into the chair next to Andy, cleanly shaven and crisp in his uniform, smelling of Old Spice. I realized in that moment that Simon was perfectly and completely in his element in service on this old riverboat. For him, the job and the classic boat had become a kind of luminous bubble that certainly seemed to hold at bay other more bothersome possibilities like imminent torture or death related to stolen gold.

"Morning gents," he said to us, holding up his heavy coffee mug for Jimmy to fill. "Jim!" he nodded to the server. "Top of the morning."

"Sir," acknowledged Jimmy. He'd been trained well, likely by Simon.

I didn't really want to toss a monkey wrench into ebullience, but the question had to be asked. "You know these guys want the gold and will torture you until you tell them where it is then kill you?"

He looked at me, smiled, like I'd told him there would be a dance on Saturday night. "I do know that," he said. "And for what it's worth, I'm sorry you've been roped in."

"Is this your way of saying you *didn't* put a message on Tundra Times, asking me to meet you at your cabin in Chatanika?"

"I did not," he said, "very definitely did not. But I will admit that I knew it had been done. I sent word ... tried to send word ... but somehow I missed you. Did you..." he hesitated, "you didn't... walk out across the ice in the dark?"

"Well..." I said.

"You didn't," said Andy.

"Well," I said again, "it turned out to be a lucky break because that's when I first noticed I was being followed. Forsythe," I said to Andy. "So all of a sudden it makes a lot more sense that he sent for me than Simon."

"I'm assuming," said Simon, with a look—a shift so slight that I couldn't read, but would remember—that all is well at my old cabin?"

"Yeah," said Andy, "if you don't count your whole yard being dug up, like it's infested with mountain beavers."

"My yard?" said Simon. "Huh! Anything else?"

"The place was pretty well ransacked," I told him. "A few floorboards pulled up. Looks like somebody planned to touch off a campfire in the middle of your floor, but it hasn't happened yet."

"Used to love that old cabin," said Simon, fishing in his uniform shirt pocket for a cigar to unwrap and clip absent-mindedly while he talked. "What you see now, all gold dredge tailings, used to be a little lake fed by a stream and filled with rainbow trout. Mining company said I only owned a little of the lake. Said they could do what they wanted with the rest, and they did. Destroyed it all. So I moved away."

"So where have you been," I asked him. He scratched a kitchen match with his thumbnail, lit the cigar, and gestured around him with the still-lit match.

"Right here," he said, "my other home, the old *Nenana*. I'm the winter watchman. She's going to Fairbanks after this voyage, though. They're building some kind of park there and they want the old girl in the middle of it. Maybe I'll move to Fairbanks," He finally remembered to blow out the match. "Maybe I'll go along to keep an eye on her."

"What's your plan?" asked Andy. Simon looked at him for a long moment, turned his head to exhale an aromatic blue cloud then watched the passing riverbank for so long I'd begun to think he forgot the question.

"I'm gonna do my job and ride this boat down the Tanana, down the Yukon all the way to the Bering one last time. I know they're coming, have known for years they were coming. None of this is a surprise." Standing, he pushed his chair back with his legs and picked up his purser's hat, regarded it fondly, and slipped it on over his crew cut. He pulled a gold watch out of a pocket at the belt line of his uniform trousers, consulted it, and said, "And my shift begins right now. Good day to you gentlemen. Enjoy the voyage. There'll never be another one just like it."

"Does he not hear what we're tellin' him?" asked Andy when Simon had gone.

"He hears," I said, "and he knows. It's not that he doesn't care. I feel like there's something else going on here and that we're the ones who don't know." We stood, pushing our chairs back. "Let's get this food back to the others, and some coffee." We each poured ourselves refills, mine 'clear,' just the way William likes, and Andy's with two teaspoons of canned milk, and one flat teaspoon of sugar, the way Evie likes.

As we left the dining room, wait staff moved in to get the table cleared off and cleaned up. I paused at the door to watch them. They wore black trousers, black shoes, and white shirts with a white protective jacket. Some wore aprons over those. They were all Athabascan with neatly trimmed hair, in their uniforms alike enough to be brothers or cousins. Three or four of them appeared well trained, but the rest were clearly new to it, less experienced and needing to be closely supervised. Not surprising I guessed, with the unexpected sailing of a boat that had been completely out of service and mothballed for two full seasons.

"Wonder how they were able to staff this boat so quickly?" I said to Andy as we balanced our coffees back along the deck to the staterooms.

175

"Lots of folks in the villages want work," he said, "especially for cash.

"Sure, and how many of those are trained up and ready to go?"

He shook his head, nearly spilling Evie's coffee. "Dunno. Tell you one thing, more Indians working this boat than most. Officers on the *Nenana* used to be mostly white. Waiters, kitchen staff, and deckhands, were Indian. Most of the crew are Indian on this trip. If that's a trend, I like it. Maybe now I can get a real job."

Reasoning that Simon would be safe in his office on his shift, Andy and I strolled the decks in the clear spring air, smelling the river and new leaves on the cottonwood and birch trees along the river edge. Under the broad, brilliant blue bowl of sky, the scenery—small leaf trees, a few low hills and miles of absolutely flat river bottom—flowed away to a distant ring of jagged snow-covered peaks.

In the meantime, back in their respective cabins, William napped after finishing his small breakfast and Evie pacing and fidgeting, chaffing under her enforced confinement.

"All fine for you boys, strolling the decks while we're stuck in here," she crabbed.

"Don't think about us strolling, think about us standing guard," said Andy, "out where the danger is, your first line of defense."

Her whole response sounded like "hah!" So we did the only thing we could, went back out to stroll around the decks some more in the clear air and guard.

"Not appreciating us," said Andy.

"I'm not surprised," I said.

By now we had a pretty good feel for who was on the boat, or at least we felt like we did. There were twenty-five crew, down from thirty-five in her glory days, according to Andy. And while she used to carry as many as thirty-five passengers, most of the staterooms appeared to be empty, with fifteen passengers, plus Andy and me and of course not counting stowaways like William and Evie.

Of the fifteen passengers, there were two couples who seemed mostly interested in themselves and not likely to be here to keep an eye on Simon or on us. Two single women traveling together seemed mostly thrilled to be on an Alaskan adventure, taking pictures of everything, and also seemed to be on board for their own reasons.

Which left nine known males to wonder about, bearing in mind there could be others keeping to their staterooms. Several seemed to be traveling, if not together, for some central purpose. "Could be oil execs," said Andy, "if William's right about his big oil strike."

"I'd bet on him," I said.

"Okay, so would I." Which left five guys who could be here to keep an eye on Jimmy keeping an eye on Simon.

"I think we're looking for a white guy," I said.

"How come?"

"They would need someone to keep an eye on Jimmy and it would be a lot harder to find a native who Jimmy didn't know."

"Maybe," said Andy. "The Territory isn't that small."

Later that afternoon, with Andy napping in anticipation of a night shift, I stepped into the purser's office to speak to Simon. "We've had someone join us on the trip and I want to get her on the manifest."

That got his attention. "Join us?" he said, looking puzzled "A hitchhiker?" He looked out his window at the passing shoreline as though there might be more of them lined up out there. "Her?" he said, peering at me over half-glasses."

"Her," I said, "Andy's cousin, Evangeline Williams. She'll be bunking in with him."

"Evie!" said Simon, with obvious delight. A wonderful girl. With Andy," he said, studying me."

"Cut it out," I said. "Yes, with Andy. She flew back with me and boarded at Manley. Her ticket was paid for but she 'missed the boat,' so to speak.

"Makes no difference," said Simon. "The whole boat is bought. Doesn't really matter how many hitchhikers we pick up; everything's been paid for by ..." he jerked a thumb toward the bow and the barge we were pushing, "the barge. There'll be a couple more of them once we hit the Yukon."

"What's the cargo," I asked him. He made a face and shook his head.

"No clue, and certainly none of my business what the National Petroleum Consortium wants to ship to the Arctic."

"Aaah," I said, because there didn't seem to be much else to say.

"Be my guest for dinner?" I said to Evie later. She looked at me. "Really? I can get out of here! She threw her arms around my neck, hesitated for a tick, then kissed me on the mouth. It was a really good kiss and I admit I helped.

Dinner proved tasty: meatloaf made of meat I couldn't identify, maybe caribou, with sides of canned potatoes, canned string beans, which I've never liked. Too much trouble getting through the strings to the bean.

For dessert it was Jimmy who brought us a small dish of canned peaches and an equally small square of white cake with no frosting. Usually unfazable, Jimmy stopped short at the sight of Evie.

"Eve!" Suddenly bashful, he looked at the floor, frozen in place with his serving tray. But then he looked back at her intently. "You shouldn't be here," he said, with feeling. He turned his head to look at me. "She shouldn't be here. It's not safe."

"He's not a bad guy," said Evie, when he had gone to get coffee. "But he's sure got himself in a bad spot. Isn't there anything we can do to help him?"

Andy looked at me. "I have an idea," he said. As it turned out, we weren't the only ones.

We steamed on through the evening, the sun setting after midnight. With William sleeping or prowling, the three of us didn't have much to do but endlessly circle the decks, far preferable to sitting in our tiny staterooms watching the walls. So we watched other riders and the parade of riverbank sights: animals, small cabins, fish wheels, and the occasional canoe or kicker-driven work boat. The *Nenana* moved along just fast enough to discourage the season's first mosquitoes.

The river didn't seem to know what to make of itself. In a valley so flat that some geographers and mapmakers called the whole area a bog, the river freely reinvented itself mile by mile. Sometimes it formed a single channel, narrowing to maybe a quarter of a mile—still a good-sized river—and sometimes it expanded to run so wide and slow it almost looked like a lake. Still other times the river sprawled across the broad sandy bottomland, cutting large and small channels and then braiding them. How the pilots knew which channel to keep to mystified me.

Finally, near midnight, I said goodnight to Andy and Evie, she kissing my cheek but he declined with a laugh, and I crawled off to my rack. There were no springs on this bed, just a solid wood shelf barely long enough and wide enough to contain a three-inch mattress, with a wooden lip to keep the mattress in place. Luckily I'm neither tall nor wide so found the bed only mildly uncomfortable. William, on the other hand, claimed to have to sleep twisted over like a pretzel. He said it was torture and with one or two more nights trying to sleep on it, he'd be ready to tell every secret he knew.

Waking sometime after two, I heard the rattle of the key in the door and the lockworks turn as William sneaked quietly in. "I'm awake," I said, without opening my eyes. When he didn't answer and the door didn't close, an electricity of something being not right brought me—not just awake—but twisting and half up off the bunk. That's when they grabbed me, three of them, two large men, unidentifiable wearing masks—both big and bulky enough to be my old 'friend,' Clyde—

Forsythe's brother—plus hapless Jimmy, unmasked.

"Sorry, Father," he said, which earned him a whack up the side of his head from the bigger of the two thugs.

I opened my mouth and drew a breath to shout, ending up with a rag in it. Jimmy quickly secured it with duct tape as the others easily snatched me out of the rack, hauled me out of the room and down the deck sternward. I struggled to get rid of the mouth rag, to breathe, trying to break free or to land a punch, all with no success. When I realized where they were taking me, I struggled even harder, but it didn't matter.

Pausing, just above the spinning, churning paddle wheel, one of them laughed, saying, "The old man has gotta love this one!" Then they pushed me up and over the tall bulkhead, right down into the bight of the wheel, down to die in the muddy Tanana.

As they dropped me, one of the paddles came around and caught me, forcing me down, slamming me into water that had been flowing ice only the week before. Paddle after deadly paddle thrashed the water, throwing a corrugated chop of wake out behind.

Instinct wants to bring you back up quickly, and nothing seemed quite so important as driving with all the force in my arms and legs up out of the murkiness to reach the surface. But in midthrust, better sense took over and I forced myself to dive deeper in the cold dark water, images of snags and quicksand, whirlpools and all the goblins of this known-to-be deadly river picking at me. Down I went and down, twisted and flopped in the rage of conflicting currents and, even underwater, the thunder of the lethal paddlewheel.

My only hope of surviving would be to dive deep, stay deep and swim with everything I had to somehow surface outside the churning wake.

I had to make it. I had to live! I didn't want guys this bad to win; and I didn't want to be found dead on the riverbank in my underwear.

CHAPTER 22

*W*hen I couldn't stay down another second, holding my nose to keep from breathing, lights flickering behind my eyes from lack of oxygen, I drove for the surface. Ripping off the tape and spitting out the gag, I drank in cool sweet air like an elixir, filling my lungs with it, in and out as I was swept along the Tanana in the Alaska twilight.

Down the river, stern lights of the *Nenana*, and the crashing water of the huge red wheel receded then disappeared as she swept around a broad bend and out of sight. I remember actually thinking *good riddance*, as though I wasn't now all alone, almost dead center in the vast wilderness of central Alaska with no clothes, no food ... no nothing. No pockets in my underwear.

The current carried me and I didn't have to swim much, just aim. Now that I'd been in the water awhile, the air felt cold—an illusion—I didn't have too many minutes left in the water before I'd start shivering uncontrollably, lapse into unconsciousness and this whole mess would all be behind me. But the wrongness of it rose as rage and resolve from someplace inside me. They'd done this twice that I knew of—probably more—and needed to be stopped!

But before I could get even, I needed to get out of the river. *I need help*, I said aloud, a prayer to God and to the river. Almost immediately one of those large, round life rings from the *Nenana* came floating up to me, doubtless tossed out by Jimmy as a last, desperate "Sorry, Father."

"It's o-k-kay Jimmy," I said through chattering teeth. "H-help is on the w-way."

A few hundred yards downstream, the river gently stubbed me up on a vast flat sandbar, unfortunately one that appeared to be an island in the middle of the stream, so I'd ultimately have to put myself back into the river to walk out to anywhere from here, if that were even possible.

So I crawled up, numb and shivering and sat on the riverbank, wearing only my T-shirt and 'tighty-whities,' watching the predawn light grow in the northeast as the sun came back around. I dried off pretty quickly in a light breeze that also chilled me, so I found a snag to serve as windbreak and sat with my knees up, shivering, arms wrapped around them, trying to preserve what might be left of my body's core temperature. Only one or two mosquitoes found me—a blessing. I'd heard stories of large animals farther north, like caribou, sucked completely dry by voracious swarms of the hellish creatures. *Why would God create a mosquito?* I wondered.

Exposed as I was, even the first of the sun's rays brought warmth—though not enough—and I began my morning prayers with teeth chattering.

"D-d-d-dear G-G-G-God," I said, "please protect my friends, Evie, Andy, William, Simon ... and Jimmy! Keep them safe and out of the paddle wheel! Give them the strength and wisdom to get to the bottom of this whole thing ... and beat the bad guys, whoever they really are ... and make them pay!

That last part just sort of popped in, unbidden. Before I could go back to amend my request, the small buzzing sound I'd been hearing unconsciously through the filter of my own thoughts and teeth chattering, burst into my consciousness as a DeHavilland Beaver, following the river at an altitude of about fifty feet eased around a river bend into full view and with full thunder.

I lunged awkwardly to my feet, doing a kind of slow-motion jumping jack for visibility. I could easily make out the face of Len "Petey" Samuels and immediately saw the wings waggle. "He sees me!" I shouted, marveling at the amazing sight of the airplane, already wondering what could possibly happen next.

I was supposing he might radio for a boat, or that he might drop a blanket—already worrying that it could fall into the river. Maybe some C rations? Suddenly I felt ravenous. I thought of all the things he might possibly do to help me except the very thing he did. He flew a big loop back around into the breeze, ramped ever lower and easily landed the Beaver, with its balloon-ey tires, on my large, flat sand bar.

As the plane stopped, I tried to take a step, but couldn't. The cold had suddenly stiffened me up so badly I could scarcely move. Samuels cut the engine, pushed open the door and climbed down bearing a blanket and blessedly, a *Three Musketeers* candy bar that I couldn't make my fingers work to unwrap.

"Well, Father," he said, "we meet again. Let me help you with that." He slung the blanket around my shoulders and unwrapped the candy bar. Then straightening up to look at me, he said "Oh heck," and snatched me up with some ease, somehow grabbing the life ring and simultaneously tossing me over his shoulder in a fireman's carry, hauling my nearly frozen self to the airplane.

"Th-th-thanks!" I said, when he'd set me down by the door.

"All part of the service," he said, placing my foot on the air step, boosting me up and in.

"Sure glad to see you here alive," he said, climbing in through the pilot door. "And maybe a bit surprised." His face clouded. "How'd you come to fall overboard?"

"I h-had h-elp." I chattered.

"I wondered," he said. He started the engine turning, then fingered down the dual magneto switches for spark. The engine fired immediately, blowing a large blue-white exhaust cloud back and in through the still open door. "Sorry, Father," he said closing the door, and began to taxi around for his take off. "Lucky you drifted up here, there's not another decent landing spot for miles. Not sure what else I could have done. Dropped you the blanket, maybe. This is better."

When airborne, he handed me a headset. "So somebody wants you dead," he said when I had gotten it in place, not a question.

"It sure looks that way. Not sure who yet. Lucky you were flying out this way in the middle of the night."

"Lucky, hell," said Samuels. "Sorry, Father. I had little Clifford beating on my door," he looked at his watch, "about an hour ago. Somebody called, from Fairbanks, I think. Beats all. How did someone in

Fairbanks know that you were swimming around out here? In the middle of the night. I don't get it. I don't even get why anybody was up at this hour to hear the radio call."

"From Fairbanks?" I said. "I don't get it, either."

"So now, the question is, where do you want me to take you? I could have you back in Nenana in time for Rosie to serve us breakfast." He actually licked his lips. "Good-lookin' woman," he said. "Good pancakes, too. So how about it?" he asked, hopeful.

"I've got to get back to the boat," I said. "My friends are in danger. They don't have any idea what happened to me.

"I was afraid of that." He turned the Beaver, the compass dial swinging west. "Your best bet is Tanana. The boat'll be there sometime this morning, I imagine. You gonna sneak back on like your friend Stolz?"

"It does make sense," I said, "to be there and have them think I'm not."

"You know," he said, "no offense, Father, but you're not really a cop, and this feels like cop business. Maybe it's time to call the marshal, and get him involved. I think you're in over your head. Way over." He looked out at the river. "Literally."

I thought about what Samuels said as we flew on. Below us the river caught the rising sun, gleaming, snaking through the flat wilderness, gold plated in the early light. We flew over the *Nenana*, no one on deck that I could see and I imagined them all in their beds, sleeping, with no idea what a dangerous mess we had gotten ourselves into.

This couldn't finish well, and yet we kept coming back to it, as though 'good' or 'right' would somehow prevail. So far, the other side had managed to 'kill' two of us, and we still didn't even really know who 'they' were. Maybe Samuels was right. Breakfast in Nenana at the Coffee Cup? Nah.

We landed at the Tanana airport well before anybody was up or out, with nobody in yet at the CAA office. Samuels lent me spare clothing from his emergency pack so I didn't have to show up at the Tanana St. James Mission in my underwear. So instead, I showed up barefoot in clothes at least three sizes too large. I looked like nothing so much as a small boy out in his dad's clothing.

I knew pretty, red-haired Helen Martin, the rector's wife, only slightly from the outbound missionary conference in Connecticut, which now seemed like another world. She looked me up and down, her smile both a welcome and a question. Her husband, Franklin, had gone off for the week, flying with the bishop, but she greeted us warmly and fed us coffee and sourdough biscuits "just out the oven." Then she helped me rummage through the mission barrel for clothes that would fit. Finding shoes was a struggle—while Samuels had "just one more biscuit."

"Here's a hat," she said, pulling a floppy-brimmed, brown felt hat from a box. It fit large, which was okay, covering more of my face. She also found a two-toned jacket with a collar that stood up around my jaw. "We're all out of floppy mustaches," she joked. Yes, picking out a disguise to sneak back on a riverboat where people would only try to kill me again, if they spotted me, did seem surreal.

Later, as we walked Samuels back to the plane, Helen said, "You came to the right place, you know." I must have looked quizzical. "St. James," she pointed at the small log church.

"Brother of John the Baptist," I said, "Apostle of Jesus ... James the Greater."

"He and his brother shared a nickname." she reminded me, "Sons of Thunder." They wanted Jesus to rain down fire on their enemies." She shook hands with Samuels. "So good to see you again, Petey," then she kissed me gently on the cheek. Off in the distance we could hear the steamboat whistle, and then the rattle of the wheel, "Go with God," she said with a grin, "and rain down fire."

Hers was a gentle but effective pep talk and I admit I went out to make things right. When I shook hands with Samuels he said, "Hate to send you back alone. Feels like you might be outgunned. Not that I want to come aboard and let people try to kill me, too. Hope to see you again, soon, and not in any kind of trouble."

"Thanks, Petey," I said.

He shook his head in mock disgust. "Not you too. That name hasn't been cute since I was five."

It took a while to get the *Nenana* snubbed up to shore, the gangplank winched into place, and the strenuous process of loading what looked like a mile of cordwood under way. There didn't seem any sense hurrying aboard. And it seemed smart to give anyone observing the chance to get tired of the chore and let their attention drift.

So maybe an hour into the process—no wristwatch—with my hat brim down and collar up, I threw my shoulder into helping propel a groaning wood cart to the gangway and down, then stepping aside quickly, hopefully unobserved, climbed the stairs and walked the few feet to my stateroom door.

Turning the knob, I found the door unlocked and quickly stepped inside, the room unlit and dim after bright sunlight shining on the white boat, eyes adjusting slowly. There were three people in the room, the three I had expected, and three guns pointed at me, one of them my own snub-nosed thirty-eight, held in Evie's hand, her knuckles squeezed white on the grip.

"Honey," I said to the three, "I'm home."

CHAPTER 23

*A*ndy shot Jimmy Lucas just at sunset on our third day on the boat. He said Jimmy didn't even look surprised. I couldn't quite see it from where I was hiding but Evie said her cousin aimed my thirty-eight at the center of Jimmy's chest and fired point blank. Jimmy looked at Andy, his mouth a kind of *O*, then looked down and clapped his hand on his chest, the hand pulling away leaving a bright trail of red smear down his white server's jacket as he went over the side.

"So long, Jimmy," I said to William.

"One down," he replied quietly.

A few minutes after Jimmy disappeared, his two shadows—big men, one of them Forsythe's brother Clyde—finally came crawling out of their worm hole, as William said, just three doors down on the port side. "How do you remember which is port?" I asked him.

"Port and left are the short words," he said. "Starboard and right are longer."

"Even I knew that," said Evie.

Clyde and his buddy went to the rail and peered out into the twilight. Seeing nothing, hearing nothing, shaking their heads, somehow managing to hide their 'sorrow,' they shambled back to cover.

"They don't seem too broken up," said Andy, joining us to watch Clyde and his buddy.

"They are probably wondering who will now bring them their breakfast," said William.

"Won't be me," said Jimmy, rubbing his wet hair with a towel. "Ugh, I'm all gritty."

"Scared heck out of me with that red stuff," said Andy. "After all the time I spent pullin' that bullet apart, thought maybe I fired one with a slug after all."

"Saw it on a movie," said Jimmy. "It looked pretty good on the white coat, didn't it? Good idea about tying the rope to my ankle. I'd a been swept right under the barge otherwise." He shuddered. "Thanks for pulling me out," he said to William.

It had all been William's plan: tie a rope to Jimmy from the far side of the vessel—out of sight—and run it around just under the bow. Then shoot Jimmy and let him fall overboard where William could grab him and pull him into a small work skiff close beneath the overhang of the bow. It helped that Clyde and his big buddy weren't two of the brighter bulbs in the package.

"Now can I shoot one of the others?" asked Andy. He laughed at my expression. "I jokes!"

Out on the river at the time of the 'shooting,' we still hadn't departed Tanana. They spent the whole day loading firewood, then most of the evening the boat shifted up and down the waterfront adding barges to push—now a total of four—with the help of a small river tug. Just above town we had seen the last of the Tanana River, and now were steamboating on the legendary Yukon.

With four barges on, the *Nenana* see-sawed back into her moorage in front of the town, I supposed to finish loading the last of the wood. But with the last of the wood loaded she still sat by the beach, chuffing quietly, not moving, not preparing to move, just waiting—for something or someone. With the cabin light switched off, Evie and I took up a watch of the gangplank from behind the curtains in my stateroom, the first time we'd been alone together since my return.

"I thought you were dead," she said, still facing out the curtain. "I spent the whole night trying to figure out how life could go on without you. And I couldn't," she said, turning her face to me. "And then in the morning we hear steps and actually think they're coming for us. Then the knob turns, in you walk, and say something stupid."

"I thought it was at least humorous."

"Yeah, if you're *Lucy*."

"I… I thought you'd all be still asleep and not even have missed me yet. That was the difficult part about being out on the sandbar in the middle of the night. I didn't think anybody even knew I was gone. I thought you were all still sleeping. Come to think of it, why weren't you sleeping?"

"Jimmy," said Evie. "After those creeps made him help throw you overboard, he tossed you the life preserver then scribbled a note and stuck it under my door. I heard a quick knock, got up and found the note, so we knew just minutes after you hit the water. Andy and William went out to look for you, here on the boat, in case it was a trick and found the life ring missing. They found Jimmy and offered to shoot him. Since he was on the bow crying, they were pretty sure it was true. So we just sat together saying nice things about you until morning. Then we heard footsteps outside the door."

She took my hand in both of hers, her hands darker than mine, warm, strong-looking, nice to hold. "I've been spending a lot of my alone time thinking about what people will say, in the village, or in the States someday if we were to get together and then you decide to try life somewhere other than Alaska. Last night I realized I've been spending too much time worrying about that. Way too much. I just want to say I'm not going to do that anymore. Well, I'm going to *try* not to do that anymore. Last night it broke my heart to believe I'd missed all my chances with you. So I'm just saying, I'm here. I'm ready. I'm... yours, if that's how it goes."

That's when I kissed her, or she kissed me, but then we had to pull away quickly when we heard the key turn and the door opened to admit Andy. He looked at us closely, his eyebrows hooding with mock suspicion.

"I can't leave you two alone for a minute!" Then more seriously, "Someone's coming. I think it's whoever we been waitin' for." He reached over and pulled the curtain aside.

Three figures approached in the gathering twilight, one being pushed in a wheelchair. The one in the lead had his arm in a sling, obviously Forsythe. The smaller one at the back looked female and she strained to push the wheelchair across the unpaved ground toward the gangway.

I had a pretty good idea who we were about to see, but her face remained shadowed in a dark scarf until she crossed the gangplank into the glow of one of the deck lights. She flipped the scarf back off her head revealing what I suspected—Ellen!

Trim, shapely, alluring, even without the Pan American uniform.

"Is *that* Ellen?" breathed Evie beside me. "That's *got* to be Ellen! I recognize her from the breathless description of her when they had me locked up on the *Lizzie Ann*. Okay, I can see what's the big deal with her. Hubba, hubba!" She leaned over to kiss me on the cheek, even with Andy in the room. "She's the one you *didn't* sleep with?"

"I'm not even keen on women," said Andy, "and I can see she'd be hard to resist. Hey, you coulda *made up* stuff about gold—until morning anyway."

"Very funny," I said.

"Although," he added brightly, "it could be like the black widow spider that mates then kills."

"That's not true," said Evie. "It's an old wives' tale."

"About spiders, or this one?" He pointed out the window. "Wonder who the old guy in the wheelchair is."

"I think it's the original Forsythe," I said, puzzled. "He's the dad, returning to the scene of the crime. But why? Why bring him all this way? Oh! And I just this minute figured out who Ellen is!"

"*Who* she is?" said Evie. "Who *is* she?"

Andy guessed. "She's the sister."

CHAPTER 24

I need a place to keep Jimmy," I told Simon the next morning. "Someplace safe and out of the way. Is that possible?"

"So he is alive," said Simon. "I wondered. Yes, it's very possible." He looked at me directly. "Do you trust him?"

"I do," I said.

It turned out, although the *Nenana* had been assembled and launched in 1933—after Prohibition—the original blueprints included what Simon called a 'hidey-hole.' Somehow totally enclosed and lost in the structure of the third deck, it measured about ten feet long and no wider than its built-in bunk. The hidey-hole had been built in the hopes of hauling contraband cargo, mostly bootleg whiskey, and had done so for some years, according to Simon, as there were some Indian and Eskimo villages to this day that are still 'dry.' There were no windows and no electrical wires that could be "followed" but the room had its own ventilator that let in both fresh air and a little daylight. A clever kind of sliding door arrangement made it hard to get into quickly and impossible to sneak into.

Jimmy would be difficult or impossible to find or attack here, and it would both keep him safe at night and get him off the floor of my stateroom and generally out from under foot.

Simon chuckled to himself. "There's people worked on this boat season after season, that don't know about this little room. I worked for Captain Rufus Edmonton, and this was his *private* space. He would 'entertain' in here," Simon explained delicately. "The Captain had women would come aboard when we tied up in the larger towns—Fairbanks, Nenana, Fort Yukon—was my job to show 'em in here, open the bubbly. Nothin' but the best for Captain Rufus. Man, if these walls could talk, you'd have to be over eighteen to listen!"

I had knocked on Simon's door just a few minutes after six. Already up, Simon looked relaxed, dapper, smooth, even stylish. I was surprised to find that, as an officer, he still shared a room. From a chair by the small table, his roommate, a stocky young Athabascan named Leonard, looked up from a worn paperback with a pulp-magazine illustrated cover of a young woman in peril with bright red lipstick and plenty of cleavage.

He saw me looking. "Good story?"

He turned the book to look at the cover. "Not nearly as good as the cover," he said, and went back to it.

Shaving, Simon wore his black uniform pants, a polished black belt, and a ribbed undershirt that showed off his darker skin and his slim fitness, for a man possibly in his sixties. He greeted me warmly, I declined the offered cigar, and he went back to his safety razor at the tiny sink as I perched on the edge of his bunk behind him. "A good time to talk?" I asked. He nodded and I proceeded to bring him up to the moment on all that had been happening on his boat.

I might have been telling him about a weekend getaway to Circle Hot Springs for all the reaction he showed, except when I told him about being thrown into the wheel. I saw his razor hand jerk. "Ouch," he said, quietly. "Nicked myself." And he bled. All the while, I could see him watching me in the mirror. "You're a lucky man. Most people don't survive being thrown into the wheel."

"Hand me that towel," he said, and I did, not quite missing what might have been a look between Simon and Leonard, something I mentioned later to Andy.

"Is Simon homosexual?"

"Gay," he corrected automatically. Then he scowled. "You think because I'm gay I know everybody else who is? You think they hand out membership cards and a secret handshake or a wink and we all know each other?" Then he smiled a little. "I've heard stories about Simon and I can tell you none of them included another man. I think it's safe to say Simon is *not* gay. You know, some men who are not gay do share secrets."

"And maybe I imagined the exchanged looks," I said, but didn't think so.

"Father," Simon had said, drying his face on the towel, "don't you think it's time for you folks, Evie particularly, and Andy, to get off the boat? These are bad people, especially old Forsythe—the worst. With them on board, and what you're telling me has already happened, it isn't safe for you here."

"Safe for me!" I said. "What about you?" I felt alarmed and probably looked it. "They're not here for me; I just happen to be in their way. They're here for you!"

Simon just smiled.

"Where could I be safer than on the *Nenana*? This is my boat. My ..." he hesitated, "my ... universe. I have everything I need right here."

When I left the cabin, not at all sure I'd convinced him of the present threat level, he shook my hand and thanked me. "Sorry you got caught in the middle of this thing, Father," he said. "I'm betting it will all blow over. We'll laugh about his later." But he wasn't laughing. For once he wasn't even smiling.

"All blow over?" said Andy later. "Depends on how you define *blow*, but I don't think so."

❖

"It is oil gear for drilling and pumping," said William the next morning, smiling slightly in my direction because he'd been right and I'd been skeptical. "All four barges." During what had been a mostly sleepless night for me, with the boat underway, William prowled the barges, slicing into canvas wrapping and sometimes actually crawling inside the packaging to examine the machinery.

"Of course I am on the front side at all times, safe from the view of the pilot and crew, but to be sure, I placed my lit flashlight inside one, then crawled back out to check. No sign of the light inside. It is heavy canvas. Someone went to much trouble to conceal what is being shipped."

"So it *is* oil," I said. That would change things. The Alaskan arctic, forming the north slope of the Brooks Range, traditionally belonged to Eskimos, who still had to hunt and fish to stay alive. "I can't even imagine what Eskimo life will be like when they're all rich."

William snorted. "Rich? They will be lucky to see nickels when dollars are flowing out like rivers to the men who paid for this equipment."

"But that's not fair," I said. He wouldn't even dignify my naiveté with a comment, just 'humphed.' I knew I deserved it.

Midmorning, we gathered in William's and my stateroom, including Jimmy. Of five of us aboard, three were believed to be dead—Jimmy, William, and me.

"More dead than alive," said Andy, then looked around. "I jokes," he said, laughing too much. No one ever enjoyed his humor as much as he did.

Only Evie and Andy had gone to breakfast, reporting back with a pot of coffee, spare mugs and whatever breakfast they could get into their pockets: halves of apples and about a half dozen disks of pilot bread—what some old-timers still call hardtack—a big, round bread-sized cracker prized as a staple in interior Alaska. The stuff would keep nearly forever and many of the old timers still thought they were in heaven if they could enjoy a piece of pilot bread smeared with lard. I preferred a smear of Sunny Jim peanut butter, another Alaska staple.

"Anybody see you," I asked Jimmy.

"Nobody out," he answered, crunching happily.

"How is it in there?" inquired William.

"Great," said Jimmy, smiling with pilot bread in his teeth. "Sure never thought I'd get a cabin of my own." I had to smile at his optimism.

"So what are we going to do?" asked Andy. "We can't just all hole up in here all the way down the Yukon." That's when I told them what I thought we ought to do next.

The second phase of my plan was the simplest, and not dangerous: radio or telegraph the marshal next time we stopped anywhere with communication. That would be the easy part. In the meantime, I thought we needed to do something to discourage whatever would be the Forsythe's next move with Simon. "Get him off the boat," I said, in answer to a question from Andy. "I'm afraid the younger Forsythe's government work has more than prepared him for getting the answers he needs from Simon. That's probably why he's here."

"Get Simon off the boat? Didn't you hear what he told you? He's not goin'. This boat is his 'universe,' whatever that actually means."

"It means he thinks he's safe here."

"So what will we do?" inquired William. "What *is* your plan?"

"Eat lunch," I told them.

In the absence of Jimmy, Simon had pressed himself into service in the ship's mahogany-paneled dining room, pouring coffee, helping to serve, chatting and smiling all the while to a passenger count that now, after Tanana, numbered nearly thirty. His turning out to serve surprised me a little, especially since I counted no less than eight other waitstaff, including servers and bus boys in the room.

The dining room had an unexpected elegant look for a frontier riverboat with place settings precise on pressed white tablecloths, neatly arranged with what looked to be polished glassware and silverware.

Two rows of tables ran most of the length of the room, and the Forsythe group sat all on a side at the center of the far table from where we entered, all five of them, relaxed and expansive, smiling. Casually but attentively, collectively, they eyed Simon like nothing so much as big cats on a savannah observing an orphan wildebeest, happily flicking their tails, licking their lips and biding their time.

Third through the door behind Evie and Andy I could see their easy smiles freeze on faces abruptly stiffened with surprise and a crackling electricity of anger, becoming only more intense at the sight of each of our three 'dead' faces: William's, Jimmy's and mine.

Our entrance caught Ellen midlaugh, her laughter choking off through the round *O* of a mouth she forgot to close. From one heartbeat to the next, they sat erect, clenched as a group—like a fist— and grew visibly angry with us for being there and being alive; and angry with each other for their failures, which allowed us to be here, alive. Even across the room and through the muted clatter of lunch we heard muttering staccato jabs of recrimination, the words indistinct but the meaning unmistakable.

Sensing the shift at their table, Simon turned and saw us, something shifting on his face, too. But he wasn't surprised. He leaned to say something to stocky Leonard, who also turned, though impassively, to look at us. Leonard, all shoulders and thick neck, working close at Simon's elbow, looked more like a body builder than a waiter. Selecting a tray and arranging it with five filled water glasses, he moved smoothly to seat us.

Watching their reactions, pushing in Evie's chair and settling into my own, accepting a water glass from Leonard, the mental equation shifted and I saw that the effect of our entrance ran far deeper than just a shift to even the numbers. The summation of their group failure twisted their features with anger and embarrassment, making them—even Ellen—ugly with it. I had to guess they'd been tasked with two simple chores: kill William and kill me. Now we had the bad form to both show up alive and to reveal and magnify what they had been unable to accomplish.

I can't say that any of us enjoyed, or even noticed our meal. I didn't notice what I ate, let alone how it tasted. What did I think would happen? I don't know, but when Ellen pushed her chair back—so quickly it toppled—and stood, I knew it had begun. I watched as she deliberately came around the end of her table to stand at ours, next to Evie.

She looked at me and sneered, then looked down at Evie. "He begged me for sex," she said. "Told me he wasn't getting any." The last thing I had ever imagined we'd be talking about here was sex, it took me completely off guard and made me instantly and unreasonably angry. I might have jumped to my feet but for Andy's hand on my shoulder and Evie's firm squeeze on my thigh as Ellen turned slowly to look at me. "Ahh," she said, "so that's how it is."

Emboldened, misreading my red face for embarrassment, Ellen went on, playing to the room now, louder and nastier.

"All night," she said to Evie. "And I said to him, 'what about your Indian bitch?'" Ellen looked around, pleased at her effect on a room that had now gone completely silent, all eyes riveted on her. Somehow she had missed comprehending that three-quarters of the people listening were Athabascan.

But Evie just smiled at her and also spoke a little louder. "He showed you the three bullet holes, didn't he, right up his chest, machine gun wounds from Pearl Harbor? To make you all sympathetic?"

I saw Ellen's eyes flicker. This wasn't what she had expected. "Yes," she said, a little uncertainly, then louder and a bit triumphant, "he did!"

That's when Evie stood up too, every eye in the room now fixed on her.

"Except that he didn't serve in the Pacific, he served in France, and as far as I've been told wasn't wounded and therefore doesn't have any bullet scars. Which makes you," she said, leaning slightly forward, "at least a liar."

Ellen's mouth opened, she looked a little wild-eyed. Behind her, big Clyde's chair went scraping back as he stood up, on his way. Off to my right I saw Leonard start in our direction with a tray of desserts.

"Indian slut!" said Ellen.

Evie smiled slightly and slapped Ellen so hard her head turned as she fell back a step. In the same breath Clyde charged the table but before any of us could stand or move, was deflected by Leonard,

204

arriving with the tray, somehow shouldering Clyde off in another direction while not even upsetting the desserts.

"Oh, excuse me sir," said Leonard, as Clyde ricocheted hard into his own table, slamming it back against the others in his group and against the wheelchair.

By then we were all on our feet, even the elder Forsythe, his wheelchair scooting back to thump against the wall behind him. In fact, in that moment, most of the people in the room stood, with the general racket of chairs scraping and dishes rattling.

Unarmed, I watched as Dave, Clyde, and Clyde's shadow all seemed to be reaching for concealed weapons. None of this had been part of my plan. But before things could get any worse, all eight of Simon's waitstaff, plus Simon himself, flooded into the space between the two tables, adjusting chair placement, clearing place settings, and offering coffee and dessert at both tables, deftly defusing those critical seconds with the motion and activity of formal dining room routine.

That was lucky, I thought, until I caught a look from Simon. And when I looked back at the room, waitstaff were helping Forsythe back into his chair and rolling him out. Dave Forsythe had his crying sister by the elbow, guiding her away as she worked her sore jaw, the bright pink glow of Evie's handprint still clear on the side of her face.

As we turned to file out, faces uniformly grim with the knowledge of tragedy so narrowly averted, only Evie smiled.

"Well," she said, "that was refreshing."

CHAPTER 25

G"ood plan," said Andy walking back along the deck. "Lunch, Too bad it didn't work. Nearly got us all shot. Lucky Big Clyde 'stumbled' on—what's his name—Leonard, or we might've all been shot! I wasn't even carrying the thirty-eight.

"Just for the record," I said, "some of it worked. They now know that Simon isn't just here for the taking. And I think the old man Forsythe is here now because his thugs told him they'd eliminated William and me.

"Like, come out," said Andy, "the coast is clear."

"Right, and then it turns out the coast isn't clear."

"And the goons look like screw-ups."

We paused to lean on the rail, watching thickets of birch trees slip by, already almost fully leafed out. A bull moose, drinking from the river, raised his head with its massive spread of rack to watch us pass. He didn't seem concerned.

"Don't know how they hold those things up," said Andy, nodding at the four or five foot expanse of bone the moose carried on his head."

"Practice," I told him.

"Must have a neck like Leonard," he mused. "Never saw a guy, an Athabascan anyway, so built up. Looks like he could lift a truck. Seems funny to have a guy with so many muscles waiting tables. But I guess a job's a job." He watched the shoreline sweep by for a few moments, then said, "Maybe I could be a waiter."

"And take Rosie's job?" I said, and then, "I jokes."

"Funny." "I could be an Italian waiter. Shouldn't be too hard, right? Just learn the Italian on the menu; bring food. I think I might enjoy that. He turned to me and looked intently into my eyes.

"*Dov'e´ il bagno?*"

"That sounded good. What did you say?"

"Where is the bathroom? But you get the idea."

"You'll go far."

Then out of the blue it occurred to me. "Leonard is Simon's bodyguard!"

"Makes sense," said Andy. "He ricocheted big Clyde like a pool ball into the side pocket. Made it look easy, too. But is one bodyguard going to be enough against the bunch of them?"

"Let's hope we don't have to find out."

Standing with the warmth of the sun at our backs, we watched the moving shadow of the boat on the swirling water with its paddlewheel turning, watched us rounding a bend in an already wide stretch as the river expanded to what looked like most of a mile. I'd never seen a river this wide, including the Mississippi in Tennessee. All around us the land still lay very flat, ringed in the distance by snow caps. It would have been a near-perfect day except for the people on the boat who would like us all dead.

For the next forty-eight hours we didn't see the Forsythes at all, not any of them. Not on deck, not at meals. It was as if they'd gotten off the boat, maybe decided their party was spoiled and they'd just walk home to teach us a lesson. Yeah, I know, fat chance.

The tiny village of Ruby came and went. While the crew loaded cordwood I held a small, outdoor communion service on a quiet stretch of riverbank and visited and blessed an old Athabascan man who was mostly just sick of being old.

"I am down to my last days," he said somewhat pathetically. "What does God want me to do now that I am almost at the end?"

"What would you do," I asked him, "if you were just twenty-four years old and didn't know you were going to die on your twenty-fifth birthday?"

He smiled wistfully. "I'd get up every morning smiling, and hunt and fish, break trail—maybe go into Fairbanks and raise hell—sorry, Father," he said. "But I wouldn't know the day ..."

"Well, you don't know the day now, do you? So as much as you can, I think God wants you get up every morning smiling, to hunt and fish, break new trails, maybe even go into Fairbanks and kick up your heels."

"But not sit around here being old, huh?"

"That's what I think."

"Okay," he said, smiling for the first time. "I guess."

"It takes guts to get old," I told him. "You got 'em?"

"Hell, yes," he said, sitting up straighter. Then like every former mission kid, "Sorry, Father."

❖

Breakfast on the fourth day featured home-made wild blueberry pancakes, except that they didn't have any blueberries in them—too early for blueberries—our waiter said with Alaska logic. *And not made anywhere near home*, I thought.

William and I sat finishing our coffee, definitely not the Italian stuff, when Dave Forsythe came through the door, not wearing his sling.

"I come in peace," he said, back to wearing his schoolboy smile. He nodded a greeting in William's direction. "Stolz."

"He wants something," murmured William as Forsythe approached, also reading and judging the smile.

"Have a chair," I said turning over one of the heavy coffee mugs and shoving it in his direction. By the time he got his hand on it, one of the waiters had appeared to fill it while one of the busboys began clearing away our dirty dishes.

"Blueberry pancakes, sir?" said the waiter to Forsythe. He declined.

"Sounds good, though," he said.

"Too early for blueberries," said William.

"I have an idea," said Forsythe, cutting to the chase, "before somebody else gets hurt." Involuntarily he gestured with his wounded hand, the bullet hole scabbed over but still bright red. Very slowly he clenched the hand, still not nearly able to form a fist, wincing.

"So what is your idea?" asked William.

"That we—interview—Simon in your presence, see if he knows what we want to know. All we have is our old man's version of what happened. All the newspaper accounts of the original robbery, and all the rumors on the street have the gold being thrown overboard somewhere in the Tanana, with a floating marker of some kind that must've broke off and drifted away." Dave made a face shrug. "Maybe Simon knows something, maybe he doesn't. Either way, after we talk to him you have my word we'll move along and let you people alone. So what do you say?" he asked, grinning, all boyish charm. Give us a shot at Simon?" William just stared at him until Forsythe actually reddened.

"Okay," he said, "poor word choice, but you know what I mean." Forsythe pushed his chair back, the legs scraping on the wooden floor. "Talk it over," he said, "and get back to me. I'm in thirty-four. Don't knock on thirty-five—that's the old man." Standing smoothly, he headed out one of the heavy doors that whooshed softly and clunked shut behind him.

"Interesting," said William.

"His proposal?" I asked.

"I think we are both aware that this man's—'idea'—is a trick. No, it is watching him work that is interesting. His arrogance. A professional liar who believes he is at the top of his game."

"Yeah, you know when he's lying when his lips are moving."

"Liars have a thing they do," William said, "like poker players, called a 'tell.' It might be a twitch or a blink, or unconsciously touching their face. This one employs a charming smile, very childlike, which won him pats on the head as a child. You saw it now. He is lying. He means to kill all of us when he has the opportunity."

"So I guess that means you don't want to give him the benefit of the doubt," I said, tongue in cheek.

"Father," he said, "this is the man who looked me in the eyes and smiled as he shot me."

He had a point.

Turned out, nobody liked Forsythe's offer except Simon, who appeared oddly unsurprised by it when I told him.

"We can meet in the dining room after dinner, and after the other passengers have cleared out. The crew'll still be clearing tables and setting up for breakfast, but we can talk, if that's what they really want. I'm not sure what they think I'll say. Back in '38, I told my story in Fairbanks court. It hasn't changed."

"What do you think happened to the gold?" I asked him, after the others had gone and we left his office, taking a turn on the deck.

It would be warm this afternoon, another perfect Alaskan day with the sun high and clear in an arch of blue, cloudless sky. Moving downstream with the current gave the old boat a feeling of effortless speed, the engine chuffing gently, the paddlewheel turning, but not too fast, sunlight dancing on the ripples and riffles of the great river. The air smelled like cool, clear water and cottonwood trees, which lined the bank along here, ready to bloom.

He smiled and reached for a cigar. "You know," he said, peeling off the cellophane and stuffing it in his trousers' pocket then cutting the cigar end, "I saw the gold come aboard. I think I told you they let the crew file through to admire it all stacked up in the stateroom, number 17 there, right at the top of forward stairs, nearest the gangway. "They even let us touch it." He expertly lit the cigar, even in the river breeze, and drew his lungs full of the exotic-smelling smoke—really very nice on the fresh river air, like a little bit of wood smoke smells on a brisk autumn day.

"They knew we'd never see gold again, oh, maybe a little dust. We were laborers ... Indians ... poor folk. They thought it was a kindness to show us something so rare. As though it was *theirs*, as though they weren't just running the steamboat that carried it." He shook his head, still clearly perplexed.

"Forsythe stood guard with a rifle as I passed. Remember, these were solid bars, all stacked up. It looked like pirate treasure from one of those N.C. Wyeth illustrations of *Treasure Island*. It was a sight to see!"

"I'm surprised they let you touch them," I said.

"Well, me too. But I worked personally for Captain Rufus Edmonton. The captain stuck his head in at the door, saw Forsythe with his carbine and ordered him to stand down. Then he came in like he owned the boat—course he darn near did—picked up one of those gold bars and handed it right to me."

"Squeeze one of these," he says. "So I got to hold one of those bars, not too big, but *heavy*, quite heavy for its size. What I remember most is the coolness of it, and the deep, soft, nearly liquid shine. I remember thinking how beautiful it looked with a little bit of river light reflecting on it."

"By then, the captain had gone out, so Forsythe jabbed at me with the rifle barrel. He said, 'Time's up, nigger,' which was what he called anybody with dark skin. Nigger. I really did want to kill him," he said, matter-of-factly. "Still do." Then Simon turned to look at me. "I think the gold still exists, but trust me on this, no Forsythe will *ever* profit by it."

Walking the deck with Evie later that same afternoon, had a surreal quality. On the one hand, there are men on the boat that meant to kill us, had already given it their all, failing through no fault of their own.

On the other hand, the sun shining and river breeze soft on our faces and in her hair, made strolling the deck together and having the chance to just be us, irresistible. The chance of anyone rushing out to grab us and pitch us over the rail seemed remote, too.

Walking, the backs of our hands brushed. It felt very nice. Back in Chandelar, we went out of our way to not seem too chummy, though I sometimes sensed that we were fooling mostly ourselves.

Last December, at the Christmas dance in the Civic Center, one of my older parishioners had hauled someone by the hand across the floor, saying, "Here Father, dance with this one." When she stepped aside, instead of whichever victim I thought she dragged over to dance with the single priest, I found she had brought me Evie. So it was Christmas and we danced in front of God and everyone, and generally had a great time. No one seemed surprised or offended.

Now, several hundred miles down the Tanana and Yukon from Chandelar, there were no parishioners about, except the ones we'd brought along ourselves—Andy and William—so why not?

I took her hand, and after the tiniest fraction of a second of delay, she took mine as we strolled along the deck. I felt like the whole wide world, in that moment, was okay, which it certainly wasn't.

"I don't like him, don't trust him," Evie said. "Don't know why we're even going to consider his *idea*." Just the way she said the word made it sound bogus.

"It's Simon's choice," I said. "With him willing to meet, who cares if we say no? Whatever is going to happen will happen. All we can do is be there and try to make it turn out okay."

"You're such an optimist," she said. "Do you believe in the Easter Bunny, too?"

"Well, actually ..." I started. She squeezed my hand.

"It's okay," she said. "It's one of the things I like about you."

CHAPTER 26

Simon set the meeting for that same evening at nine. He reminded all concerned that we wouldn't be alone in the dining room. Cleaning up and setting up would be going on around us, but that we could talk. None of us liked the idea of meeting under any circumstances, but it was his decision and in this, at least, his boat.

We were there early, drinking the last of the coffee—which was terrible—but filled the cups and the moments as they ticked up to nine o'clock. I counted about twenty other passengers at dinner that evening, tourists, businessmen, unaware and unconcerned about anything but their business or their journey, or as with one couple, with each other. I envied them. The afternoon's gentle moments with Evie only made me desire more of them.

At a few minutes after nine the Forsythes rolled in, the old man pushing his own wheels in a determined fashion, his face set. Dave followed, then Clyde, as unlike as two men could be. Different mothers looked like a sure thing. Then sulky, sullen Ellen, followed by the other big guy. By the bulgy look of them, everyone—even Ellen—carried a marginally concealed handgun.

"They are rather well armed for a conversation," observed William.

On our side of the table, only William, with his sleeve derringer—and whatever else—and Andy with my thirty-eight, were armed. Jimmy, not so thrilled anymore with the isolation of his 'personal stateroom' had asked to come. Evie sat between Jimmy and me.

When Forsythe had wheeled himself into place, Simon, who had been working and instructing his waitstaff, slid into the opposite chair. Although not smiling, he appeared much as usual. With every reason to be frightened and cautious, he seemed totally in his element, focused, even cordial. And while the Forsythes emitted darkness and anger—rumpled and unshaven—Simon in his uniform, radiated cleanliness, order, and efficiency.

He had no more than scooted his chair in than he reached for a cigar, tore the wrapper, cut the tip almost without looking, struck the wooden match with a thumbnail and inhaled deeply. Only then did he lock eyes with the elder Forsythe, signaling that the meeting could now begin. Forsythe blinked. This was *not* the confrontation he had imagined all these years. This should have been the pick-the-meat-off-Simon's-bones time, but it wasn't and Forsythe sensed it. He didn't understand it, and he didn't like it.

"I want my gold," he growled, straight to the point.

Simon inhaled again, smiled, and I saw him settle a bit in his chair. "It was never your gold," he said.

He might as well have slapped Forsythe, just as Evie had slapped Ellen. Color, a deep kind of unhealthy purple suffused Forsythe's face. Only a force of will held him in a chair that he longed to spring from and batter a man he considered his inferior.

"Uppity," he said, the word forced through clenched teeth.

"That's what you said about Nolan Sam," Simon replied. "Uppity. You remember Nolan, don't you?"

But Forsythe didn't. He hadn't expected to be answering any questions, especially that Simon might be asking. The flash of insecurity made it clear that he didn't remember any Nolan Sam and resented being asked.

"The busboy you and your goons tossed into the wheel one night."

Forsythe relaxed a little and he actually bent his face into something like a smile.

"Oh, *that* nigger," he said. "Yeah, uppity. Stole my shoes."

Simon exhaled a cloud of cigar smoke across the table, thick enough that Forsythe gave a little cough and Ellen fanned it from in front of her face.

"Yeah," said Forsythe, "the boy screamed. He was a screamer. Why are we talkin' about him? He was nobody and he's been dead for nearly twenty years ... and nobody cares."

"Well see, that's the problem," said Simon. "I saw the whole thing, and after all these years, I can still see the terror on his face. He was only sixteen! I still wake up at night hearing him scream, and you laughing, wondering if I might have done something to save him. 'Course, you'da thrown me in too, and I'd not be sitting here talking to you now. But it's wrong to say that nobody cares."

"His mother and father are still alive and they care. His brother Albert—remember the state-room guard who disappeared?—he cares. Albert's eight sons care. They speak of their uncle often—

of his loss—and of their desire to balance the scale."

"Balance?" said Forsythe. His chair rolled back slightly, as if unintended.

"Uh-oh," said Evie.

"What?" I whispered.

"The waitstaff," she said. "There are eight of them., You were right about them looking like brothers."

I missed Simon's signal, but so did the Forsythes. In a single instant, with a single motion, all eight of the white-jacketed Athabascans produced short, deadly-looking shotguns, with both shoulder stocks and barrels sawed off. Shotguns came out of drawers, from under tables, from under at least one long apron.

"Take 'em," growled Forsythe, making a feint toward his shoulder, as if for his own weapon. But no one else moved. In fact, they stood as if frozen.

With the cigar tucked under his index finger, Simon waved Forsythe's hand back, a little like an orchestra conductor. "Not such a good idea," he said. "It would take us all night to clean up the mess that you will become. So I must ask you all to hold very, very still." And then he turned his head to look at us. "And Father, I must ask the same favor of your group. No moves." A small shift at the corner of my eye turned out to be Jimmy, also training a previously unrevealed handgun on us.

"Not a brother?" I said to him. He shook his head.

"Cousin."

"Handy to have you on the inside."

"Oh yeah," he replied. "Sorry to ..." he hesitated, "rat you out, Father. But this all started a long time before you got here. I'm just glad it didn't kill you."

"I'm glad too, Jimmy." I turned my head back to center stage. Thick-necked Leonard was frisking the Forsythes, including Ellen—unabashedly—passing to a brother what soon became a small mountain of blue steel at the center of a white-clothed table among silver cutlery and polished glass.

"So," said Simon to Forsythe's offspring, "we're not here to talk about gold. We're here to talk about the cruel death of Nolan Sam at the hands of your ... father ... and about payback."

"Simon," I began, but he waved me off.

"You are a kind and decent man," he said to me, "and you'll want to remind me of the civil law, and the holy law, and my sense of human decency. Okay, I'm reminded. Thank you. But when I go to God and he says, 'Did you avenge your friend?' I'm willing to stand up and say ... proudly ... yes, I did. And if that *is* really a sin, I'm willing to pay."

Simon turned back to Forsythe. "So tonight," he looked at his wristwatch, "in ten or fifteen minutes, you will die. Or maybe you won't. Maybe you are too evil for even the wheel or the river to kill. So be it." He gestured at the rest of the Forsythes. "If there are things left unsaid, this is your chance. A chance Nolan Sam never had."

"You don't have the guts," snarled Forsythe, but without much conviction. He half turned, half rolled his chair to better face his support group. "Well?" he demanded. "Do something!"

With one exception, the group shrank from him, a small but perceptible motion away. Only Ellen rose to face him.

"You raped me," she said, dry-eyed, "age twelve on. My whole life I've hoped and prayed something like this would happen to you. I'm only here for the gold. I don't love you, never loved you, don't even like you and I hope you rot in hell."

Dave rose, but spoke to Simon instead of his father. "Take him," he said casually, managing to hide his sorrow.

But the realization of imminent loss hit big Clyde like a blackjack to the soul. He let out a cry of anguish, clapped both hands to his contorted face and collapsed to the deck moaning.

"Oh my God!" said the old man, clearly discomfited and disgusted at the display. "Get up!"

Clyde rose like a crankcase piston, his mighty paw clenching a tiny pistol, likely from his boot, aimed at Simon's heart. I saw the trigger pull but the cap-pistol report of it disappeared in the roar of one of the shotguns. Clyde folded over his gut and sat down hard, both hands washed red with his blood, clutching himself tightly, as if holding body and soul together. It wasn't enough. I saw the light bulb of life go out in his eyes as suddenly as if the string had been pulled. He fell over sideways on the floor, already dead, but his legs still flexing, kicked a few more seconds until he lay still.

I pushed back my chair to stand, ignoring the sweep of shotguns in my direction and approached the corpse. "You keep away from him with your mumbo jumbo," warned the old man. I looked to Simon, who nodded. Approaching, I dropped to one knee and made the sign of the cross. "May God Almighty have mercy upon thee, forgive thee thy sins and bring thee to everlasting life." Last rites. *Poor Clyde*, I thought. He was not as mean as the old man, but with almost equal measures of big, brave, and stupid. And now, in just seconds, all done, finished with his life, and moved on. To something better, I hoped.

I stood up from the corpse and backed away, cautious about sudden moves, glad to regain my seat next to Evie. Simon had been shot. He was still standing, not seeming in much pain, with a tolerant look on his face as Leonard yanked out his shirt tail and examined the wound. The red of blood was extra shocking on Simon's crisp, white shirt.

"I'll live," he said dryly. Then he looked at Forsythe. "But you won't." He looked at the other big guy. "You in on this?" Clyde's buddy shook his head, saying nothing, and raised his hands. Simon waved them back down. "Just no guns," he said. He looked down at the remains of Clyde. "Hard to believe this one was your kin," he said to the elder Forsythe. "Heart like an ox. You never had one at all." He looked at the group. "No more tearful goodbyes? Okay." He waved his crew toward Forsythe in his wheelchair then nodded at me. "Sorry to do this to you but we need you along. And yes, we understand that if it comes to court, you'll have to testify. Frankly, we don't care."

Eight black-haired men in white jackets grabbed Forsythe while Simon and Jimmy stood guard. The eight lifted him out of his wheel chair, carried him easily, shoulder high, through the door and along the deck toward the stern while I trailed along in the wake. He didn't cry out and he didn't struggle. They paused next to the bulkhead that shielded the churning wheel and I saw Forsythe look around at the lowering sun, the river, the golding light on trees. Did he have a kind thought? Hard to know. I admit it seemed unlikely. He said nothing.

"Simon," I shouted, to be heard above the rush of the wheel, "you don't have to do this."

He looked at me and smiled genuinely. "I *do* have to do this," he said. "This is a day that I,"—he gestured at the young Athabascan men—"along with Nolan's family, have planned and prepared for their whole lives. After today, I can retire and die satisfied. I can ... do *anything* ... with this old debt paid." He nodded at the men crowding the bulkhead above the middle of the wheel, still holding Forsythe shoulder high. "My only real regret," he added, "is that Nolan's life turned out so short, and this one has gotten to live so long. On three," he said to them. "One, two ..." On three, they pitched him over the bulkhead and down into the wheel, into the water and into hell in their minds, I supposed. Then they turned from their work with smiles on their faces, shaking hands, some even hugging, and as a group headed back to clean up the mess that had been Clyde. Simon lingered only a moment.

"I didn't think he'd want blessing," he said, "but you never know. Sorry to put you through this."

"What am I to do with this?" I asked him.

He pursed his lips and shook his head. "Any darn thing you want. Report it as a crime if you need to. Do what you need to do. That's what we did. Far as I'm concerned it's all even now." He patted me on the shoulder as he turned to go, already pulling the next cigar from his chest pocket. "I would like it," he said, "in spite of Forsythe, to have you say the blessing. A blessing shouldn't be conditional." And he left me to it.

I stood by the thrashing rail in gathering twilight pondering what had all just happened. Simon, along with Nolan's nephews had just murdered a man, or executed him, in my presence, and I hadn't raised a finger to save him. Not that I could have. And now Simon, a murderer—and devout Christian—had sincerely asked me to bless the man he murdered. I felt battered by it all, unworthy, unable, nearly weepy. I felt diminished by Alaska, by the near presence of such evil, and by such faith. I reached out to the rail and held on to steady myself for long moments until Evie came to stand by me.

"You okay?"

I looked at her dumbly. "No." She nodded and stood by me. I crossed myself, and she seeing, crossed herself, and we turned to the river. "May God Almighty have mercy upon thee, forgive thee thy sins and bring thee to everlasting life," I said.

And Evie whispered, "Amen."

Then she told me that Forsythe—Dave Forsythe, the son—had gone over the side. "He escaped. Gone."

Escaped maybe, I thought, *but gone? I don't think so.* Which is why I told her with certainty, "We'll see him again."

CHAPTER 27

A completely abashed Ellen came and sat at my table after breakfast as I finished my coffee. She sat penitently on the front of her wooden chair staring down at her clasped hands.

"I'm sorry," she said. "Sorry for everything. I ... my life is such a mess."

I didn't say anything. If she was looking for an argument she had come to the wrong place.

"But my offer still stands," she added, shifting gears, that moment of introspection now in the past. "You and me." She dialed up her warm look. "The two of us. You know, I can make you happier than Evelyn."

"Evie," I said.

"Whoever."

"You need to leave."

She looked confused. "Leave?"

"The chair, the room, the boat if necessary. Leaving Alaska would be okay, too."

"But," she protested, "you're not sleeping with her, and you could be sleeping with me!" She leaned closer. "I admit it's not so easy on this ... *boat.*" She said the word like it was a contemptible thing. "And then when we get back to your ... village," I noticed she said that like it was a contemptible thing, too. "we can do whatever we want."

"There's a problem," I said.

"There is?"

"Actually, there are more problems than the two of us together can number."

"But..."

"But the *main* problem," I continued firmly, "is that I'm doing what I want, and Evie is the person I want to do it with."

She pondered this. "Well, what if we *didn't* sleep together then, if that's the way you *really* want it. What if we looked for the gold together? This Simon seems to trust you. You could tell him I'm okay and I could—you know—get him to tell me where the gold is." She looked up. "I'm pretty good at that."

"Did you love your dad," I asked. Her warm and honeyed face changed instantly into a fierce look of revulsion.

"I hated him," she nearly hissed. "I hated the sight of him, his smell, his touch, his smile when he wanted something and thought you didn't know he wanted it. If there was anything about him I didn't hate ..." she paused, "I don't even know what it is."

I leaned forward meeting her eyes, speaking softly, hoping to make this a moment she could remember. "Then," I said, "from this moment, you need to do everything you can to not be like him."

"Be like him?" she nearly shouted, jumping to her feet, dumping the chair. "Be like him?" she said again, smacking both palms hard on the table top, this time making no effort not to shout. Several of the busboys paused, dishes or utensils halfway to somewhere. "You!" she shouted, drawing back her arm as if to strike me, though with a table between us, she didn't have the reach.

"I hate you," she said through clenched teeth. "And I hate Evelyn ... *all* of you! You killed my father and now my brother has abandoned me. I'm going to kill you, and her, and all of you. You're going to beg me to not kill you, but I'm still going to kill you anyway ... and I'm going to get the gold. I'm going to be successful, and live in a big house, and have a *life*. And ... and you can beg all you want, but I'm never sleeping with you again!"

"You never slept with me before," I pointed out.

"Well get used to it," she said, and spun and stomped out.

Unnoticed by either of us, Andy had come back into the dining room. He set right Ellen's chair and slid into the one next to me. "How do you do that?"

"Do what?"

"Your *woman thing*. What is it you do that makes them warm up to you like that? You managed to not sleep with this babe already once. If I was a hetero, I'd sure want to study up on what you got, because you really got it! She went from wanting to feed your dogs to wanting to kill 'em in just a sentence or two. That's kind of amazing."

"Thanks, I think." I said. "Dogs?"

He waved me off. "Just an expression."

With Dave gone, Ellen not speaking, and the other big guy retired—who turned out to be a fairly amiable Italian from Boston by the name of Alphonse—days settled into a routine of running down the river, stopping for wood, or delivering light freight to an occasional homestead. It turned out we carried mail, too. And, of course, I held informal communion services to parishioners along the way. Otherwise, moving west we had an amazing succession of sunny, peaceful days that made it easy to begin to forget about all the nastiness that hovered like a dirty halo over the legend of lost steamboat gold.

Jimmy moved out of his hidey-hole to an empty stateroom, now that it seemed no one would be trying to kill him. "I got a window," he told me with visible pride, "and a light."

"Does it *get* any better?" said Andy with a grin.

Only William prowled, guard ever up. "This is not over," he told me. "Is not nearly over. Forsythe still believes that Simon knows what he needs to. He will be back for Simon."

I sighed heavily. "You're right, of course."

"And there is another thing."

"Do I want to hear this?"

"Whether Forsythe wants the gold for himself," as his relatives have believed, "or whether he is on government assignment, seeking gold for the Federal Government to claim, he could make use of other resources."

"But not telling the family," I said, seeing the possibility. "Wouldn't *that* be a nasty shock!"

"His sister would very definitely kill him," William said. "Although she might have to stand in line for the opportunity."

For the most part, the *Nenana* steamed 'round the clock, as had been her way when this was an established summer freight route. But on this trip, with supplies of firewood uncertain, we sometimes tied up overnight at a tiny village or even a fishcamp site while cutters hauled in wood.

"I forget places like this still exist," said Evie, leaning on the rail with me at one such stop.

"Like this?" I said.

"These fishcamps, like the one at the Mission when I was a kid, where I cut fish and learned to sharpen knives. Those are drying racks over there, filled with dog salmon split up to the tail. It's winter food for the dog teams. And that place back there, closed up, is the smoke house. It smells *so* good in there."

I'd been in salmon smokehouses and had to agree. Even now, at a distance, the memory made me salivate.

She pointed at the fish wheel, spinning slowly in the current. It alternated paddles with chicken-wire baskets to catch the current and scoop salmon out of the river. As we watched, the wheel turned up a wriggling fish and dropped it down a wooden chute into a box with others.

"I wasn't much bigger than the fish when it became my job to empty the box and wheelbarrow the fish up to the cutting table. This was before I was big enough to stand at the table and cut. I was a "fetcher." My first wheelbarrow only had two fish in it. It was all I could push. Over the next couple of summers I built up to a whole wheelbarrow load of fish, which is why I'm stronger today than people expect. Later, when I was a teen, I stood with a knife gutting fish for hours, with blood and scales drying on my arms, flies and mosquitoes landing on me, and my nose always itching because my hands were too gunky to scratch it. I used to hate it all."

"But now?"

"I still hate it, but somehow I feel a little nostalgic about it." She looked around, as if just starting to see where she was. "Maybe I do belong here," she said softly.

At William's urging, we divided the day into six four-hour watches, shared between William, Andy, Evie and me. And then when Jimmy figured out what we were doing, he demanded a shift, too.

"You don't trust me anymore," said Jimmy to Andy and me, "and after all I've done for you."

"Well," said Andy, "not really. Actually, I never trusted you," he added.

"I saved him, twice," said Jimmy, nodding in my direction.

"Well yeah," Andy agreed sarcastically, "while tryin' to kill him."

"That was just coincidence," said Jimmy. "Here's the deal. I'm workin' for Simon. I've always been workin' for Simon. You guys are protecting Simon so I'm in. So is Leonard. And maybe we can get one of his brothers, too."

"Workin' for Simon," said Andy after Jimmy had gone. "That's interesting."

So with the extra manpower, around the clock, two of us rode the top deck, one looking ahead of the boat, downriver, and one looking behind the boat, upriver, for any sign of Forsythe or anybody else trying to come aboard.

"You know this only works," said William, "if they are coming by boat." With Jimmy and Evie keeping watch up top, William, Andy and I met for dinner around Yukon River salmon, which was delicious.

"How else could anyone get aboard?" I asked.

"A man like Forsythe, with his Viet Nam experience and training, might swim."

"Swim in the Tanana?" Andy and I said, pretty much together.

"There is a program, in your U.S. Navy—somewhat secret—called Scouts and Raiders, actually begun in World War II. It was Scouts and Raiders who blew holes in the beaches at Normandy. If Forsythe has been telling the truth about Viet Nam service, then there is a good possibility that he has had this specialized training and would think nothing at all of swimming in the Tanana."

"Oh good," said Andy. "Train 'em for overseas so they can be extra dangerous at home."

"Well *you* are," said William. "You who can shoot a button off a vest at half a mile."

"Well, yeah, but ..."

"But not psychopathic," said William.

Andy shot a look in my direction, eyebrows raised like question marks nearly to his hairline. "I think I had shots for that," he said, "whatever it is."

"It's what you see in Forsythe," I explained, "a textbook case. Highly antisocial behavior with diminished capacity for empathy."

"Oh," said Andy. "Forsythe, to a tee."

"No feelings," I said. "If someone like you hurts someone else, you feel bad for them. If he hurts someone it's just another day in the office.

"I get it," said Andy. "The father and sister, too."

William agreed. "Yes, it is very clear he was not adopted, nor Ellen. How do you say it? This apple is not falling far from the tree."

"Now apples?" Andy pushed back his chair. "I'm out. I'm gonna go find someone to talk to about guns or moose or outboard motors. You guys jump around too much."

"Jimmy wants to know what's the deal with us," said Evie later. Her four-hour watch ended, she came tapping at my stateroom door, whispering, "You awake?"

"Yep, just lying here trying to make sense of this whole thing." She closed the door quietly, and I noticed she clicked the bolt. Then she perched next to me on the narrow hard shelf of bed, the room lit only by deck light through the window. With a watch coming up, I hadn't even bothered to undress, just threw myself down, tired, but apparently not yet ready to sleep.

"Did you explain it to him?"

"Gosh," she said, "I don't even know what to tell myself. I told him I never met anybody like you. And then Jimmy said, 'He's white, you know.' like I might have missed it. It always comes back to that, doesn't it?"

"Seems to. I don't think of it, do you?"

"Not moment to moment. You and I are color-less in my heart. But if I try to imagine the future ... well, you know how that goes."

"I do," I said. "It's just skin."

"Yeah," she said, and then, "scootch over." She pushed me lightly, and when I 'scootched' and turned on my side in the narrow bunk, she lay down beside me and put her arm over me.

"This is nice," I said. She wriggled around in a vain attempt to get more comfortable.

"The deaconess at the Mission used to talk about her 'bed of pain,'" Evie said. "I think we've found it." We laughed about that, and then about other things, and lay there chuckling to ourselves in semidarkness as the *Nenana* bore us steadily

231

west through the sub-arctic twilight. In a little while we drifted off to sleep together, just that way, she before me. The last thought I remember is that it did feel very nice.

As luck would have it, Andy came rapping on the door at four a.m. to wake us for the next shift. Since, Evie had the outside position on the bunk, it was she who opened the door, blinking and squinting in the morning light, pushing her hair back out of her face and looking just a bit embarrassed to find Andy standing there. William would have been easier.

"Thought I might find you here," he said, "hoped I would, since you obviously weren't sleeping in your own bunk. Glad to see you're already dressed."

He wasn't hard to read. "*Still* dressed," she said. "Hope you guys just know what you're doin'."

"Me too," she said after he had gone. Slipping on shoes, she bent to kiss my cheek. "I guess we're up, sleepy head." I rolled out, and we were.

❖

Back on watch with Andy the next afternoon, me just below the pilothouse and Andy at the stern, atop what the crew called the hurricane deck, from my hard chair I could see for thirty miles in three directions across the flat, sparse Yukon River bottoms. A part of me wanted to see and memorize everything, knowing this would be the last run for the *Nenana*, the last of Alaska's great river steamboats. But not the last riverboat, by any means.

Just a few years back, the Alaska Railroad got out of the riverboat business, selling all its gear to an outfit called Yutana Barge Lines, running steel screw-driven, diesel boats. In fact, we passed the modern, *M.V. Tanana* just west of Manley, both vessels hooting and whistling, with passengers and crew lined up along the rails. *We're making history*, I thought, and we were.

I could also see Jimmy walking with Evie, below me, in endless circles on the saloon deck. They'd go out of sight all along the covered sides of the boat, emerging from the overhang at the bow. Every now and again Jimmy's radiant face smiled up at me, stuck on the hurricane deck, while he finally got to make time with the girl he had loved since he was five years old and she helped him adjust his suspenders. Sure, that would be magic! At first I felt a little jealous of the two, but remembered my own quiet time with Evie through the night, her arm wrapped around me as we talked and then slept. And then I smiled back at him, wholeheartedly.

The river narrows below Galena. It's one of the few tall places on that part of the river—called Bishop's Rock—where a piece of hillside drops steeply to the water's edge. To get around, especially pushing a string of barges, the pilot sends a man with a sounding stick to the front barge, then slows the boat to little more than drift speed and eases around the bend, not more than twenty feet from shore.

It was there, with Jimmy and Evie leaning on the rail at the bow, talking and laughing, that Dave Forsythe stood up out of low brush, almost level with the two. Left-handed, he aimed his pistol at Evie and pulled the trigger quickly three times. I

watched the shooting from above, his bullets stopping my heart.

CHAPTER 28

*E*vie-e-e!" I heard someone shout a warning—I figured out later it was me—but too late, far too late and too slow. To this day, in my dreams, it's still always too late.

Evie had her head back, laughing. She didn't see Forsythe, just heard the too-close boom, boom, boom of the pistol firing. I saw her and Jimmy pitch backward hard, landing all piled up on the deck.

Jimmy had been telling a story from the Mission school about a time the late and universally unlamented six-year-old Frankie got himself stuck in river silt at the edge of the water. Instead of calling for help, as anyone might, little Frankie stood shouting, "If someone doesn't get me out of here *quick* there's gonna be trouble!" Every kid within earshot stopped what they were doing to point, laugh—and as one—walk away. Finally, when he had blustered and sunk himself nearly to his knees, Evie went back down to help him out. Then she had to endure Frankie's tiny raging nastiness for seeing him helpless. One of the last times. Though forgotten by Evie, the moment had long been nurtured by Jimmy, and some twenty-five years later he could hardly retell the story without laughing until he wept.

Also from way back at the stern—even above the rhythmic whacking of the waterwheel—Andy heard the shots and knew them. A combat sniper in France and Northern Italy, he still heard shooting in his dreams. "Sometimes I wake up, middle of the night," he told me, "crouched by the side of my bed, ducked and covered." Though we had shared a laugh about it, in the early years after the war with those memories way too fresh, only alcohol took the edge off those moments to put him under and let him get some rest, until the sound of shooting became a smaller problem than being a drunk.

But Andy still had sniper-quick instincts. With the echo in play, vibrations only just headed back across the river from the stark face of Bishop Rock, Andy sprinted forward from the stern while pulling the two-inch-barreled .38 Special. In that single motion, straight-armed, sighting, he emptied all five cylinders at Forsythe on the shore—Bang! Bang! Bang! Bang! Bang! a spray of tiny bits of steel, completely unexpected by Forsythe—and even at a distance—deadly.

Focused in this, his triumphant moment, I could easily imagine Forsythe already savoring his delight with Evie bleeding out on the deck and 'that bastard Hardy' unable to pray his way out—or whatever voodoo I had so far used to hold off harm. The virtual squall of bullets stunned and, by the look of it, panicked him. Bullets ripping at his sleeve, pinging off rocks and tree stumps, snapping off a branch inches from his left ear—thudding into the ground, and a whining ricochet all conspired to push him off balance and tip him abruptly out of his triumphant moment. It sent him scurrying back into deeper brush like a small, frightened animal.

I descended the narrow forward ladder in about three big steps, dreading what I'd find. Mary's death in the iron lung had been a release, a blessing, the answer to my prayer. Blue-lipped, gasping, I watched her ease over to another kinder shore and I could imagine her smiling there, strolling, even laughing.

But Evie's death—the tight grouping of bullet holes I already imagined in her chest—was no blessing. My prayers, even in the scarcely controlled drop from above, were simple: *Let me say goodbye, let her not suffer!*

What I found stunned me.

Evie, seemingly untouched, knelt on the deck, legs folded under her, cradling Jimmy, bleeding, dying. "Doesn't hurt," he murmured, as I dropped to my hands and knees and placed my hand on his forehead for the blessing. "Bury me at Nenana," he said to me, "on the hill."

His eyes shifted to Evie. "Happiest day of my life," he said, coughing a little then went quiet forever.

CHAPTER 29

*H*e stepped in front of me," she sobbed, "pulled me back so hard I lost my balance, then we fell. As I rolled over to get up, I said, 'That was lucky!' B-but it w-wasn't." And she put her hands over her face, her whole body shaking as she wept.

We were seated around an unset table in the dining room with Evie, Simon, Leonard, William and Andy. Simon had conjured coffee from the galley but I noticed we mostly held the heavy, cooling mugs, too numb to sip. Still, it felt comforting.

Leonard wanted to form up a posse of himself and his brothers with their deadly sawed-off shotguns and go hunting; an idea William and Andy opposed.

"He's wearing camouflage," Andy said. "even had his face painted. Hard to see until it's too late.

"He is an expert at running, hiding and ambushing," added William. "One by one he will pick you off,. It will be Christmas for him."

"We've gotta do *something*," sniffed Leonard, a little teary. "Seems like, his whole life, Jimmy couldn't catch a break. His folks died. He was sent to the Mission. Grew up without family. It was only about five years ago I found out I even had a cousin.

"At first," Leonard admitted with a little shrug, "I didn't think much of him, kinda small and quiet. But he was one of the bravest guys I ever met." He looked at Evie. "And you know, he was crazy about you."

That set Evie, who had settled a bit, to sobbing anew. "I do," she said. "I do know that. I've always known that." I put my arm around her and she leaned in to my shoulder. "He saved my life. Twice! He deliberately gave away his life to save mine. Why would he do that? Who willingly stops living so someone else can?"

"That's the whole conundrum of Christianity," I said. "Someone filled with love. You heard him ... *the happiest day of his life.*"

In the moments after the shooting and death, after Andy had tried—with no success—to lead Evie away, the three of us, with Simon, Leonard and some of his cousins, stretched Jimmy out flat on the deck, closing his eyes and arranging his hands and arms neatly. Evie brushed his shiny black hair back from his forehead, letting her hand linger, lips moving slightly in her own private prayer.

"Where can we put him?" I asked Simon. "No matter how he goes back we're still quite a ways from Nenana and burial."

"He'll be okay in the cool room," said Simon, with a slight sideward glance at Evie. "Not the first one to ride there," he paused, "but might be the last. We'll get it set with sawhorses and planks and he'll be covered." Simon looked at Evie directly. "He'll be okay in there." She nodded, unable to speak.

Back in my own room, I suddenly found myself sobbing, my body shaking, face pressed into my hands, trying to make no sound, remembering again that crying is more than tears. When the door opened quietly, it was Evie's face that peered in at me, her own eyes red, and whatever makeup she started with smeared around them raccoon-like.

"Oh Hardy," she said, came in, closed the door and we held each other for a time. Until she straightened in my embrace.

"He was wet!" she said. I admit to being a little mentally blurry. I thought about what she'd said, came to the conclusion I had no idea what she was talking about, and said the only reasonable thing.

"Huh?"

"Forsythe. He had to swim to get to where he could shoot at us. And when you think about it, how did he get there at all. There are no roads. It's not like he could grab a bus or hitchhike."

"You're right," I said, my brain finally coming back over to my side. "The only way to get from upriver where he went off—to here, is by boat."

"This one!" she exclaimed. "He went over the side but never left the boat. He's been hiding on the *Nenana* or on one of the barges the whole time."

Although I'd stopped to rinse my face in cold water, Andy gave me a double-take when we found him with William, back at their watch posts on the hurricane deck.

"Wet," repeated William, absorbed in specula-tion. He pressed his lips together. "So he is on the boat somewhere."

I noticed it took a lot less time for him to reach the obvious conclusion than for me.

"It makes sense," I said. "Otherwise he is afoot in the wilderness. Not only no way to strike at us, but no way to get supplies or to get out. "Maybe find a fish camp and steal a boat but that doesn't feel like Forsythe's style."

"So we have to search for him," said Andy, "search the boat, search the barges."

"It is very dangerous," said William. "*He* is very dangerous, especially up close. And the problem is" that this is his game. He waits, he strikes, the timing, the setting, is all his. We could search all the equipment bundles on the barges and I have no doubt that we would find him. But at least one more of us will die. He has made that very clear. I am afraid," he hesitated, "that it is time for the three of us—and for Simon—to leave the boat. Otherwise, more will die."

No one liked his suggestion. Andy didn't like running away, which was how he saw it. Evie didn't say so directly, but she didn't like leaving Jimmy, alone in the cool room. And she didn't much like running away, either.

"If leaving now would be the end of it," she reasoned, "but he'll just turn up again until he gets what he came for ..."

"At least now we know where he is," Andy finished her thought. "That gives us a slight advantage."

I didn't like the idea of any more of us dying. There wasn't enough gold in the world to be worth losing one of us—or anybody on the boat. Still, I had to admit they had a point.

"Maybe we could get Simon off," I suggested half-heartedly. "He's the target."

"Fat chance," said Andy.

"Maybe," said Evie, "since we're all pretty certain Simon won't leave without a fight, there's something else we can do with him."

"Huh?" I said.

"Stake him out," said William, sensing Evie's drift and going with it.

I didn't get it. I turned to Andy who translated.

"Bait," he said.

Simon liked the idea. What was there to not like? He got to stay on the boat with no trouble from us and keep doing what he liked to do and what he wanted to do, his job and his life on the river.

But Leonard tried to talk him out of it.

"We can't protect you here Uncle." He turned to me. "He'd be a sitting duck! You should be talking him *out* of staying," he protested angrily.

"What are the chances?" I asked him.

I watched him deflate, and his anger dissipate.

"About zip," he conceded. "We've already had this talk a bunch. "So what's the plan?"

"Let Simon keep precisely to his routine, be really predictable. But he needs a room alone. You need to move out, like you think the danger is past.

Leonard bristled. "I'm supposed to be in there protecting him."

"We need to make it look easy. It doesn't look that easy if he has to go through you."

Mollified, Leonard took a breath, relaxed a bit. "Okay, but how are we going to protect him when Forsythe shows up?"

"For one thing, by not letting him sleep in there. He can sleep somewhere harder to find."

"So, who *will* sleep in there?"

"Nobody. We'll build it up to look like someone is. Less chance of anybody getting hurt."

Leonard shook his head, unconvinced. "I don't know. I'd rather just go barge to barge, find him, shoot him, and have the whole thing over." But in the end he agreed to the plan.

To make the plan work we assumed that Forsythe wasn't on the *Nenana*, but instead had found himself a hiding spot on one of the barges—or maybe a hiding spot on each of them. His appearance in cammo even suggested he had hidden supplies there in advance, just in case.

So we'd spend more time watching forward, toward the bow and the barges, and not bother with the stern watch at all. Besides, swimming up to the paddle wheel and trying to get on board back at the stern appeared all but impossible, even for Forsythe.

When evening came, Simon would go through the routine of closing his office, checking the dining room, looking in on the pilot, and finally heading for his stateroom. He'd go in and close the door after Leonard had checked it for any unauthorized 'visitors.' Then, on the first river curve to port, when Simon's door went out of view from the vantage of any of the barges, he'd slip out, head to the stern, down the stern ladder and make his way unseen to the Captain Rufus Edmonton memorial 'hidey-hole,' where, as he said later, he slept like a baby.

In that way, day eight uneventfully became day nine, and finally day ten as we approached the vast Yukon River Delta.

"About the size of Oregon," Evie said of the delta as we neared Marshall, the *Nenana's* western port of call. From there, other more seaworthy boats and delta-savvy pilots would take the barges the hundred-or-so miles on to the saltwater of the Bering Sea.

"This is it," said Andy, as the two of us stood by the bow rail, watching the village of Marshall grow from a distant downriver smudge to a small river town. "We made it."

"You thought we wouldn't?"

"A time or two," he admitted. "Like when you were out swimming in the middle of the night and we found Jimmy crying. I'd never known Jimmy to be an easy crier."

"Poor Jimmy," I said, and he nodded.

Two tugboats met us to pick up our barges. Instead of tying up to meet them at the Marshall waterfront, we joined up out in the middle of the Yukon—by the look of it, about a mile wide—where in a matter of minutes they rafted up to our barges. We cut loose, the sternwheel slowing to a stop then battering up in reverse to pull us free. The old boat turned to head back upriver the mile or so we'd drifted below town.

"You thinking what I'm thinking?" asked Andy.

"You mean that we just sent Forsythe on to the Bering Sea?"

"Something like that. I hope he brought a sweater!" He laughed, the first time in a while any of us had done any laughing. "Time to get home," he said.

Snubbed up to the riverbank at Marshall, the inevitable wood loading began for the turnaround trip back upriver—the last trip this steamer would ever make. Although I had tried to get Simon to fly back with us, there wasn't a single chance he would miss the old steamboat's last-ever leg.

"I've got Leonard and the boys to keep me company," he said. "And we'll be on the lookout, just in case Forsythe figures out how to catch up, but he doesn't have many options." He smiled and took a long draw on his cigar. "No place to get off out there, and pretty darn wide. Too bad."

Still sulky, Ellen also left the boat, now with Alphonse trailing like a Great Dane in her wake. She stopped on the riverbank to look up and down, as though expecting someone to meet her. Seeing no one, she filed along with the rest of us to the gravel airfield where a good-sized Wien airlines DC-3 just in on a route from Nome, was already firing up its engines. Apparently it had been waiting for us. Only in Alaska!

Of the four of us, only Evie hesitated. "I just don't feel like I should leave him," she said. We had made arrangements to have Jimmy—now in a canvas body bag with straps and handles for easy carrying—moved up to the cold storage where he could remain until one of the airplanes had enough cargo space to fly him back to Fairbanks.

"He's gone on," I said gently, "to a better place."

"I know," she said. "I just keep thinking of "little Jimmy" by himself. What if he needs a suspender adjusted, or something?" She gave me a close-to-tears look that made it impossible to not take her in my arms and hold her.

So the four of us tossed our gear on the cart, William ever watchful at the rear, and filed up the rolling stairs to find seats, smelling fresh coffee brewing. In moments the airplane "slipped the surly bonds of earth," hurling itself into the air with an ear-splitting roar, to swoop a broad curve over Marshall giving us our last look at the Yukon. It felt good to be bound for Fairbanks, and for home.

Not so good to know we had—maybe a week or two until a killer came calling.

CHAPTER 30

*I*n a dream, I saw myself walking along a sparkling, clear-water trout stream holding the hand of a little girl. I didn't know her but she knew me. She called me Hardy and had brown hair and hazel eyes that showed mostly green by the water.

"What's your name?" I asked her, and she answered, but I couldn't hear what she said over the pounding, which I first thought was river noise until I figured out it was pounding on my door. "Wait a minute," I said to her, waking up to answer the door—which I now kept solidly bolted at night.

"I'll be right here," she assured me seriously. But in the next second she and the river had vanished, leaving me thrashing around in my squeaky bed trying to wake up to answer a door that could only mean trouble. My round-faced ticking alarm clock read ten minutes after three. No one comes to the door at three a.m. for anything but trouble.

So I opened the door with my foot against it and the .38 in my hand, held slightly behind my leg. In my small entryway I found Maxine, the public health nurse, a small, sturdy woman in her forties or maybe early fifties, her impossibly curly, sandy-colored hair tied down tight with a blue bandana. She usually just barged in at these hours to shake me awake.

"Good," she said, "you're home! I heard you were somewhere downriver. When did you start locking your door?"

"When people kept waking me," I said with a sleepy grin. She glanced at the .38 and snorted a sort of laugh.

"Yeah, I'll bet," she said.

"What have you got?"

"A bad one. It's a gunshot. I haven't had one of those for a while."

"You're lucky," I said, thrust instantly back to thinking about my riverboat ride and Jimmy. "How bad?"

"The *worst*, is what I'm told." I let go the door and she followed me in and down the hallway to discreetly lean against the wall—just out of sight of me dressing—and talk to me as I yanked on my clothing.

"Do we know the shooter?" In my mind it was already something do with Forsythe.

"Yeah," she said, exasperated. "*Shooters!* We know 'em. A couple of the regulars at the Bide-A-While showed up packing. When the argument started, this guy got in the middle. The story is they both fired, one hit."

"Why were they armed? In bar brawls they usually just black each other's eyes and get to wake up in the morning. Who's the victim?"

"The new school teacher," she said. "Picking up some extra cash as the night bouncer. Stepped right in like he was back on the playground. He won't do that again." She drew in a sharp breath. "This wouldn't happen if they'd pay those people what they're worth." Satisfied I was really awake and moving, she sprang away from the wall, headed for the door. "Now finish getting dressed, *quick* and meet me at the Bide-Awhile. Bring your bag."

"I'm dressed, see?" Stepping out, I finished pulling a cotton sweater over my head.

But she had already made it out the door, leaving it ajar, and I could see her in the driveway with her bicycle, nudging the kickstand with her toe. Although she had a car, a late '40s Dodge, she preferred the blue Sears bike as her summer in-town mode of transportation. She rode the girl's model with the low front bar and a large woven-wood basket containing her medical supplies mounted above the front fender. "Hurry," she urged. "He could be a bleeder."

I threw on a jacket, grabbed my army-issue medical bag and was ready to head out the door in less than five minutes. Then I stopped with my hand on the knob, retraced my steps and called Fairbanks to scramble the military rescue helicopter. They'd be surly if he died before they got here. "We're not a hearse," they had been known to say.

"On our way," said a distant voice, tinny but precise. "About an hour."

"An hour," I thought, jogging the two blocks or so from the rectory to the wide main street. 'Uptown,' the locals called it.

So that would be the challenge, keeping the schoolteacher alive while Army Rescue flew the sixty miles to reach us. Good luck to us!

Pushing through the door at the Bide-Awhile I took it all in: the low light reflecting dully off the polished, honey-colored knotty pine walls; six trophy moose heads that sometimes wore party hats, and the long, gleaming bar. A few die-hard drinkers still clustered around one table, reluctant to leave beer on the table. The long room hung thick with smells of Lysol, decades of cigarette smoke, and overtones of vomit, urine and, of course, beer.

I recognized the teacher. He had stopped by the rectory to introduce himself earlier in the summer, a man named Brad Young, from somewhere in Ohio. "I'm anxious to get started teaching the natives," he had said, "and to get out fly-fishing."

Now he would do neither. He had taken a hit low to the gut and lay stretched out on the floor, pants undone and belt buckle flopped over, lying in a small pool of blood. I took the small amount of blood—less than a pint—for a possible good sign. Unless the rest of it was pouring out on the inside.

He opened his eyes. "Call my wife," he whispered.

"She's on her way," said Maxine, whose eyes met mine. I knew the look. This guy didn't have a chance. But we set to work, my first task, a small dab of holy oil to make the sign of the cross on his forehead.

"May God Almighty have mercy upon thee, forgive thee thy sins and bring thee to everlasting life," I said. His eyes fluttered open.

"It's that bad," he said, not a question.

"A precaution," I told him, "but yes, it's bad."

"Damn," he said, softly. "My wife ... ?"

"Any minute," I told him, willing her to hurry. Nothing in Chandelar, including the teacherage where they lived, was more than a ten-minute walk from this spot. Then the door opened, hesitantly. "She's here," I told him.

She stepped in quietly, a tiny blond woman—couldn't have been five feet tall—dressed in jeans and plaid flannel shirt, with a scarf tied around her short bobbed hair. Behind tortoise-shell rims she had serious, nearly bottle green eyes that quickly took in the room. "I *told* you," she said, darting an angry look at her husband.

His eyes opened again but looked like he might be having trouble focusing. "You made it," he said. And then, "I'm cold." Maxine produced a blanket and handed it to me. I looked at the wife.

"Help me?"

She pressed her lips together but came around to grab one side of the folded wool army blanket and we arranged it over the top half of Young's body and tucked the sides under.

"Better." He murmured. She looked at me, her eyes asking the question.

"It's serious," I said. "He's had last rites—just in case—and the helicopter is on its way from Eielson Airforce Base in Fairbanks."

She nodded once, and just looked at me, her eyes into my eyes. It was as if I could read the whole frustrating story of her life, or of their life at least, in that long gaze.

"I asked him not to do this," she said bitterly. "I begged him not to come up here, to this ... *place*. And now he's going to die and I'm going to be alone here and have to figure out how to get home!"

Young opened his eyes to look at her. The pain in them wrenched my heart. It had nothing to do with his gut wound. He opened his mouth like he might say something, then closed it, and closed his eyes. This was apparently old ground.

"Don't worry about that now," I told her. "Brad's young and healthy. He has a chance." She stood up and went to sit on a chair. In a few minutes the bartender came to ask her if she wanted anything.

"Well," she said, "a martini would be nice but I guess I'd better stay with coffee for now. She looked around at Maxine and I trying to keep her husband from bleeding to death. You'd better get coffee for them. They're going to need it."

I didn't notice when the room grew silent, or when singly or in pairs people filtered in to claim a bar stool or heavy chrome chair to sit quietly and watch. And to drink, Maxine told me later. By the time we heard the *thwok, thwok, thwok* of the Huey, every seat had filled and the bartender scurried quietly, chair to chair, taking orders and collecting money.

The door opened, admitting an extra blast of helicopter thunder and blowing dust into the room, the graveled main street out front plenty wide enough for the chopper.

Andy burst in, looked at me, looked at the chopper and then at the soon-to-be-grieving widow. "Drinkin' a martini," he said later, "just pullin' out the olive and eatin' it when I got there!"

"He'd been awake anyway, another of the products of his World War II service in Italy. He knew well the sound of an Army helicopter and came running when he heard it, following the noise. He looked at me, looked at Young; I looked at him, he nodded slightly and went to start gathering the "grieving" wife for her helicopter ride.

Someone led the four medics in, with their stretcher and gear. "Wow," said one of them to us, "good work." And then to Young, who had opened his eyes, "Good care here, you're a lucky guy. Let's get you out of here." Within about two minutes the four medics had him blanketed on a wire stretcher basket, had an oxygen mask on him, and had him out the door to the Huey. Andy brought up the rear supporting a now not-too-steady Mrs. Young.

At the chopper door she paused and turned to Andy. "I need you to stay with me," she said, having quickly 'bonded.'

"You'll be fine," he hollered, reassuringly, to be heard above the loop of spinning rotor and whine of the engine. He handed her, disappointed, to one of the medics who drew her smoothly through the door, her feet and the helicopter leaving the ground in just about the same instant. In sixty seconds the helicopter and Mr. and Mrs. Young were all just a memory and an echo. I looked at my watch: 4:10 a.m.

"Will he make Fairbanks?" asked Andy.

"It's not how I'd bet," I told him.

"When I first saw him lying there I thought it was Forsythe. Thought our troubles were over."

Together with Maxine we packed up, cleaned up, and cleared out.

"Last call," said the bartender, but with the main act finished and gone, had no takers. "Well," he said to me, "it was a pretty good night for business, anyway." Then he surprised me with a wad of cash. "Give this to the little blond, she's gonna need it. And tell her if she wants to work ..." His eyes met mine and his voice sort of trailed away.

"I'll see she gets it," I said, and Andy and I went out, watched Maxine straddle her bike and pedal off into the dawn.

"Coffee?" asked Andy, and I thought about the cozy, squeaky bed I'd left—and for the first time since waking—the mysterious little girl.

"Sure," I said, "some of the good stuff."

"I have an idea," he said, when events of the early morning had begun to fade and we had settled into our accustomed places around my kitchen table, mugs of Italian-roasted coffee hot in our hands.

"About Forsythe?"

"Well, no. About me."

"You?"

"It's like this," he said. "I got no job and no hope of one around here. I don't have enough money to go back to Italy and besides, I miss you and Evie ... Rosie ... the village ... when I'm so far away, so I been thinking." He drew a breath. "Thinking of opening a restaurant, an Italian restaurant. Makin' my own job."

"Here?" I asked, sounding doubtful.

He looked at me like I might be nuts. "Nah, Fairbanks." But then a knock on my front door interrupted him, and the sound of someone pushing on the bolted door, rattling the latch, then knocking again."

Andy shot me a look. "Forsythe?"

"Forsythe doesn't knock," I told him, and went to unbolt the door for Evie.

"You're locking your door," she said. "Good!" She stepped in, closed the door behind her, and re-bolted it.

"We're in ... here ..." I said, except that catching my arm she turned me back to her.

"I know where you are," she said, and put her arms around me and kissed me a long time, very nicely.

"Welcome happy morning," I said, quoting the old Fortunatus Easter hymn."

"'Age to age shall say,'" she said, never at a loss for a quote. She put her hands on the back of my shoulders and leaned her head against my neck as we single-filed down the narrow hallway to Andy.

"I heard the chopper and smelled the coffee," she said, "and hurried right over." She smiled at her cousin. "I knew you'd be here. Is the teacher gonna make it?"

"Too close to call," said Andy.

"So Andy is thinking of opening an Italian restaurant in Fairbanks," I told her, ready to stop thinking about bullet wounds, blood and death. "But you probably know this already?"

Her brown eyes widened. "First *I've* heard. In Fairbanks? What are you gonna call it?"

"Andrea's," he said, happily, "Italian for Andrew. Pronounced, *Ahn*-dray's. That's what they call me back home in Vernazza. From the Greek, meaning manhood or valor, which is me, all over." He struck an appropriate pose. She laughed.

"What?!" Andy exclaimed, feigning insult.

"*You're* going to cook?" I asked. He shook his head.

"I'll hire a cook. At least to get going. It'll be a family place, where you can sit at a long wooden table like Italians do, drinking wine and singing."

"Singing?" said Evie, sounding doubtful. Like me, she was imagining a table full of shy, quiet

255

Athabascans who would be unlikely to sing in public even if they had been drinking wine.

"Maybe the singing will come later," said Andy, as if sensing our thoughts. "But just wait until you taste the food! I collected menus and recipes all over the Cinque Terre, but I didn't exactly know why. Now I do! It's gonna be..." he kissed his tented fingertips in a torrent of unfamiliar Italian enthusiasm, "*molto magnifico!*"

CHAPTER 31

*M*arshal Frank Jacobs, angry, was not a pretty sight.

"So this dead body," he said, "just shows up, C.O.D. The Airline phones and says come get your stiff—and pay us $23.97. So I go out there and find Jimmy Lucas in a body bag—and he *is* stiff! Frozen solid, flown in from ... from somewhere."

In my office, shuffling papers by nine o'clock, I had heard Frank knock and let himself in, heard his footsteps as he walked through my frontroom—recognized his authoritative 'hello,' and watched him carefully position himself on my guest chair, shifting his gun belt for a more comfortable sit, then pop back up to head for the kitchen. "I smell coffee," he called back, suddenly sociable. "Bring you some?"

"I got some, but bring the pot."

So I told him about my Yukon River voyage, leaving out almost everything.

"That's your story?" he said. "You better work on that in case there's an inquest. You must have been absent the day they covered 'Lying to the Law' in seminary. So it's been about three weeks and no sign of the man Forsythe, and it looks like you're still packing that little gun there in your jacket pocket, so I guess you're still expecting him."

I admit I looked from the marshal to where I kept the gun in my right jacket pocket. "You're good," I said.

"Aw shucks," he answered, feigning modesty. "And no sign of the gold?"

"Gold?" I said.

"Yeah, right." He sipped his coffee from my new mug, the one that said 'Fly Pan Am' in Italian, and allowed himself a brief lean against the chair back. "You should be dead," he said, "maybe three times over. I don't have any idea why that's not you in the body bag instead of poor dumb brave Jimmy. I heard somebody on the *Nenana* went overboard. News like that travels. Had no idea it was you." He nodded to himself and sipped again. "Should have known." His eyes met mine over the mug rim. "I've got a warrant out for your buddy Forsythe," he said. "Got a witness who makes him for the Stolz shooting. Armed and extremely dangerous. The warrant gives us more eyes."

"He claims to be some kind of spy," I said.

"Heard that. It may give him a license to kill—somewhere—but not here."

When my ten o'clock arrived, the marshal showed himself out as a sheep rancher dressed like a cowboy, from south of here on the railroad, showed himself in. Leaning his Winchester lever-action carbine and a backpack in the corner, he pulled out some paper and handed it to me.

"I could use a little help with my income tax," he said. His whole self—from high boots worn outside his pants to a big-brimmed hat, which he left on his head—was a uniform shade of brown dust that lifted off him in little updrafts, and sparkled in sunbeams from the window. A working man, he wore the smell of horses, sheep, rank sweat, and God knows whatever else like an outer garment. It permeated my small office and had me breathing shallowly before he even hit the guest chair. It had been a long time since any part of this cowboy had gotten anywhere near soap and water. And, I guessed, that smell would linger long after we'd figured out he couldn't possibly owe anything because he hadn't *made* anything.

He looked at me with bright blue eyes, and a wide-open grin with a couple of teeth missing.

"Hopin' for a refund," he said.

CHAPTER 32

*W*eeks went by with no sign of Forsythe. And yes, I began to relax a little.

Somewhat predictably, Brad Young didn't make it. He hung on most of two more days with his small blond wife, Alice—as it turned out—at his side, before slipping away. After making arrangements to ship him back to the States, Alice hitched a ride back to Chandelar, moving out of the teacherage and into to a small cabin close by, taking the job at the Bide-A-While. "You sure about this," I asked her. She hesitated.

"I married Brad in college and we only ever did what he wanted. Now I get to choose what I want. For right here and right now, I choose this."

The *Nenana* made it back upriver uneventfully, laying over to take on wood for the final leg of her working life, the voyage to Fairbanks and her new life in some kind of park the City had planned. "Gonna be the jewel in the crown," someone said to me. Part of that idea bothered me a little. Burning to the waterline or weathering to pieces like the rest of her kind seemed more dignified, more in keeping with who and what she had been.

A big chunk of June had zipped by almost unnoticed as we voyaged down the Yukon. Now, steaming rapidly through July, I could already begin to imagine the glaze of ice on ponds and leaves yellowing as winter came striding back.

We buried Jimmy on the hill across the river from Nenana, Tortella Hill, the translation from an

Athabascan word I had yet to say correctly. Viewed from out in the valley, a huge Celtic cross marks the grave of a deaconess at the mission school who gave her life for her students, Jimmy among them. It was what he had wanted. "Bury me on the hill," he said. Standing by the grave I helped dig, rubbing a sore shoveling shoulder, I thought of the quote from the Robert Lewis Stevenson tomb. "Home is the sailor, home from the sea, and the hunter home from the hill." Okay, more like home *to* the hill, but it's what I thought of.

Evie cried, but had grown philosophical with time. "I believe we'll meet again," was what she said. I believed that too.

A couple of days later, with things settled down, the school superintendent and his wife invited me for dinner at the teacherage, out of the blue. I did everything I could to come up with a reason to not go. While I didn't mind her, I had never known him not to be snobby and stuffy. To make matters worse, the wife, Delores, took my hand in both of hers and said, "… and bring someone."

When I told Evie about this, she looked directly into my eyes and said, "Are you asking?" I hadn't been. I didn't want to go with her because I didn't want to go at all. "Because if you *are* asking, and you're still serious about the idea of … us … I'll go. I admit it's a little scary though, taking the lid off our secret life."

She walked over that afternoon, to meet me, and stood knocking until I answered. Swinging open the door, I was stunned. I knew how I felt about her, had spent a good deal of time around her recently, and had somehow forgotten she was beautiful—and fashionable. She wore a white blouse under a sky-blue cotton cardigan, a coffee-colored skirt to mid-calf, saddle shoes and what they call bobby sox. She also wore lipstick in a pinkish shade that made me want to say, "the heck with dinner, let's just hang around the cabin and smooch," and a bit of eye makeup rendered her dark eyes bottomless.

"You're stunning," was all I could say.

"I was hoping you'd think so."

I came out, she took my arm, and for the first time, we walked the six blocks or so through town together, smiling, a couple, for all the world to see.

If Delores was surprised to see her, she didn't let on. Her husband, stuffy Edmund, was less smooth, unable to keep his woolly caterpillar eyebrows from arching at the sight of us. But he shook hands amiably with both of us and saw us to comfortable stuffed chairs in a homey, old-fashioned living room for a round of small talk before dinner.

"A little wine?" Delores produced a lightly sweet red wine in small, stemmed glasses.

Evie held her glass up to the light and swirled it, then to her nose, testing the aroma. "Delicious," she said, and it was.

"This may surprise you," said Edmund, "but this wine is from grapes grown in Oregon." It did surprise me, though I knew a few grapes were being grown in California, I still thought most of the wine grapes in the world came from France.

"Some people think Americans can't grow grapes," said Edmund. "And *certainly* can't make wine!"

"Viticulture," said Evie. "With Oregon and Bordeaux on the same latitude, I'm not surprised."

"But it's the grapes, dear, don't you think," said Delores.

"Those French grapes are partly American," said Evie. "When the French grapevines were wiped out in the 1850s, it was American rootstock the vintners grafted to French varieties that got European vinyards going again."

To be honest, I didn't even have to open my mouth at dinner, except to fill it. To say that the conversation flowed, on a wide range of topics, would be an understatement. I think we took a run at every possible topic, with Evie in her glory. Politics, history, philosophy, education—all those years of sitting alone in her cabin reading paid off. But it didn't come sharply into focus until the evening seemed to be winding down.

"I understand," said Edmund to Evie," that you've been attending the University in Seattle."

"Just the semester. I had to leave a few days early, and still have projects to complete, but my professors all gave me grades anyway."

"Education," asked Edmund.

"Yes," said Evie, "I've been a reader all my life. I thought I might like to try teaching."

"So you must have had Professor Hobson?"

"Oh yes! He was amazing."

"Funny," said Edmund.

We both looked at him quizzically.

"Why funny?" I asked.

"Because that's what he said about Evie. Amazing. He wrote me a letter and said he'd never had a student to match you, and he's been around a while."

"He's older than dirt," confided Delores, with a little help from the wine.

Her husband gazed at her, fondly I thought, and I began to feel better about him. "So here's my situation," said Edmund. "Brad Young is dead, as you know, and I have a second/third split without a teacher. About twelve students. Hobson says you're my man. Well, woman. And you're Athabascan. You'd be Chandelar's first Athabascan teacher, and a good one, I think. You'll need to continue to work toward your degree, but what do you say? Will you take the job?"

"Teaching," said Evie, and then said nothing. For the first time all evening she fell absolutely speechless.

Edmund continued. "The salary is $8,000 for the nine months and includes an apartment here in the teacherage, if you want. You'd be helping us out, immeasurably."

"I..." she said. "Yes, of course!" They shook hands on it and we drank another half glass of the fine Oregon wine.

We were halfway home, walking down the road hand in hand, before she spoke again. "I have a job," she said, and then again, "I have a *job!* I'm a *teacher*. I'm thrilled."

"Me too," I said, because it was true.

A few minutes farther along, taking my arm she pulled us close and said, "It was a setup."

"Huh?"

"They knew you'd bring me. They knew all along. They knew we were *us*." We walked along, both very happy to be *us*, and apparently not much of a secret to anyone.

CHAPTER 33

*H*eard you and Evie were walkin' around town all dressed up and smiling," said Andy the next morning, also smiling.

"Good grief! You heard that, really?"

"Well, maybe I jokes. Actually, I saw Evie at the Coffee Cup this morning, and she told me. A job, teaching, right here in Chandelar. Do you have any idea how happy that makes her? She was there drinkin' coffee, studyin', annoying Rosie by being only one at a table. Rosie made me sit with her."

"I know exactly how happy," I said, having been present for the goodnight kiss she gave me when I walked her home. It had definitely been a happy kiss.

"Heard something else," he said, the smile fading. "Heard at the Coffee Cup there's some white man holed up out in the Chandelar flats, wearin' cammo, changing camps every night, holding real still when people come near, as though people who've lived on on *this* land for thousands of years can't hear him, can't smell his smoke fire or his body odor!"

"William says Forsythe's training is all for the jungle, so he can outfox the Vietnamese. Maybe the muskeg is throwing him off," I said.

"Bet they know he's there, too," said Andy. "Smoke is smoke. A metal fork on the edge of a metal pan is still a clang out there. No bird makes that sound."

I refilled his coffee mug.

"So what do you want to do about him, is the question," said Andy. "Time to go hunting? I can put a bullet in him from so far away he'll be dead a day before he even notices."

"That feels a lot like murder."

"It's what he'd do."

"Boy," I said, "if he'd do it that tells us right off the top it's not something we should be doing."

"Okay, good point. But what *do* we do? He's just killin' time until he can crawl out from under his rock and kill one of us, or all of us."

"In a couple of weeks," I said, "there'll be frost on his drinking water and leaves falling off the trees. He'll be really cold and really tired of this game with darn little cover left, and he'll have to pull out and move on."

"Leave his gold?" said Andy, "I don't think so. He's already killed for that gold, and he's just waitin' around to kill again and collect."

"I'll call the marshal," I said. "We'll see how Forsythe likes a regular U.S. Marshal patrol flying over him."

"I like that idea," said Andy.

Even though the calendar said late July, the days bright and warm, we were already hearing that whisper of something that happens in the far north: the first promise of winter on the way, something in the slant of light and something on the breeze. Here and there around town the first chain saws fired up, the rich exhaust of mixed gas mingled in the air with the scent of fresh-cut trees and the high keening echo of rackety chain saw moans.

People had sleds upside down in their yards, waxing runners, steaming wood to refashion and replace the broken parts, taping up fresh plastic window coverings and stuffing newspaper in the cabin cracks.

I had a checklist. First I rewrapped my water pipes using unsold garments from the church rummage sale. I would cut and tear into strips such garments as a seersucker blazer—that no one in Chandelar would pay a quarter for in a million years—to keep my pipes from freezing. I also put a new light bulb in the plywood outdoor case that houses my propane bottle—at thirty-five or forty below, just enough heat to keep the gas flowing. Together, Andy and I finally repaired the bullet hole one of my clients shot in my office roof, the one that leaked all season from rain or snow melt.

We had moose meat sandwiches for lunch, the moose meat cool and unspoiled right out of my new, brilliantly-white, black-bear-sized Amana refrigerator. We'd finally moved it over from its previous home in the teacherage. I noticed Andy still sniffing the canned milk for spoilage. Old habits die hard.

Bible school came and went. This year's pair of Bible-school girls, college girls up from the States, arrived just as cute, perky and primed for summer adventure and romance as those previous. They attracted the town's handful of wholly undesirable single men—some twice their age and some with wives elsewhere—like flies to a grizzly bear, and the girls reveled in it. They'd apparently never been this sought after back home. For me, being the widowed priest with an obvious girlfriend went a lot easier this year than last. Back then I appeared just so lonely, with hair that needed cutting and buttons that called out to be sewn on. They hadn't known whether to try to flirt with me or adopt me. And my black-bear-sized refrigerator turned out to be perfect for Bible-school Cool-Aid.

Dressing in the morning, I still combed my hair, strapped on my wristwatch and dropped the .38 into my pocket, odd for a priest. And I still double-checked both my front and back door bolts before turning in, plus the one kitchen window that would actually open. But as days turned into weeks and July slid over into August, I could feel myself sliding back into the routine of *not* being alarmed, of not thinking each day that something bad might happen. Soon I knew I would debate with myself about carrying the gun, which was wearing serious thin spots in my various pockets. Andy suggested a holster but I didn't like the image of a priest visibly 'packing.'

"No sign of him," said Andy, when I asked about further Forsythe sightings.

"Maybe he moved on," I ventured.

"Not a chance."

Andy had been spending time in Fairbanks, bunking with a cousin there, and scouting space for his Italian restaurant. Although he planned to hire a cook, he also began trying out some of the recipes he'd brought back from Italy, usually in my kitchen, which was delightful. He clearly had a knack for it. His biggest problem was where to get fresh herbs like basil, rosemary, and oregano in the middle of the Alaska Territory. The answer was 'nowhere.' But he persevered, found ways to get and use dried herbs, and the results, even relative failures, were highly edible.

"I want to be an investor," I told him.

"You?"

"Well, actually the Frankie Slick Memorial Endowment Fund." He laughed. The so-called memorial endowment had been the estate of a murdered loan shark and thug who had made a career of sucking the lifeblood out of the entire valley. Through some Evie sleight of hand, his bookkeeper, I had inherited the whole pot. When I wasn't buying myself—and the church—things like refrigerators, I had dedicated the fund to pumping the lifeblood back. Andy's new restaurant with employment and training for local people would be perfect.

"Already have one investor," he said.

"Evie," I said. He nodded. "I'll give you a better rate."

"Interest?" he asked. "How do you beat totally free?"

"I dunno. I guess I could pay you to take the money."

"No wonder people go into business," he said. "People giving me money to take money. This is great. Wish I'd thought of it sooner."

"You're a natural," I agreed. In the year I'd known him, I'd never seen him so happy.

When my phone rang one morning, I walked down the hallway into my office feeling all the usual dread, counting the kinds of trouble, including misery and death, my phone calls tended to represent. Happily, picking up the receiver I heard Andy's voice with news that he'd found a place, an old saloon that turned out to have a good-sized kitchen at the back, though it hadn't been used for awhile. "Can you come up," he asked. "Bring Evie and William if he's around. Need help getting this place dug out."

"Sure," I told him, hanging up the phone, happy. I'd gotten so little good news on this phone I'd begun to think part of it might be broken.

I found Evie studying at the Coffee Cup.

"Hope you're planning to sit with her," said Rosie, handing me a coffee mug. "Can't have just one person at every table. You'll put me out of business."

"And good morning to *you*," I said.

"I mean," she said, "I was pretty sure you'd want to sit with her anyway, beings you two are an item now."

"An item?" I said to her back as she rushed away. A reminder that this was life in a tiny river town with little to do for entertainment but speculate on the neighbors.

"Good morning, sweetie," said Evie, and—for the first time, right out in front of God and everybody—raised her face and her lips for a quick kiss. Yes, it made me smile. Rosie raced over with the coffee pot to fill me and top her.

"None of that stuff in here, you crazy kids," she said, and smiled.

"Sure," said Evie, she'd drive along to Fairbanks with me and spend a couple of days cleaning out an ancient kitchen that likely hadn't seen soap or a wash rag for a quarter of a century. What else did she have to do but try to cram a whole year's

271

worth of teacher ed into the next three weeks or so? "It'll be a hoot!"

After breakfast, I left her at her cabin to pack, and walked the several blocks toward where William lived, near the school. I saw his axe stuck in the top of his chopping block, like maybe he'd just gone inside from splitting his morning firewood. Of course the door stood unlocked. Inside I saw his bag of Italian coffee on the counter by his water-filled coffee pot, but no fire in the stove, no lights on, no sign of him at all.

His rifles still hung on their rack, pocket change and a few bills lay on his dresser, like he'd just stepped out. It was all a bit puzzling but nothing that quite raised an alarm. Still, I walked back to the rectory feeling that first little trickle of uncertainty—and maybe fear—of something not quite right.

Unlike William, I still locked my door both at night and when I went out. Now I unlocked my door with the .38 in my hand, deliberately closed and locked it behind me. I cautiously walked through to check the whole place for signs of someone who didn't belong, or something out of place. I found nothing.

I packed quickly and answered the door for Evie when she knocked. "What?" she said, reading my expression.

"Probably nothing." I related my visit to William's cabin.

"Maybe at the school?" she said. "You know he's been extra busy getting the windows washed and floors polished. Maybe he just went in early."

"Without coffee?"

"That's not good." Should we drive around and look for him?"

"You know I'm probably just spooking myself, spooking you. He's probably out doing whatever it is he does—spying—and us driving around looking for him would be silly. Let's just leave him a note and head on. When he gets back from wherever, he can come along or not."

"Okay," she said, "good idea." Then she looked at me. "But you're still worried, aren't you?"

"Just a little, but it's the natural result of having a trained killer on the loose and after us. I'll get over it."

"Yes," she said, and a bit uncharacteristically, "I'll get over it, too, when someone puts a bullet in him,"

Jimmy's death still on her mind.

The drive seemed much shorter together. It took just a few minutes to reach Nenana where we drove onto the tiny river ferry. We were the only ones aboard that midmorning. From the river we drove an hour north on the highway to Fairbanks. The road lay dry and dusty, graveled but smooth in this season, with few potholes. We made good time, at 45 to 50 miles per hour over most of it. We mostly talked about Evie's teaching job and the sudden appearance of new chances and how it made us both feel, which wasn't anything but happy.

Nearing the city, the flat, boggy river bottom lined with small alder trees and stunted swamp spruce gave way to green rolling hills feathered with stands of birch and aspen, famed for turning spectacularly to gold after the first frost. We had

273

no trouble knowing when we neared Fairbanks, flagged as it was by a brown haze of fine river dust thrown up by traffic on streets that were little more than packed beach sand.

"Ah, the glory of the city," said Evie, surveying the dust cloud from a near hill. "So much to see and do."

"Like ..." I said.

"Woolworths! And the big Northern Commercial Company—about ten times the size of the one in Nenana—and you know there's a bakery here. Maple bars!" Salivating, we drove on.

The future home of Andrea's, probably built around the turn of the century, featured an old time saloon false front and for the time being, plywood nailed over all the windows. It had a worn dusty look on the outside matched by a worn dusty look on the inside, except for a spectacular bar, much of it hand-carved, running for nearly thirty feet. A long dusty portrait above the bar showed a well-endowed young lady dressed in lavender but not much. "She's a grandma by now," said Evie, which failed to dim my appreciation.

At the back of the main room, someone had recently converted a pantry or storage area into two new rest rooms. In the glory days of this place, patrons had likely gone out the back door to a privy, even at forty below, which even now made me shiver. Guiding us through, an excited Andy insisted on demonstrating all the features for us, creating a virtual chorus of the taps turned on and off, and flushing.

The surprise in all this was the kitchen, which turned out to be the 'real thing,' an old-time commercial kitchen. The floor featured hand-laid hexagonal black and white tiles, with real floor drains. Lower cabinets had been finished with countertops of additional tile or tight-grained maple cutting surfaces and above were knife racks, some knives still in place, and plenty of pot racks, some with pots. The kitchen range, five or six feet of it, appeared to be wood-fired, though Andy had been told it would also run on coal. Keeping a range that size fed would be a job in itself.

Although as narrow as the bar room, the kitchen equaled nearly half the bar room length. Some of it gleamed, where Andy had already been at work. The rest of it, what Andy needed us for, lay thickly coated with dust, cobwebs and rodent trails.

"Swell," said Evie, "mice."

Andy showed her a sack of traps. "Not for long."

So we set to, sweeping, mopping, window-washing—the insides at least—wiping the whole place down with bleach water and what my mother used to call 'elbow grease.' The more we did the more there seemed to be to do. By early evening, hungry, tired, and dusty, we went out to find food, regretfully for Andy's part. I think he had fully and unreasonably expected to be cooking in his own place by evening.

In the spirit of the amazing kitchen, and lots of talk of authentic Ligurian cuisine, we went out from our labors to find cheeseburgers, fries and Cokes to sustain us in the American style, squeezed into a burger booth while the expanding glory that would be Andrea's filled our minds and our excited talk.

We had just gotten back to Andrea's, just walked back through the bar room and swinging door into the glory that would be the kitchen, when we heard a voice, a tentative hello from out front.

"Back here," called Andy, as he looked at us, eyebrows raised. "We expecting anybody?" Then the door pushed slowly in and we found William. Unfortunately, someone else had found him first, with his hands bound at his back it looked like he'd been beaten half to death. Pushed hard from behind, he staggered, nearly fell, and that's when we saw Forsythe and the gun.

CHAPTER 34

*Y*ou're all here," said Forsythe. "Good, I hoped you would be." He smiled his disarming, college-boy smile but it didn't work anymore and I wondered if it ever would again. It didn't even look like a smile, more like a grimace or a mask of cruelty, maybe even madness, and it made me shudder.

He had a gun in each hand, a smaller .22 revolver in his injured right hand, and his own service .45, recovered from William, in his left. The guns didn't slow Evie down. She rushed forward, caught hold of William's elbow and led him gently to a chair.

"Now that's sweet," said Forsythe. And then to the rest of us, "any guns?" He looked directly at me. "That a .38 in your pocket or are you glad to see me?" Then he laughed. "Two fingers," he said, and watched me carefully as I deposited the .38 on one of the tile counters. Setting down his .22 he reached over and dumped the bullets out of my gun one-handed. They made a clattery sound hitting the tile floor.

By the look of him his weeks in the Bush hadn't been easy ones. He'd lost weight, his jawbone prominent and cheeks stretched flat over cheekbones. Mosquitoes had a field day with him and he'd been bitten everywhere that I could see—a lot.

"Sorry about your friend," he said, gesturing with the automatic to William. Had to hit him a few times with my weapon." William's nose had been broken, again, I suspected. His eyes were puffed nearly shut, with blood seeping out of a cut over one eyebrow that would want stitching. Through swollen lips, I could see he had teeth missing or broken. He obviously had been tied up when all this 'hitting' happened. I felt heat starting deep in me, and the desire to hurt Forsythe, to make him pay. I wasn't the only one.

"You bastard!" snarled Andy, and guns or not, started for Forsythe. In a single move that seemed almost casual, the man stepped back while smoothly shooting Andy with the .22 through the top of his right foot. With a cry and grimace Andy went straight to the floor, and ended up sitting, back braced to one of the cabinets, huffing with the pain, pulling off his boot and cradling the shot foot.

"I owed you that," said Forsythe, and I could tell he was enjoying this. "But don't worry, it won't bother you for long."

"Now," he turned to me. "You can tell me where the gold is. I can't find your buddy, Simon. He just seems to disappear in this god-forsaken country. But finding you isn't that difficult and I have a good feeling he told you where he hid the gold."

"He didn't," I said. "We never discussed what happened to it, only how it was obtained— stolen—by your father and his cronies."

"And then by Simon," said Forsythe, "so plenty of blame to go around. Doesn't matter now."

"I do know where it is, though," I said, "and I'm surprised you don't. Leave these people here alive, walk out with me and I'll take you right to it."

"How do I know you'll keep your word?"

"You know me, at least that well. It's what I do."

"Well, that's true, I suppose, but I also know you'd do anything for a friend. Anything! Including not keeping your word to me, to sacrifice yourself and save them. It amazes me."

"So," I said, "do we have a deal? You and me out of here?"

"Hell, no. Not a chance. You people are all going to die, and soon. And don't think it's a secret you can keep. You'll die begging to tell me. Your only bargaining chip is how quickly you get to leave the planet." He pointed at Evie. "You. Over here."

Evie straightened. She had been ministering to William's smashed-up face with cool water and a cloth. Slowly she moved to face him. Stuffing the .22 into a pocket, Forsythe reached with his left hand to the top of Evie's blouse and, with a single hard jerk, yanked his hand down spraying buttons like tiny teeth to clatter and ricochet off hard surfaces.

"No!" I said, and must have taken a step forward even though I'd already been warned pretty graphically about stepping. I found myself staring into the round, black eye of the .45, close up. Way too close.

"None of that," he cautioned. "This one will take your whole foot off."

Even in a bad situation, I had to admire Evie. She stood erect, shoulders straight, though looking terribly vulnerable with soft curves exposed in a white, sort of frilly bra against smooth dark skin.

With the barrel of the .45, Forsythe pushed against the exposed orb of her right breast, steadily, until she had to step back, and back again until her shoulders reached the wall and still he pushed, compressing the soft flesh to the breastbone. But she still stood silent, lips pressed tightly together and held like that.

To get her to make a sound, which I'm sure was what he wanted, he slapped her hard with his open left hand, bouncing her head back against the plaster wall as she let out a cry and I saw her lower lip quiver. She never looked at me, only directly at him, her gaze never wavering.

He smiled again. I think he liked sounds of pain, probably a good thing in his line of work. When at last he pulled the gun away from her breast, it left a red circle with the sharp outline of the barrel opening and front sight set in her skin. It would be a nasty bruise if she lived long enough.

"So my deal is this. Tell me now and you all get the quick bullet. She can go first so you know I'm keeping my word. Make this difficult and she goes slowly and last. And if she doesn't know where the gold is, which I doubt, it will be really, really, bad for her, if you know what I mean."

I knew exactly what he meant, I could read it in his eyes. Some *thing* or some combination of things in this man's life had made him a monster, albeit soft spoken, but a monster nonetheless. I couldn't help but wonder what use our government could have for a man this damaged.

I didn't care about the gold, had never cared about it, but knew he did, making it my only leverage to try to get us out alive. Each time Forsythe had us in a bad spot, I'd been able to stall him about the gold, until one of us saved the others.

Now the saving part of the equation was done, with Andy here, William here, and me.

"The gold is hidden out at Simon's cabin," I said. "Almost in plain sight."

"That's crazy," said Forsythe. "You saw the digging job my idiot brother Clyde and his idiot gangster pal Alphonse did out there. Strings, grids, the whole shooting match. No gold. Nada."

"It's in the cabin," I told him.

He made a frustrated sound. "There's nothing in the cabin. We even tore up some of the floorboards. Nothing but ..." I could see he suddenly 'got' it.

"Nothing but a bonfire somebody laid but didn't light," I said nodding, "supposedly to torch the place. Books, magazines, junk. I even noticed a Dashiell Hammett title, "Dead Yellow Women," but *I* didn't ... none of us ... dug through the pile or lifted any of those boards. We just walked around it, looking at it. It's there.

"Right under Clyde's nose, all our noses!" exclaimed Forsythe. "Clyde even dug through the magazines looking for pictures of women." He shook his head. "Poor dumb Clyde." It was the closest thing to a kind thought I'd seen him have.

"Okay," he said brightly. "So who's first, since I was lying about killing Evie first. I'm definitely saving her for last.

Evie attacked him. She ran at him, swinging, and he slapped her so hard she deflected off in a completely different direction, swaying, reaching for the counter and to one of the low racks to steady herself.

At the same time, I moved in, looking for a punch. I caught him with a left hook to his lips and chin that had to hurt—rocked him—and he swung at me and missed with the barrel of the .45. At the same time, through swollen lips and broken teeth, William yelled something I didn't immediately make out.

Forsythe spun on me with the gun, aimed for my face and pulled the trigger three times. *Click! Click! Click!* Nothing. As fast as a frontier gunslinger, he ejected the clip with one hand while pulling a fresh clip from his pocket with the other. With a triumphant *Ha!* He aimed again for my face and pulled the trigger three times. In my mind I was already hearing the roar, feeling the painful shock and blackness, but again, the gun clicked three times. And that's when I made out what William had yelled: *firing pin!* He had been carrying this gun for weeks, disabled, anticipating just this moment, this need.

Out of the corner of my eye, I saw Evie move, reach up, I thought to grab one of the pots, but it wasn't a pot! She grabbed a wooden-handled kitchen knife, maybe ten inches long, with a narrow, wicked-looking blade.

"Ha!" shouted Forsythe again, assuming a wider defensive stance and a look of condescending confidence. He'd been trained for hand-to-hand knife combat and I could see him already planning to take the knife away and use it on her.

"No!" I shouted, imagining her cut and bleeding. She smiled a little, holding the knife in her hand, without taking her eyes off Forsythe. She flipped it, without even looking at it, a simple, quick half turn, a move that suddenly had her holding the knife by the tip of the blade. In that flash I remembered Andy's story of Evie and the knife back at the old Mission School. "When you see her flip it," he'd said, "she's gonna throw."

Forsythe watched the knife flip, as I watched him know the game had changed. As she drew back her arm to throw, he threw up his left hand to defend, while struggling to get something from his right pants pocket.

She threw straight and very hard. I saw the knife turn over, just once in the air before it skewered Forsythe's left hand, the hilt making a sharp smacking sound hitting his palm with the blade slicing clear through. He screamed, a surprising, high-pitched mix of pain and the shock of seeing the entire blade protruding through his "good" hand.

Horrified, he examined his palm. "*Fuck!* Not again!" Then he grabbed the knife by the handle and swiftly drew it out, blood streaming freely. He screamed again, dropping the knife, and held his painful, wounded hand out in front of him.

Shooting a glance in my direction, eyes round and wild, he bolted through the swinging door and down the long saloon. He made it all the way out of the room before the reality of it caught up with me, and I spun, running to follow. Behind me Evie called, "Hardy, no, let him go!" But I didn't. I wanted to catch him. And I admit, by now I wanted to hurt him.

He made it all the way to the street before I caught him. I grabbed him by the shirt, spun him around and landed just the first of several heavy body blows, spinning him back and around, hitting the front fender of my truck. He left a bloody hand print where the wounded hand smacked down on the hood. I moved in. Although I hadn't thought about what I'd do, I was mostly thinking about what he'd done—to William, to Andy, to Evie—and I think, in that moment, I planned to beat him to death. So I went for him, fist pulled back, as he turned, bloody, knees all but buckling, pale, gasping, and leveled his small .22 revolver at my right eye.

CHAPTER 35

*F*orsythe didn't fire. "You have one chance," he croaked, "to save your friends." He clicked back the hammer on the .22, cocking it. "Because I'll go back in there right now, after I shoot you, and shoot them all. Saving them is what you've been desperate to do, be some kind of hero. Do it now. Just get in your truck and drive me to Chatanika. Heck," he said, pulling himself together, "when we get there, I'll throw away the gun. We can find the gold together. There's enough for both of us." When I hesitated, he said, "I can still shoot you and drive myself."

"Okay, don't shoot. No more shooting. Get in. Try not to bleed on the upholstery."

The cabin wasn't far, about twenty miles out, the road flat and straight, and I expected to see the Highway Patrol or U.S. Marshal overtake us on the way, but no such luck. Of course Forsythe didn't throw the gun out when we got there. I never expected him to. And he kept it pointed at me as we walked down the trail to the cabin. With one exception, the cabin and dug-up yard appeared as we'd left them. That exception: Simon, standing among the test holes as if waiting for us, smoking his cigar.

"You!" said Forsythe, coming up short, briefly aiming the gun at Simon instead of me. It might have been a Japanese fan for all the attention Simon paid.

"Bet it was you, figured it out," Simon said, nodding in my direction. He inhaled, filling his lungs with cigar smoke. "And you," he said to Forsythe, "out on the Chandelar Flats, how did that work for you?" He peered more closely at Forsythe. "Bad year for mosquitoes, for sure."

"You knew where I was?" Forsythe seemed befuddled. "I couldn't find you."

"You're not Alaskan," said Simon, again nodding my way, "like this fella."

"I want the gold," said Forsythe, cutting to the chase. "I want it now. Get it for me and I might leave you alive. Both of you."

"It's in there," said Simon, "you know where. You can get it if you want, and enjoy it. Those bars are still beautiful." Simon leaned in to look at Forsythe's wounded hand. "Ooh," he said, "nasty cut."

"But Forsythe wasn't to be distracted from the gold, now so close. "We're going to get the gold and you guys are going to load it in the truck," he said, waving the small pistol, still demanding. "And I'm going to drive away with it."

"Well," said Simon, another deep draw, "that's the part that's not going to work. You're welcome to find the gold. You and your *evil* father certainly worked hard enough to get it." The emphasis was his.

"But you're not going to drive away with it. In fact, you're not going to drive away, or walk or crawl away even without the gold. You're done. This is it." But Forsythe didn't hear him, or couldn't hear him, and went on waving the gun, blustering.

But I heard Simon and almost immediately stopped hearing Forsythe, like I had some kind of radio antenna in my brain that tuned elsewhere. I tuned to Simon, relaxed, calm, smoking. To the cabin and the woods, silent, utterly silent. No bird calling, no breeze shifting the birch.

And when I knew, I began to back away. Simon saw me, nodded almost imperceptibly, fiddled with his cigar. He was in no hurry, no strain, no sweat.

Abruptly Forsythe aimed his gun at Simon, who smiled slightly. Maybe the smile gave it away. I saw Forsythe suddenly notice the silence, the utter calm, and watched him swivel his head side to side, even letting his pistol arm relax. But then, as if deciding, he raised it quick and meant to squeeze the trigger.

From the woods, the first shot exploded his head and the rest, mostly shotguns nearly blew him to pieces, fired so closely together that the noise came back as a single echo. I had to turn away, throwing up my arms, startling back, tripping and falling, then laying there, not wanting to get up and certainly not wanting to look.

"You okay, Father?" said a voice, and I looked up to see a pair of masked men both wearing thin leather gloves and black balaclavas, reaching out to help me up.

"No," I said, raised to standing, "not okay."

"Yes," said the voice, "hard to look at this." He hesitated. "We need a blessing here." I didn't want to look, but by now had been through too much to not look. I've never been able to forget that last time I saw Forsythe. *Shot to pieces* sums it up. The creature that had been Forsythe might have been a deer or a small bear or some kind of road kill on the highway for all I could tell now.

I never wanted less to bless someone. I even thought my lips might not be able to say the words, but they did. "May God Almighty have mercy upon thee, forgive thee thy sins and bring thee to everlasting life," I said.

"Amen," said the voice.

Six more men, all wearing balaclavas came out of their concealment in the woods to glance at the remains, then drop their weapons next to the corpse and walk away.

"He'll never hurt anyone again," I said, to no one. And no one answered. They had all gone.

CHAPTER 36

I never saw Simon again, regretfully. Local gossips had him moved offshore to some small island nation, though they could never agree on which one. Because of the gold—an extremely poorly-kept secret—the one fact most of the speculators agreed on was that the island had no extradition agreement.

I didn't uncover the gold, didn't look at it. Was I curious? Sure. But in my presence, four men involved with this gold-seeking had died suddenly, violently, before my eyes, in just the last thirty-seven days. By then, I felt overtaken by death and needed desperately to put it all behind me.

I found out more about Nolan Sam, thrown to his death in the paddlewheel late that night on the old *Nenana*. Only 16 when he died, he lied about his age to get what he considered his dream job, what he hoped would be a life on the river.

"Workin' on a steamboat was all he ever wanted to do, from the time he could walk," his older brother, Albert told me. "He thought he'd made it with a job like that, then got murdered on his first voyage." He shook his head, the loss still fresh after nearly twenty years.

Because they never found Nolan's body, there had never been a funeral. So we organized a memorial at St. Mark's, in Nenana. That's when I met Albert Sam, gold guard the night of the robbery. He was also the father of eight UCLA attendees and graduates, including thick-necked Leonard, who went on to briefly hold a school record for something like pass completions. The brothers lined up, each of them shaking my hand very seriously, thanking me for all I'd done. Although they had all been on the boat working as waiters—and bodyguards—it was the first I'd spoken to several of them when they weren't wearing their black balaclavas.

At the service, Leonard read Hemmingway for his uncle:

"Best of all he loved the fall
The leaves yellow on the cottonwoods
Leaves floating on the trout streams
And above the hills
The high blue windless skies
Now he will be a part of them forever.

Although written in Idaho, it certainly felt like Alaska.

Not long after the service, I got a call from the railroad depot in Nenana.

"Your stone's here," said the voice. "Come get it."

'My' stone read, "Nolan Aaron Sam, 1922–1937. Always in our hearts." The next summer, Andy, Evie and I set the stone in concrete on the hill overlooking Nenana, sharing the view with Jimmy Lucas.

They held an inquest for Forsythe. I didn't attend, and admit I wondered why—present at his death—I hadn't been subpoenaed. Although thanks to the balaclavas, I certainly couldn't identify any of the shooters. I quit wondering when I spotted the brief account in the *Daily News Miner.* The way it read, a tourist, David A. Forsythe of Seattle Washington, had apparently been bird watching in the Chatanika area when accidentally caught in moose-hunter crossfire. Never mind that the death occurred well before moose season, and with shotguns! The article also cited a rise in moose poaching.

I've since heard more about the CIA and about spies, and know they are sometimes called 'spooks.' Spooky is a good way to describe how the ground opened up to swallow Forsythe, his deeds, victims, accomplices—his madness—his government job, the gold he killed for, to leave him just an innocent bird watcher caught in a moose-hunting escapade gone terribly wrong. It earned him less than two column inches on a newspaper back page.

It would be a month of treatment and recuperation Seattle before William made it back to Chandelar, pale, thin, gray, still moving stiffly, smiling cautiously and "desperate," he said, "for coffee—Italian coffee—the good stuff."

"Don't they have good coffee in Seattle?" I asked.

"Seattle is a coffee wasteland," William said. "I think they will never have good coffee there. And certainly not coffee roasted in Italy and hand-carried back to America by a personal friend."

On that next morning, a Saturday, Andy knocked first and let himself in through the now unlocked front door, tapping down the hall with his cane, followed shortly by Evie, who kissed us both and in a few more minutes, by William, who didn't kiss either Andy or me but briefly, gently put his arms around Evie and kissed the top of her head.

She looked up at him. "You're the father I never had."

"Why... thank you!" He beamed. "Those are the nicest words anyone has ever said to me."

And it wasn't until that moment when all the pieces fell into place and 'normal' began again, like a stopped movie that suddenly starts back into motion. It felt right and good to be finally all back together, gathered around my kitchen table, selecting mugs, circling the coffee pot, sliding into our accustomed spots on the tippy stools.

We were no more than seated, each with a mug of coffee, when Andy said, "What I don't get is what happened to the gold? I bought newspapers for a month, kept expectin' a big headline like 'Secret Gold Stash Discovered in Chatanika,' but nothin', not a word. Didn't they find at least some of the gold?"

"They found all of it," I said, "information courtesy of Marshal Jacobs. Actually they found more than all of it."

"Huh?" said Andy.

"It turns out Simon had been living on that gold all these years, also the whole Albert Sam family, including all those boys' education at UCLA. In their minds it was just payback for the loss of Nolan."

"So," said Andy, "check me on this... that should make less gold found, and not more."

"Not in Simon's world," I said. "Remember what Simon told us that morning back on the *Ne-*

nana? 'I'm not a thief!' Well," I said, "he didn't steal it—never considered keeping it or using up the stash. Instead, he *'borrowed'* it, kept track of it, and accounted for it all. He converted some of the gold to cash, invested, made a ton on munitions in the war—things like that—and when they toted it all up, the value had nearly doubled, even after educating all the Sam boys."

"And then he ran away," said Andy.

"Ran, heck," I said. "He collected a fat finder's fee from a grateful government, established a memorial scholarship at UCLA—he likes their football—and bought himself an island somewhere."

"Wow," said Evie. "But I'm with Andy. How come no headline?"

I shrugged. "You'd have to ask someone from the government about that," and I turned to William. "Care to explain?"

"No," said Andy, patiently, "it would have to be from *our* government, not a Ruskie."

"Care to explain?" I asked William again.

William looked uncomfortable, glancing around the table at each of us through his spectacles. He sighed. "I wondered when we would be having this conversation. The gold, originally stolen from the *Nenana* in 1937, came from the National Bank of Nome."

"Well, yeah," said Andy.

"It had been made illegal in the United States," said William, "for individual citizens to hoard gold, especially gold bullion, just as it remains illegal now. So this gold, bound for the repository at Fort Knox, Kentucky, had already been bought and paid for by the United States government."

293

"So the government owned the lost gold?" asked Evie. "And that's why they sent Forsythe as an agent to recover it? That's not right! It was Forsythe's father who originally stole it and who planned to kill anybody he had to, to get it back."

"No," said William. "The assignment was never Forsythe's. He had become what is called a 'rogue' agent, working only for himself. The government sent someone else to recover the gold."

"Well, who did they send?" asked Andy, "and how do you know all this?"

"Because they sent *me*," said William.

"You," said Andy, "but you're an agent from Russia."

"I am from Russia," agreed William, "and I was a Russian agent briefly after the war, but I am now an American citizen and am employed as an agent of the U.S. Treasury Department."

"No!" said Andy. "Go on!" He took a sip of his coffee, sighed. "That's a relief," because I always knew you were one of the good guys."

"And I, you," said William, saluting Andy with his coffee mug. Andy ducked his head, modestly.

"Which is how you've known Frank Jacobs for quite some time," I said.

"Why, yes," said William, "but how did you know that?"

"Len Samuels. When I told him you'd been shot, he remembered someone who looked like you flying with the marshal, and described you perfectly. But the real tip off was Frank."

"Frank told you? I am surprised."

"He didn't just out and tell me," I said. "But I knew he knew you. He's pretty formal. Until just recently he always called me Father, and Evie he called Miss Williams. Andy was Mr. Silas at first, but *you* were always 'William.' He obviously knew you well."

"He needs to work on his spycraft," chuckled William.

"I don't get it," said Andy. "The Treasury Department put you here under cover years ago to look for fifty thousand dollars of stolen gold? They've probably spent that much by now just keepin' you here. And it's not like anybody is payin' interest on gold."

"That's not accurate," said Evie. "In 1933 when the government passed the Anti-hoarding Act, making owning gold illegal, the *Nenana* gold—at just over twenty dollars an ounce—was only worth fifty-thousand dollars, but..."

"How can you know all this stuff!" exclaimed Andy.

"I read." She gave him her sweet smile. "You should try it."

William smiled at her. "Go on," he said.

"Then the government raised the value of gold to thirty-five dollars, nearly double, so suddenly the *Nenana* gold is worth closer to a hundred thousand dollars."

William nodded. "Yes, and..."

"Now they can raise its value again. Raising the gold price to seventy or eighty dollars would nearly double it again."

"Or," said William, "they could make collecting and owning gold legal again, when it suits them, and allow it to seek its own market value, like any other commodity.

"So gold might rise to a hundred dollars an ounce," said Evie, "or five-hundred dollars, or more ... *a thousand dollars* an ounce! Let's see, that would be," she calculated, "two-and-a-half *million* dollars. It's hard to even imagine that much money."

"That's crazy," said Andy. "Way crazy. That'd make the original *Nenana* gold—which was a nice little nest egg, by the way—worth a fortune, a fairy-tale fortune! That's not gonna happen."

"Are you a betting man?" asked William. Andy threw his hands up. "Not with you! You know too much."

"So the gold never left the boat, did it?" said Evie. "And after all those legends about dumping it in the river and the marker floating away—all those holes dug so hopefully—up and down the river. The gold was stolen by Forsythe's father and his buddies simply by moving it from one stateroom to another, leaving a guard in place."

"A guard who wasn't Albert Sam," said Andy, "he must've got off the boat after his brother was killed because Simon warned him."

"Okay, so Albert saw it all," said Evie, nodding. "He saw who moved the gold and where they moved it!"

"He was a dead man," agreed William. "And the only reason they did not track him down and kill him is they did not know who to look for. Albert could not read or write back then, so they let him make his mark and did not bother to ask for his last name."

"And then Simon moved the gold again," asked Evie, "instead of putting it overboard and letting people assume the marker washed away?" She looked at me. "But you knew that. *How* did you know that?"

"Simon showed me where he put it," I said. "He didn't mean to—or maybe he did—but when he showed me the 'Captain Rufus Edmonton Memorial hidey hole', he told me that few in the boat's whole history had ever known about it. He didn't say they hid the gold there, but where else? After the thieves moved it, *he* moved it."

"It was all so simple," Evie said, "and it seemed like such a mystery."

"What I want to know," I said, turning to William, "is how you got word out that I'd gone overboard when they threw me into the paddlewheel? Petey had to have been in the air within thirty minutes."

"Well, I ..." said William, shaking his head.

"It was you," I said, "but I don't get how. You'd need a pretty stout shortwave setup to reach Fairbanks, or anywhere, and I sure never saw one in your stuff."

"It's that little black box," said Evie, "isn't it? The one I saw you slip into your travel bag. But it's so small..."

William made a face. "Transistors! A new thing to replace tubes. A radio that once was as big as a breadbox will now fit in your shirt pocket.

I dialed-in one of my military frequencies that is monitored around the clock, and talked to the night operator. And—how do you say—pulled a few strings." He looked at me glumly. "But without much hope."

"And here I am," I said, "thanks to you!"

"So," said Evie, "are these transistors top-secret spy stuff that we can never mention without fear of finding cloaked agents on our doorstep?"

"Maybe they're the same ones who show up if you rip the warning tag off your pillow," suggested Andy.

"Transistors are absolutely top secret," William said, looking at his watch. "For about ten more minutes. I am told that the Christmas catalogs will be full of tiny, brightly-colored radios from Japan, made by a new company called Sony. You can already buy transistors from the Lafayette and Radio Shack electronics catalogs with no fear of government intrusion."

He smiled. "However, you should continue to be very careful with those pillows."

After William and Andy had drifted away, Evie reached across my kitchen table to take my hand.

I flashed—again—on her knife flip and throw. "You saved us all," I said, "and I'm embarrassed to admit, just after I had decided there were no *men* left to arrive in the nick of time. Humbling."

"Well, you saved *me*," she said, patting my hand. "If you hadn't made it onto that Pan Am flight to
Seattle, I'd be dead."

"When I was listening at the door on the *Lizzie Ann*, they had already decided to kill me, by sunset the next day. I prayed you could get there but knew in my heart the timing wouldn't work. You'd have to already be in Fairbanks, ready to step on the airplane.

Then when Jimmy came and told me the ice had gone out early in Nenana, I knew I was lost.

You couldn't possibly make it in time. But you did! Somehow you got up and got across the ice before it broke up. That was so dangerous," she said, squeezing my hand, "and so lucky! You must have an angel."

CHAPTER 37

*I*t took me a long time to figure out what really happened on the *Nenana*, on that long voyage, and to realize I had the whole thing backwards.

While I'd been trying to hide Simon, to protect him and keep him out of harm's way, he'd been deliberately leading old man Forsythe on, luring him back to the boat. It all fell into place one day talking to Andy.

"I hardly ever saw the captain on that voyage," Andy said. "Even with all the shooting and trouble, he never came down from the pilot house, never ... did *nothin'*!"

That's when I realized Simon had been in charge, totally in charge, probably even leasing the boat and hiring all the crew, including the captain.

"So it was a setup," concluded Andy, the light coming on.

"The whole time," I said. "The old man, thinking he had trapped Simon, neatly delivered himself to his own execution. Simon, along with the entire Sam family, had been planning and maybe even practicing the pay-back for nearly twenty years."

Dave Forsythe fell for it, too. When he found Simon alone in that dug-up clearing around the cabin, I'm sure he felt lucky, when in fact he, also, delivered himself. In spite of the beating, William *did* know where to find Simon. So when Evie telephoned the lodge at the Chatanika trading post that night, to warn Simon and get help for me, they were all staying at the lodge, as it turned out. Then Forsythe shows up at a shotgun party in his honor with a small .22, so arrogant, so full of himself and good old-fashioned greed..."

"He never knew," said Andy.

"I think he did," I said, seeing it all again. "In that last second, he looked up, finally reading the signs, knowing it was over. And when he saw how death would be for him, he made it a quick one."

❖

I had left Forsythe at the cabin, as he had fallen, and drove back very slowly to Fairbanks, gunfire ringing on in my ears. Picturing the horrifying spectacle of Forsythe's bloody remains sickened me, until I finally had to pull off, get out, and throw up.

Which helped, but I kept seeing and reliving it all again and again: Forsythe's head exploding and me cringing, falling, lying there not wanting to ever get up. But then, being helped up—made to get up—to have to play it all through again!

I didn't bother going back to the future Andrea's Restaurant. Knowing Andy had been shot and William badly beaten, I went straight to the hospital. St. Joseph's, an old wooden building, lay just a stone's throw from the sluggish Chena river.

"Visiting hours are over," stated the duty nurse, small but formidable in her starched whites and cap, letting me halfway in the front door and looking pointedly at her wristwatch. "*Long* over."

"I'm Father Hardy," I said, "priest from Chandelar."

She glanced at me oddly, and it was only then, seeing the large lobby clock, I realized I'd been gone most of six hours, arriving at the hospital about an hour after sunset, now after midnight.

"You're a priest?" asked the nurse, doubtless looking for the black clerical shirt and white collar, but seeing only a battered-looking man, unshaven, wearing a faded flannel shirt over a white T-shirt.

"I'll vouch for him," said a voice, Marshal Frank Jacobs. He looked at me in his careful lawman way but said only, "Good to see you," sounding like a worried friend. "Are you okay?" he asked, pulling me aside, checking me, as if for bullet holes.

"Yes," I said. "No. How are the others? Are they here?"

He made a face. "Yeah, they're upstairs. Evie gave me the whole story. She's worried sick about you, of course. They're going to put William on the morning jet to Seattle. Likely internal injuries, broken nose, maybe a broken cheek bone, but all recoverable, they say. Andy's going to limp a while. Lucky it was a small caliber. I put out an APB on this guy, Forsythe, which here in the Territory only means if someone accidentally steps on him they'll call it in. How'd you get away? Any idea where he's going?"

I couldn't help thinking, *To Hell*, but didn't say it. I said, "Nowhere, he's done. Dead."

"Dead?" he said, drawing back a bit, looking at me. "You do that?" All I could do was shake my head.

"Frank," I said. "Marshal, I'm happy to go over it with you but I need to go upstairs first."

"Oh!" he said, a little startled. "Sure you do. Second floor, room twenty-two."

I dragged myself up the flight of creaking wooden stairs, weary, but more. I felt crushed under the sheer tonnage of Forsythe's baggage: his evil father, pitiful, damaged sister, his poor dumb, faithful brother—and his victims worldwide. My last thought as I finally made the second-floor landing was *I can't do it anymore!*

And then I saw her.

In a tiny waiting area at the end of a long dim hall, Evie sat alone in a pool of yellow lamplight, dozing over a magazine. She opened her eyes just as I reached the landing and must have seen my figure silhouetted under the exit sign just as I saw her. She squinted a little, blinked, looked again, then rose tentatively. She'd been waiting, watching all evening, fearing the worst—that Forsythe had killed me, just as he promised. Sitting there, watching and waiting, she'd already had hopes raised by men who weren't me, coming up the stairs.

But now, becoming more certain, she began walking toward me, slowly at first then faster, in a focused, deliberate way—as though aimed—until she reached me, and stopped just at arm's length. "It's you," she said in a small voice. "You made it. I hoped you would. Oh, Hardy, I *prayed* you would! But it's been... *I've been waiting for you for so long.*"

I took her in my arms and she took me. We stood that way a long time at the top of the stairs, under the exit light, just holding on. In those few moments, I felt the weight of the world rising, shifting, becoming bearable again.

Finally stepping back, we caught hands and walked down the long corridor together toward the warmth of yellow lamplight.

ABOUT THE AUTHOR

Raised in Alaska, Jonathan Thomas Stratman infuses his novels with all the excitement, color, and adventure of life in the rugged 49th state.

Whether in his acclaimed *'Cheechako' Youth Series,* or in his *Father Hardy Mystery Series,* Stratman's characters call on

Photo by V Judy

reserves of courage, stamina and resourcefulness—not just to prevail, but to survive. No wonder so many readers say, *"I couldn't go to bed without finishing the book!"*

A NOTE FROM THE AUTHOR

Dear Reader,
If you enjoyed this book, would you please go to Amazon.com, or Goodreads, under Jonathan Thomas Stratman, and write a quick review? I'd appreciate it very much!

You can also check out my Facebook page:
'Jonathan Thomas Stratman, Author.' A "like" would be very helpful, too.

Thanks,

Jonatha

*P.S. **Holy Oil—Book 3** in the Father Hardy Mystery Series is available at Amazon.com under Jonathan Thomas Stratman.*

Made in the USA
Middletown, DE
09 August 2020